UNTIL I CLAIM YOU

CALLIE STEVENS

1

———

EDWIN

"Fuck. Get your shit together."

As I look at myself in my office mirror, adjusting my sleeves, my fingers run up against my cufflink and I pause. I trace the lion emblem, and my nerves start to settle down.

I'm Edwin Lyons, for god's sake. This night belongs to me.

I used to look forward to this. Playing happy host to our members as they indulge in the hedonistic pleasures afforded to them in the confines of my club.

However, this year, my mind is far away.

My phone buzzes on my desk.

I rush over.

Maybe it's him.

No such luck. Instead, a text from my daughter gives me the information I've been dreading.

> Nate's not coming tonight. Sorry, I did my best.

"Fuck." I know Abigail has been trying her ass off to get

her brother in touch with me. But that's not working either. *Nothing* is working.

I navigate to his contact info and call him for the umpteenth time this week. If only I had tried this hard before.

I get that nasty ringing as I wait for him to pick up. Pray that he does.

"Come on, come on, come on…"

"You've reached the mailbox of –"

I hang up and curse myself, my fist clenching around my phone so tight it may snap in half. I put the damn thing on 'Do Not Disturb' and slide it into my pocket.

There's a knock on the door.

A male voice sounds from outside. "Ed? You in there?"

Oh, good, Solomon is here.

"Come in." I try to remain on an even keel despite my uneasy mental state.

My best friend throws the door open and beams at me. The shine of his crow's-nested baldhead a close second to his white veneers. "There's the man of the hour."

I manage a poor impression of a smile.

My eyes land on the objects in his hand.

He holds one out to me. "I took the liberty of picking out yours."

I take it. "What's this supposed to be?" I turn the eye mask this way and that to try and figure it out.

The handcrafted piece of art is decorated with feathers made of wood that starts red and transitions to yellow until they're something resembling flames.

"Why, a phoenix, of course!"

"Ah, I see that now." The craftsmanship is divine. "I didn't know Hans Christian Andersen wrote about a phoenix."

The theme of tonight's masquerade is Andersen's fairytales.

"Well, it seems he did. About lots of birds, actually." His grin is nothing short of taunting. "I thought it was fitting for you."

"Now, why would you think that?"

"Because I think you're entering a new era, Edwin."

I sigh. "One can hope, my friend. One can hope. Now, what's yours?"

He holds a green, bumpy thing up to his eyes and grins. "A goblin!"

"That fits your personality to a T."

"Hey! I resent that."

I smack my friend on the arm with the back of my hand. "Just giving you a hard time."

This guy is the least goblin-like man in the Lyons Club.

Not quite an achievement since money has a way of bringing out the worst in some people.

"Although I don't know how you expect to bed someone wearing something like that."

Sol laughs and goes up to the full-length mirror in the corner. "I know you have a history of bedding women every masquerade, or close to it. I mean, in thirty-one years, you might have missed out once or twice, but is that all tonight is for you? A chance for a conquest?" He pulls the mask on, obscuring the top half of his face.

"Not *all.*"

Thirty-one fucking years. God, when will I grow up? I'm a year away from fifty and still wondering who to add to my roster next. I should have settled down years ago now. Yet, here I am, talking about girls like I'm some fucking horny frat boy.

Pathetic.

I know I'm not perfect. I've never had the emotional availability to make something work. I accepted that shortcoming for a long time.

Now, I hate myself for it. After all, look at my relationship with my firstborn.

Truth is life is empty.

The lack of personal connections has now started to take its toll on me, and my loneliness weighs so much that I almost suffocate sometimes.

I dream of finding someone to share this life with.

In these past few months, I learned that my successes are empty when there is no one there to cheer me on, and my failures cut even deeper without someone there to hold my hand. To let me know everything is going to be alright.

"Well, I'm sure you'll find someone to keep your bed warm tonight." He chuckles. Then, his eyes grow wide beneath the mask. "As long as it's not—"

"Bridget. I know. You've told me every year since she turned eighteen." As if I'd ever consider bedding his daughter.

As my finger traces the wooden grooves on my disguise for the night, I struggle to keep down a sigh. "I don't know, Sol, my mind is too full tonight. I'm not sure I'll stay longer than an hour."

Solomon puts his hands on his hips and looks me up and down. "Come on. Let's see how you feel when you put that thing on." He steps to the side of the mirror and gestures with his hands for me to come forward.

I roll my eyes but do as he asks. Whatever will get him off my case. "A phoenix..." I grumble as I slide the masterpiece on.

"Rising from the ashes..." His voice has far too much gravitas.

I sigh. "I don't know if there's much rising to be done right now, my friend."

He lays a hand on my shoulder and our eyes meet in the mirror. "Still haven't heard from Nate?"

"He's ignoring my calls."

Solomon sighs. "I can't say I'm surprised. After all, it's been, what, three years since you guys talked?"

I wince. "Yep. Three years. Since he went to California."

My friend tightens his grip on my arm. "This isn't all your fault, Edwin. He's a grown man too. I know it's hard to believe, since he's your son, but he is just as responsible for his actions as you are for yours."

"You're being...too nice." I wouldn't have said that a year ago. I'm stubborn and proud.

People apologize to me, not the other way around.

But this is my son, and I miss him. God, I'm growing soft in my age. Or maybe growing up.

"It's my fault he left and my fault he stayed away all this time."

"Fault?! No, he knows it's up to him to take up the tradition of running Lyons. Has since he was a boy. For him to act like that was brand new information is preposterous."

"Maybe." I shrug. "But my ultimatum didn't help matters either, did it? It was low of me to tell him if he turned his back on the Club, he wouldn't get his inheritance once the time comes."

And if there was any doubt, his response proved he is my son. Because after I spelled it out for him, Nate took the route of, "You can't fire me. I quit!" and left the city without a word.

"Maybe not. But still, he has to own up to his end of

things." In a softer voice, he adds, "I thought Abigail was going to rope him into coming."

"She did what she could." And I don't doubt it for one second.

"What about Jack?"

I shake my head. "Nate always responds more to Abigail than Jack."

Nate has stayed in contact with both his younger siblings through his absence, thank god. But "contact" for him means a text or call every few months.

Defeat weighs heavy on my shoulders. "I have to do nearly everything through Abigail. And believe me, I'm thankful my children are close despite each of them having a different mother, but it bugs the shit out of me when they protect each other like this." I shake my head. "If Abigail couldn't get him to come, then all hope is lost."

My friend runs his hand over his mouth as he starts to pace.

"Don't pace," I bark. "I'm already nervous enough."

"I'm just thinking."

"About?"

Solomon stops. "Why now? Why is Nate back in New York *now*?"

That's the million-dollar question. "Trust me, if I knew, you'd know too."

"I'll bet you anything he's ran out of money," Solomon grumbles.

"If he wanted money, he'd have to, you know, talk to me, wouldn't he?"

Solomon nods. "Fair point. But you know how people can be. Asking for money isn't easy when you don't have anything to give in return."

"At this point, I would pay Nate to let me be his father

again." That's a fact. "I don't care if I needed to keep him salaried until the day I die. It might be fucked up to most people, but the way my life has panned out, that would be the least fucked up thing about it."

Fuck, this hurts. "Look, can we just..." I shake my head, holding my hands up, palms facing Solomon. "We have a big night. I don't want to think about this any more than I have to."

"You're right. I'll drop it."

"And please don't say anything–"

"Edwin."

My insides lock up.

"You know I'd never say anything about it unless you wanted me to."

Besides my children, Sol is the only one who knows Nate is back in New York.

I hesitated to tell anyone about it to begin with, but even a man as hardened as me needs to have someone he can talk to. Someone to have his back no matter what.

Despite the serious way his mouth is curled, he's still wearing that awful mask, and it suddenly dawns on me we've been having this conversation as a goblin and a phoenix.

Laughter bursts out of me. "This is ridiculous."

"What?"

"Your face!"

Solomon touches his droopy wooden brows. "Oh! That. Ha! Well, let these serve as a good reminder to you. Tonight isn't real life. It's a fantasy. That's what the masquerade is all about, isn't it?"

He's right. The masquerade has been a tradition in the Lyons Club from the beginning. Has become the most sought-after event. Because it allows all of these powerful people to be pretty much anyone, an anonymous face in the crowd for one night a year.

"You're right." I sigh and pull on the lapels of my jacket.

"So, you're going to go out there, forget about all the stuff with Nate, and you're going to live a little, goddammit."

Fuck it. Tonight, I'm not Edwin. I'm a phoenix, rising from the ashes.

And if tomorrow everything catches fire again, so be it. Because I'm going to make this a night to remember.

2

SONIA

"What do you mean, you're in New York?!" I yell into the phone, causing a group of guys idling outside the bodega I'm passing to look at me with far more intrigue than I'd like.

Nate sighs. "What else would 'I'm in New York' mean, Sonia?"

I don't have time for this shit.

"Well, I don't see what that has to do with me," I grumble, looking down the alley I'm passing as a chill runs up my spine.

This is New York. So much darker than sunny California.

And sure, there are millions of people in this city, but I just got here, and I'm still learning my way around.

Besides, you know what they say, it's a small world. And the last thing I'd want is to run into my ex-boyfriend when all I want is the chance to start my life over.

"You know why I'm here."

I take a turn. I should be almost there. "I told you already—"

"I know! But I'm trying to be—"

"What?! Romantic? I swear to god, Nathan Lyons, you've got another thing coming if you think following a woman who wants nothing to do with you to another state is romantic."

Nate is quiet for a moment.

"You want nothing to do with me?"

I look up, and I'm there.

Lyons Court, named after the club and the family who owns it.

The Lyons Pride façade is something to look at with its grand columns and arched windows up a series of wide, shallow steps, flanked by marble lions. It's almost like a slightly smaller replica of the New York Library.

Luxurious black cars and limos are already starting to pull into the round cul-de-sac, stopping in front of the majestic nightclub. Guests of tonight's masquerade.

"Sonia?" Nate's voice in my ear pulls me out of my reverie.

I take a deep breath. "Goodbye, Nate. Please don't call me again."

Nate starts balking before I hang up the phone and put it into my clutch.

Lifting my head high, I put on a smile, and do my best model walk up to the front of the Lyons Pride.

Thank god, my job provides me with a stipend to afford a more appropriate wardrobe. And given that my first time here is at this masquerade, I splurged on a white off-the-shoulder number with a high slit up the side that was a bargain on sale.

Still! This is more than I've spent on anything in a long time. And way more than I should.

However, amidst the entering guests, I feel like everyone can see how cheap I am.

The dress might be expensive, but the heels are old favorites from DSW, and the clutch is a complimentary makeup bag from the Estée Lauder counter.

I follow the train of a woman whose dress seems to be emblazoned with Swarovski crystals up the stairs and inside. My jaw almost drops at the foyer alone.

There's an incredible crystal chandelier over the entryway that looks like it's crying tears of glass and to the left is a rounded staircase leading up to a second level.

This is like no nightclub I've ever been to.

To the right is a table full of masquerade masks. They look almost too beautiful to touch.

Each person who passes picks one up, some taking the time to choose one, some with abandon. And just like that, their faces become ensconced in fantasy.

When it is my turn at the table, I peruse the masks, taking my time. I want to be concealed, but I also still want to be beautiful. No trolls or dragons for me.

My eyes settle on a piece with white feathers and sparkles with an elegant beak fitted for the nose.

I take it, examining it for a moment. My heart fills with a strange amount of love for the mask. That's how I know it's mine.

A male voice comes from the top of the stairs. "Ah, the lady of the hour!"

My eyes follow the sound to the man I recognize from all our Zoom meetings. Farley Axford.

He's...smaller in person. He came across as larger than life, or maybe I was intimidated before since he held my future in his hands.

Farley navigates the stairs as easily as Fred Astaire and comes to meet me. "Sonia Hill, how are you, darling?"

He kisses me on both cheeks and then eyes my mask. "Ah! The swan. Good choice. Goes with your—" He gasps as he takes me in. "Stunning outfit! Do a turn for me."

I do so, trying to ignore any other eyes that might be looking my way.

"You look divine."

"I wasn't sure if I should choose one or…"

"Of course, you should, why wouldn't you?"

I try to smile, but I'm not sure it doesn't come off as a grimace instead. "I'm working tonight, aren't I?"

"First of all…" Farley touches my shoulders, adjusting me toward the closed double doors across the entryway. "Everyone is required to wear a mask tonight. It's part of the mystique."

I nod. "The mystique, of course."

"And second of all…"

Through the doors, the sounds of a live jazz band hit me for the first time. And as the doors open, my chin falls. The lights make the nightclub look like a smoky cabaret right out of the twenties.

"No, you aren't working tonight. You're our guest." Farley pats my shoulder.

I do a double-take. "Seriously? I thought you…"

"I want you to get a feel for the club, for the people you'll be dealing with." His smile is mischievous. "This is your welcome to New York. Now come on, put on your mask…"

I do so, allowing the "mystique" to take over.

"Perfect. Now, go get yourself a drink, and I'll catch up with you later. Remember, tonight we're anonymous. Masquerade and all. Ha! So, for as long as this lasts, you are..." His hands slide down my arms. He guides my wing-span away from my dress and marvels at me with an excited smile. "The Swan Princess!"

I giggle. "Is that how I should introduce myself?" I have no idea what is going on, but this is the man who hired me, so I'll play by his rules tonight.

"Yes. For this one night a year, we are only who we portray. I'll be asking around for you later, princess." Another kiss to both my cheeks. "Ciao, bella."

And Farley is gone. I watch him go, marveling at what a character he is.

Is everyone larger than life here?

I look back to the open doors.

It's now or never, Sonia. Let's do this.

The second I step into the club proper, I am transported.

The doors open up into a well of conversation couches and cabaret tables facing a giant stage. At the center of it all is a dance floor where people are clinging together, enjoying the freedom found through their hidden identities. A long bar flanks one wall, behind which bartenders flit around like they're doing a choreographed ballet. A metal balcony rims the room.

To my left, another staircase also leads upstairs to what appears to be a secluded VIP area that seems to have open access tonight.

"Cocktail?" A server bends a tray my way. A garden of champagne flutes full of red, bubbling liquid.

"What...what is it?"

"Lion's Roar," he says without further explanation.

I grab a glass and thank him, even though I'm a bit concerned about the contents of the flute.

After taking a sniff at the drink, my mouth waters a bit,

so I take a sip, and holy heaven, it's delicious. Bubbles of champagne, tart of cranberry, heat of cinnamon, and... Is that whisky?

This drink is dangerous.

If I indulge too fast, I'm going to be wobbling all over the place.

Now wielding my cocktail, I guess it's time to mingle. But I don't know what to try first or where I would even fit in. Although that's the power of the mask, I suppose. I fit right in anywhere simply because tonight, we're all free to be whoever we want to be.

If only that were my life every day.

No, I refuse to think about my problems, I refuse to drown under the weight of my life.

Happy thoughts, Sonia. Happy thoughts.

It's been so long since I've been able to have those.

The dream is to be free. Free to live the way I want, to be able to go out and grab a coffee wherever and whenever I feel like it. God, wouldn't that be the life...

How crazy is it that something as simple as going to grab a cup of coffee is my definition of having a life?

Oh, and finding love.

The sigh that escapes me is soul deep.

There is no way I can let anyone in my life, let alone my heart any time soon.

But this is a fantasy time, a fantasy place, and even if just for tonight, I can dream. I can hope.

My eyes start to blur as reality tries to crash this bubble, so I lean my head back.

No crying tonight. This is a happy day. I have a new job. I may be able to solve my problems more easily. I may be even able to—

Two men descending the staircase grab my attention. One in a bumpy green mask and the other...

Good god, the other.

Though his face is obscured by a mask of fiery feathers, something pulls me to him. He's the definition of tall, dark, and handsome, looking like he stepped out of the pages of *Vogue*.

Despite the low lighting, the slight salt of gray at his temples is clear.

To my shock, when he reaches the bottom step and surveys the club, his eyes snap to me.

Obsidian eyes that might as well have been uprooted from the Earth's core.

The corner of his lips turns upward.

My heart starts to sink into my stomach. And even further down.

I've never felt so much want for a man I haven't even spoken to, but goddamn, something about him...

His smirk is interrupted when the man following him down the stairs smacks right into his back. My firebird turns around and they start to bicker.

My firebird? What the...

Get it together, Sonia. The last thing I'm here for is a dalliance with one of the club members.

It's no crime to look, but one look from him warmed my insides to an impossible degree. That man, whoever he is, is dangerous.

I need to walk away, fast.

I straighten my back and start walking to the dance floor where I can disappear into the masked mass of people. It is also where I can learn about the VIP crew attending this exclusive masquerade as well as what makes the Lyons

Club tick. There is no better time to learn so I can be at my best when I start tomorrow morning.

However, the more of this Lion's Roar I drink, the harder it is to quell the heat that one look from a dark-eyed man set off inside me.

3

EDWIN

The swan disappeared right after I saw her.

I could tell she was a bird based on the detailing of feathers so much like my own. The white stood out even further against her black waves of hair. Combined with her whole air of elegance and beauty, there would be no other bird she could be than a swan.

Of course, Solomon had to bungle all that by slamming into my back and setting me off-kilter.

I guess it's my fault I couldn't contain my temper enough not to snap at him. Because by the time I turned back around, my swan was gone.

You'd think a woman in all white wouldn't be hard to find in our little club where most everyone gravitates toward dark tones and gaudy glitter. However, no matter how hard I try, I can't seem to spot her.

She may as well have been a figment of my imagination.

"Brooding, are we?"

I look into the face of a younger man, who despite his princely mask, I recognize as Mason Lotts. My son's best friend of many years.

Something happened back then that had Mason follow Nate out to California. Now he is also back, but unlike Nate, Mason has ingratiated himself right back into the Lyons Club without batting an eye.

It's good to see him again. But how I'd kill for one single message from my son.

I smile. "Enjoying the party?"

"Always." Mason takes a seat on the bar stool beside me.

Still, after all these years, I can't get used to him being here as a full-fledged member. Feels like yesterday he and Nate were scraping on the Persian rug with *Teletubbies* on in the background. "Sounds like you're finding ways to keep yourself entertained."

"At the Lyons Club, it's hard to be bored." He leans back on the bar and surveys the scene. "I was just partaking in some of the antics of The Underground. The girls you have down there tonight are..." Mason whistles.

"They came at the recommendation of Michael Carnaby," I say. "Haven't been down there yet but glad to know his recommendation is up to snuff."

"You ought to go down there. Then your shoulders might fall away from your ears, huh?"

I give him a sidelong glance.

The Underground is our dungeon. Where our members in the BDSM lifestyle can get their needs met.

Tonight, we've hired a slew of burlesque dancers to entertain down there, and there's no lack of both subs and Doms for all tastes in case some unattached members want to indulge in a little fun.

Everything that happens down there, stays down there.

Mason twists his lips to the side. "Look, I'm sorry I couldn't come through with you on Nate."

I swig my whisky. "No apology necessary."

"I did my best, but you know him," Mason says, continuing an apology that is truly not necessary. "Abigail and Jack did what they could. I know Abigail is feeling really broken up about it, but—"

"Mason, I'm a grown man. Nathan is my son. No one else but me is responsible for..." I don't even know. Rebuilding our relationship? Our trust?

He's my son. This feels so ass-backward.

Mason clicks his tongue. "I know, I know. We all just want to help..."

I can't believe my eyes.

Mason's voice fades away as a figure in white appears beside him, leaning over the bar to catch the eye of a bartender.

It's her. My swan.

I don't even think she notices me on the other side of Mason.

He does a double-take in the direction I'm looking. A smile creeps over his face. "Have you found something of interest, Edwin?"

"It still freaks me out when you call me by my first name," I grumble, then lean over the bar and snap at one of the bartenders, Kelsey, who is peeling oranges for garnish.

The bartender's head shoots up, her blue spikes of hair visible over the crown of her scaly mask. Some sort of fish. Maybe the Little Mermaid.

I gesture toward my swan.

The swan looks my way.

I hold my breath.

Her eyes are like molten gold, sparkling even in the dim light of the club.

In the background, an upbeat bass throbs.

And so do I.

She starts to smile, to thank me, but Kelsey grabs her attention before I can reciprocate. My own damn fault.

"You're such a good host," Mason teases.

I pat my son's friend on the shoulder. "Mason, you know I love you, but get the fuck out of here, would you?"

He grins. "Whatever you say." The younger man gets to his feet and trips off into the hoopla of the floor.

I watch the swan wait for her drink. And I wait for her to look at me.

Her head dips down, looking at her hands.

I take stock of every little detail about her. The severe lines of her cheekbones and jaw, her ear lobe that is decorated with a dangling pearl and a golden stud, plus a hoop at the very top of her ear.

I can't place her. And I can place pretty much everyone despite their masks.

However, this is one of the only events of the year where our members can bring as many guests as they like. She could be a friend of a friend of a friend. Someone I might never see again.

Which means it's all the more important I close the gap between us.

"A swan, hm?"

Wow. Smooth, Edwin.

The woman lifts her face toward mine. She's young. "Yes. And you are?"

I lift my chin. "Guess."

Kelsey returns with the woman's drink. Another of the evening's signature cocktails.

Farley came up with that one.

I thought it was a little too cheeky, but I've seen the Lion's Roars flowing all night.

The swan takes a sip, then looks at me once more. "Hmm..."

"You need a hint?"

"No, no." Another sip. She tilts herself back, leaning on the bar, showing off the deep well of her clavicle.

My god, she's stunning. She's probably a model. I think I've seen her before on the cover of...something. Or maybe that's wishful thinking.

"Hmmm..." The way her lips fold to hum makes my insides vibrate.

Shit, this isn't good.

"Rooster?" she ventures.

I jut my chin forward, eyes widening. "Rooster?!"

She giggles, bringing her drink toward her mouth. "Am I wrong?"

"I'm—I'm—I'm—" *Dammit, Solomon.* "A phoenix! I'm a phoenix."

The swan flushes. Imagine that, a blushing swan. "Oh! I see it now! The flames on the—"

I touch the crown of my mask. "Yeah, they're flames."

Leaning forward, she examines my mask. She's so close I could grab her and kiss her. Although that would surely get me slapped.

I want to, though. Almost to the point of despair.

Her finger comes up as if to touch the mask, me, but she drops her hand before I get that lucky. "And the bottom is all black like it's been charred. Huh. That's beautiful..."

You're the beautiful one.

Suddenly, she withdraws, tilts her drink in my direction. "Cheers."

Before I can say another thing, she floats off as easily as a swan on a placid lake.

I stare after her, mouth ajar.

Did she really call me a rooster and then walk away?

How dare she make me feel like this, leave my body all hard and wanting, and then walk away from me?

I clear my throat, down my whisky, and then get Kelsey's attention.

"Another. Make it a double."

OVER THE NEXT HOUR OR SO, I KEEP HAVING BRUSHES with the swan. I interrupt a conversation she has with another man, we brush past one another as she returns from the billiards room where I catch a whiff of her perfume, I watch her bobbing her head and hips to a song as she eats a canapé in the corner.

I watch her with all the wanting I have in me. And when I see her bobbing to the music all alone when she should be swept across the dance floor in the arms of a man, i.e. me, I give up this game of cat and mouse.

I might be a rooster in her eyes, but here, at the Lyons Club, I am the cock of the walk.

She doesn't need to know who I am or what I do here to feel my confidence and pride pouring off me.

As I cross toward her, her gaze shifts to me as if she is able to feel me coming. I'd like her to feel me coming in so many ways, but I'll settle for this for now.

She wipes her hand on a cocktail napkin, knocks back the rest of her drink, then dabs her mouth.

"You're all alone," I say, planting my feet beneath me and sliding my hands into my pockets.

She looks side to side and shrugs. "Guess so."

I hold out my hand to her.

She looks at it. "What's that for?"

I ignore her question and grab her hand.

She does not resist, letting me guide her toward the dance floor at the center of the room.

"What's going—"

"Has a man never asked you to dance before?"

"Well, usually, they use their words," she says with a playful, glinting smile.

We find a plot of land on the dance floor.

I adjust to slide my hand around her waist, pulling her only an inch closer to me. I'm not going to give her everything at once. Don't want to scare the poor girl. "I think you'll find there's nothing about me that is usual, Swan."

Her lips perk up at the nickname. Or name, I should say. I have no other way of referring to her and I'm not about to ask. I want this encounter to remain shrouded in mystery.

Why learn names when we'll never see each other again, most likely?

We adjust our dancing posture and begin to sway across the floor to the swooning melody the band plays. Our form is prim and proper to start. However, the music makes it impossible to stay apart for too long.

I find our hips pulling together as our eyes remain locked.

We are both silent. And yet so much is communicated. A mutual want. A yearning.

I lean toward her ear. "You're not letting me lead."

"I don't normally dance with strangers," she says in return. "I have to maintain some semblance of control."

I chuckle, eyes falling to her pink, glossy lips. "With me, you don't have to worry about loss of control." I congratulate myself for that one.

Except she laughs. Loud. Head thrown back.

People look at her. And what a sight she is.

"My god, you're a flirt, aren't you?"

My mouth opens and closes, trying to figure out what to say.

"You say that to all the girls, I bet."

She has my number down pat. My charms and platitudes aren't going to work against her if I remain cliché. "I don't talk to girls, I only talk to women."

"I bet you say that one too." Her gaze scans the dance floor around us.

I clutch her hand tighter in mine, her warm palm sending sparks through me.

I spread my hand across her lower back as I pull her hips closer to mine.

She doesn't resist. Which means even though she's giving me shit, she still wants this.

"Have you seen me dancing with anyone else tonight?"

"Do you think I've been watching only you tonight, Phoenix?"

I grin. "I know you have."

Her determination falters only a little, but I've been watching her enough tonight that I can catch all of her minute emotions.

"I've felt your eyes on me since I walked in."

"You say that as if you haven't had your eyes on me."

I shake my head. "No, no. The difference between you and me, Swan..." My hips brush against her and my half-hardened cock goes full tilt to an erection. I'm not even embarrassed.

The smile on her lips tells me everything I need to know.

I lean again toward her ear, this time letting my lip

brush up against her dangling pearl earring. "I'm not afraid to admit when I've been watching."

Swan holds her breath. Waiting with anticipation for me to speak.

"And I've been watching you very closely." I press my hips into hers. "Waiting for the right moment to come get you."

This is the make-or-break-it moment. If she's a runner, this will be too intense for her. She'll skitter off and hide in the dark recesses of the party until she can make her exit, or she'll sic the man she was flirting with earlier on me as some sort of defense.

Except when he realizes who I am, he'll back down.

However, Swan doesn't pull away. She draws her face toward mine. Our mouths are only inches apart.

"So, now that you got me..." she murmurs. "What are you going to do with me?"

If I lean in and kiss her, my fate is sealed for the night.

My mind races. I have so many ideas I don't know where to begin. Kiss her, touch her, fuck her into oblivion.

Devour her.

Wreck her.

I don't get a chance to even give her a friendly peck when I'm interrupted by an intent tapping on my arm. "Edwin!"

Seth. I grimace. "Excuse me for a moment, would you?"

Against everything my body wants, I release my swan and turn around to face Seth Vance, Solomon's son.

Well, stepson. Although that doesn't matter. Solomon treats him as the son he never had.

Seth's got a look on his face that has me worried.

"What is it, Seth?"

"It's Solomon," he says, pain in his blue eyes. "I don't

know what happened, but he's tripping. Hard. Like, hallucinating."

I raise an eyebrow. "Do you know what he had to drink?"

"No, but I think Quinn Puckett's daughter—"

"Carina," I growl. Carina Puckett is notorious for having her boutique "candies" at all the parties, aka hallucinogens and party drugs. I'm sure Solomon mistook one of her little "mints" for a real candy and is now doubled over staring into a light thinking it's a star person. "Where is he?"

"Upstairs bathroom."

"Okay, I'll be there in a second. Let me—" As I turn back to Swan, I'm stunned to find the space on the dance floor before me empty.

I look around.

She's gone. Disappeared just as quickly as she arrived in my life. I'm used to being abandoned, but not by women. I'm the one that abandons them.

It's not something I'm proud of, a bad habit I've never managed to wipe away.

Now Swan has gone and flipped the script. Maybe it's what I deserve. To be abandoned, not only by my boy, but a strange enchantress in the night too.

"Never mind," I say, coldness sliding through my veins. "Take me to him, Seth."

4

———————

SONIA

I STUMBLE INTO THE WOMEN'S BATHROOM, CLUTCHING at my chest to catch my breath.

What. The hell. Was that?

That man. His touch. His voice. His body.

My god.

Being in his arms was like some sort of drug, except I'm not sure you can get anything like that, even in the blackest of markets.

It's why I had to run away. All the way upstairs. As far as I could go without outright leaving. I wasn't sure I'd be able to control myself if I stayed a moment longer.

"Warm towel?"

I look over at the bathroom attendant, who is a smiley woman, hidden behind a mask made of flower petals. God, what is the *theme* tonight anyway? Things you find in nature? This is ridiculous! "No, I'm good. I'm just...hot."

"Mm. Here. You need a wipe." She holds out a little wipe packet to me, her smile never fading for a second.

"Thank you."

"Here, sit, sit. Take a rest." She guides me to a poofy ottoman in the middle of the room and sits me down.

I feel like I'm some sort of nineteenth-century maiden, the way she's treating me. As if I can't stand upright and might suffer a fainting spell anytime now.

Once I'm settled on the ottoman, I split open the packaging on the wipe and pat my face and neck. The cool, cucumber-melon-infused wipe brings down the heat level inside me. Thank god.

When I'm done, I take stock of my surroundings for the first time.

The bathroom is just as lush and beautiful as every other part of the club. *Why am I not surprised?* Gilded crown molding, marble sinks, crimson carpet, mirrors that I swear you could step through to walk centuries into the past.

I could stay here the rest of the night.

And I just might if it will help me stay out of the gaze of the Phoenix.

Don't get me wrong, I want him. I was dancing with him after all, letting our bodies drift closer and closer together until we all but became one.

However. That's not why I'm here.

That man doesn't look like a mere guest of the club. He walks around like owns the place. I don't want him to spread rumors about the unprofessional manager to other members.

But just because we can't see the top half of everyone's face doesn't mean we wouldn't be able to recognize them in the light of day.

The attendant touches my hand. "You can take off your mask." She has a kind smile. "I won't tell."

That might be just what I need. Sweat is building up under the layer of the mask.

Whoever made these cares much more about the aesthetic and less about how it feels to wear them.

"Thank you." I slide the mask up over my face. And just like that, I can breathe again. The air cools my skin. I pad the sweat away with the wipe. "Gets stuffy in there, doesn't it?"

From behind me, a toilet flushes.

As I turn around, another maskless woman emerges. She smiles when she sees me, eyes widening. "It's you!"

I point to myself, looking between her and the attendant. "M-me?"

She giggles and goes to wash her hands. "I've been seeing you around, wondering who the hell you are."

Her eyes flick up to meet mine in the mirror, an astonishing combination of blue and green. Pouty lips, pert nose, big eyes. She's the definition of everything I've ever wanted to look like.

The only thing we have in common is our dark hair, although hers is closer to brown than black.

Mine is raven, through and through.

"Oh. I'm Sonia—" I throw my hand over my mouth. "Shit, I wasn't supposed to tell you that."

The woman turns around, throwing her head back with laughter. Her lilac dress floats around her like she's some fairy princess. "It's okay, it's just the two of us. And Glenda."

Glenda holds a paper towel out to the woman.

She takes it and wipes her hands. "I'm Bridget."

"Nice to meet you." I smile at her.

"You as well." Instead of wafting toward the door in her beautiful gown, she comes over and takes a seat beside me on the big, round ottoman, holding up her mask. "It can be so stifling out there in these, huh?"

I nod. "I didn't even realize how sweaty my face was until I sat down."

"Mm..." Bridget eyes my mask. "You got a nice one."

"What's yours?"

She holds up her mask, showing off a green and brown mask with sticks jutting off of it. "I think it's a dryad..."

"Okay, that's it. I'm totally lost. What is the theme supposed to be?!"

Bridget laughs. "Hans Christian Andersen fairytales, but it turns out there are *a lot* of them and most are just plain weird." Bridget drops her mask into her lap.

I can tell she comes from money, not just by the quality of her clothes, but by that action alone.

I wouldn't dare drop this mask for fear I might ruin it.

For her, this is just another year, another masquerade ball.

Although, if all goes my way, this is my first of many to come.

"Anyway, I saw you getting cozy on the dance floor." Bridget smirks.

My face gets hot again, this time without the mask. "Oh, god. I didn't realize I was sticking out so much."

"Well, you look like an angel out there amidst all the black and gray. Hard to miss you."

Fucking great.

She pats my hand. "Don't look so sour, it's a compliment."

"Thanks." I smile. "Your dress is nice too."

Bridget shrugs. "Eh, it's a bit out of season."

"Right." I try not to portray how humorous I find her

passé attitude. If I had dresses like that in my closet, I'd feel like a queen.

"Anyway, who did you come with?"

I look at Glenda who is minding her beeswax in the corner and then back at Bridget. "Can I tell you a secret?"

"Oooh! I love secrets." She claps her hands and leans in, her full focus on me.

With all the confidentiality of a CIA agent, I whisper, "I'm actually the new operations manager."

Bridget grabs my arm as if we've been friends for years. "No wonder you stick out! You're new here!"

"Yeah, exactly."

"Well, I hope I've made a good impression. I'm Bridget Vance. My dad, Solomon, is very involved here at the club. So, I'm sure you'll meet him soon. And don't worry, he's not nearly as stodgy as some of the old guys around here. He's as friendly as they come."

My heart warms. "That's good to know."

"Anyway, I *don't* work here, so if you ever need someone to complain about all the goings on around here, you should text me. Here, give me your number."

I might be hesitant toward getting physical with a member of the club, but surely making a friend wouldn't hurt. I give Bridget my number.

She hugs me goodbye, slips on her dryad mask, and goes to the door. "You better not stay cooped up in here tonight. I know Lyons can be a lot, but..." She shrugs. "Try to have some fun."

Then, she slips out into the hallway.

Lyons *can* be a lot. I've barely even started to explore, barely met a handful of members, and I'm already feeling overwhelmed.

Not to mention...my Phoenix.

Though I'm terrified of what might become of me if I give into these intense, primal feelings I've had since I laid eyes on him only a couple of hours ago, his memory brings me comfort.

His body felt so good and safe against mine.

Yet, he's a total stranger. I shouldn't feel safe with a stranger.

But I did. And I haven't felt safe in a very long time.

"Okay, I'm going out there, Glenda."

"Nice to meet you, boss."

I give her a look.

So, she *was* listening.

I can't blame her, though. A job like this is perfect for someone who is just a little nosy. "Just call me Sonia. No need for any formalities with me."

She grins. "You got it. And if you need a wipe or a piece of gum or–"

"I'll come to you first, don't you worry!" I say over my shoulder as I go out the door.

I look back down the hall toward the stairs leading to the main part of the club where all the dancing and partying has only gotten louder throughout the night as people have gotten drunker. Then, I look the other way. The hall keeps going, drops off at a set of stairs.

This up here is the VIP area, so regular club-goers won't have access. Can this stairway lead to a different part of the club downstairs?

I only remember the stairways in the foyer and right by the door, which merge into one up here. But maybe this is another way down.

Shrugging, I walk down the hallway. I approach it, tentative and careful. I'd hate to go somewhere I'm not supposed to go.

I'm going to be the manager, for god's sake, I might as well know the ins and outs of this place.

As I reach the top, I look down, to a leather door with metal studs decorating it.

Huh.

I bathe in the silence.

Should I keep going? What is beyond that door?

Before I can make up my mind, someone grabs me by the arm and yanks me back. The scream that threatens to rip out of my throat gets silenced by a hand over my mouth.

"Sh-sh-sh...It's just me."

The voice of the Phoenix.

The hand against my mouth suddenly becomes... welcomed.

He presses me up against a recess in the wall where we are just out of view from those who might be coming and going. He releases his hand from my mouth, but his eyes are glued to my lips. "You ran away from me."

I gasp as he presses his pelvis up against me. "Y-you were needed."

"More than *you* needed me?"

I scoff. "I don't need you."

"Is that a fact?"

Though we are bathed in shadow, I can still see the glinting of his dark eyes.

My resolve dwindles. I can't be sure that I don't need him. That's why I ran away from him, so that I couldn't fall off the edge of the cliff into this man. This *stranger.*

"I said, *is that a fact,* Swan?"

His hands slide down my waist, stopping right at my hips.

I tilt my head back, letting out a tiny moan. "God..."

"You aren't answering my question."

"I don't know what to say." Desperation builds inside me. I'm an inch away from breaking.

If he doesn't let me go soon, I'll let him take me. Right here. Right now. For as long as he wants.

Phoenix slides his hand around the back of my head, piercing my soul with his gaze for a long minute. "Let me see your face."

"I can't."

"Then give me your name."

I shake my head. "No."

"You won't give me what I want?"

God, his lips are so close to mine, their energy so intense that they're caressing mine even from a distance.

"Aren't we supposed to be strangers tonight? Nameless, faceless. Anonymous?" It's a lame excuse, but it's the only one I got.

His hand slides from the back of my head to my chin, his thumb resting right under my lip. "I want to know who I'm kissing."

"You don't always get what you want." My murmur comes out deeper than I've ever heard it.

Phoenix's thumb drifts back and forth under my lower lip. "I suppose..."

My eyes flutter shut as I prepare for his lips to land against mine.

The build-up is killing me. Melting me. Burning me.

Instead, he releases me, stepping away, and backs out into the hallway.

I stare at him, confused.

He clears his throat, runs his hand down the front of his jacket, trying to look as polished and professional as he was before our bodies began to tangle together. "I'll respect your wishes." Phoenix nods. "I won't pry."

"I..." Don't know what to say.

We're all allowed boundaries. Perhaps ours are conflicting.

He needs to know who I am, and I need to remain anonymous.

Or maybe he's changed his mind. Maybe my breath smells weird. Maybe when he saw me up close, he realized I'm nowhere near as perfect as all the other women around here can afford to be.

"You're...a beautiful woman." His hesitation is endearing.

This man doesn't seem to be the type to be at a loss for words. Ever. Perhaps this is just a rare moment for him.

"Goodnight." He nods again, leaving in the direction of the staircase. His shoes clinking against the metal, going down, down, until...nothing.

I gasp, breathing again after having the air sucked out of me, mind racing and reeling. What the hell was that?

I brace myself against the wall for balance.

It's for the best that he left me. Regardless, we could never be truly anonymous.

And this job...I need it to work. I need it to stick.

I'm already going to be spread thin trying to get all my debts paid, even with the six-figure salary. I can't do anything to jeopardize my role at the Lyons Club.

If I want to avoid doing anything else stupid, I think it's time I make my exit.

I hurry down the hallway back to the stairway leading to the main room and down, wade through all the drunken members who are dancing, hollering, touching, laughing, and I don't stop rushing until I'm bathed in moonlight on Lyons Court where the noise of the club is but a distant memory.

I rip off my mask and look down on it.
Phoenix met Swan. He didn't meet Sonia.
Sonia doesn't do things like that.
My night of fantasy is over.
Time to face the crushing reality.

5

EDWIN

Solomon is at my office door. Coffee cups in his hands. My friend smiles as he lowers his head, eyes avoiding mine for a second. "I owed you a thank you for saving my ass last night."

I laugh, swiping my coffee from him. "All I did was pick you up off the bathroom floor and walk you out back to your driver. Nothing to it."

I should have gone with him instead of coming back inside.

Then I wouldn't have found Swan looking at the stairway down to Lyons Club.

I wouldn't have felt powerless to her as I pictured her in The Underground. I wouldn't have cornered her, wouldn't have almost kissed her. And wouldn't have looked like a fool when I walked away from her.

"Yes, well, Seth told me I was screaming because I thought his tie was a snake."

"You know what? That part *is* true, yes."

Solomon winces. "How embarrassing."

"It was only me, Seth, and Rocky who saw it."

Poor Rocky, the bathroom attendant, was doing his best to come up with remedies for Seth's hallucinations.

I frown at my friend. "But you need to learn to never eat a piece of candy at a party attended by Carina Puckett."

"I know, I know. I've learned my lesson." Solomon sighs. "Anyway, what about you? Did you have a good night?"

I shrug. "Fine."

Solomon eyes me. "Just *fine?*"

"Yes. Just fine. Now if you'll excuse me..." I slide past Solomon and exit my office. "I have a meeting to get to."

Big day today.

I'm meeting the new operations manager for the club. I tasked Farley with the hiring process, but I'm prepared to fire them on the spot if he's made a bad choice.

Solomon follows me down the hall. "I heard Seth interrupted you getting close with someone on the dance floor."

"Oh, it was nothing."

"Didn't sound like nothing."

I roll my eyes as we take a sharp right.

The second floor of the Lyons Pride is the VIP area for the nightclub and where we have all our offices. It is also the entry point from the nightclub to the club proper, which can only be accessed by our members.

Farley's office is toward the front of the building.

"I didn't end up going home with anyone if that's what you're wondering."

"I think I need to get you checked out by a doctor, Edwin."

"Oh, shut up."

"Or at least a psychiatrist. You can't let this Nate stuff prevent you from–"

Farley pokes his head out of his office. "Edwin, perfect timing! Sonia just walked in."

So, Farley's gone and hired a woman, huh? Our clientele will like that. Perhaps a little too much...

"Come inside, come inside."

Solomon gives me a cheeky grin. "We'll talk later."

I glare at him. "We will not. *Goodbye.*" I stride into Farley's office and have never been more grateful to see a door slam in someone's face. "Anyway..."

My eyes land on the face of our new operations manager.

And I've never seen a more beautiful woman, ever. I swear on my life.

The first thing I notice is the line of her dark brows and her sharp nose. These features alone could make her intimidating, but her lips are perked in what looks to be a perpetual smile. Delicate and easy.

Farley gestures between us. "Edwin Lyons, meet Sonia Hill. Our new operations manager."

"A pleasure to meet you." I keep my deepest, most professional-sounding voice as I hold my hand out to her, eager to feel her touch.

"You as well, Mr. Lyons."

"Please, call me..." I lose my train of thought when her eyes lock in mine. Gold. Molten gold. A near copy of my Swan.

Then she grabs my hand, sending shocks through my arm. Her touch...familiar too.

"Edwin." My voice cracks. Hasn't done that since my teen years.

Fuck.

"Call me Edwin."

"Alright, then please, call me Sonia."

I have trouble releasing her hand. I'm too stunned to know what to do with myself. I'd be foolish to believe this is the woman I was dancing with last night.

Why would she hide behind that mask and try and blend in with the common folk when she's anything but?

After what feels like too long, but not long enough, I let go and try to give her a winning smile. "Welcome to Lyons Club."

"Thank you. It's amazing. I'm so excited to get started." She smiles at me and then at Farley.

With her hair swept out of her face and tucked into a bun, her ear is on full display to me. And though she's not wearing a pearl earring today, it doesn't matter.

Two gold studs and that hoop at the helix of her ear.

My god. It *is* Swan.

Sonia Hill, the new operations manager of *my* club, is the woman from last night, the one I wanted with my heart and soul.

Without her mask, that feeling has increased tenfold. Which means...I don't know how I'm going to control myself.

From her serene smile, I'm not sure she recognizes me the way I recognize her.

And if she does, she's not letting on.

This is all for the best. We should strike last night from the record and act as if we're meeting for the first time. After all, we will be working way too close together for anything to be possible between us.

Still though...I crave her. My insides boil with want for her. *Need.* "Well, why don't we sit and –"

Farley waves his hand. "Oh no, Sonia and I are already well acquainted, and all her paperwork has been taken care of. All she needs now is a tour of the space and to get acquainted with our owner."

My eyes meet Sonia's. But I can't look for too long. Because I've already *been* acquainted with Sonia. In more ways than one.

And so much of me would like to continue to be *acquainted* with her.

However, that can never happen. I'm her superior and I don't make a habit of sleeping with my employees. Plus, I still can't get a read on if she recognizes me the way I recognize her.

My mouth is hot, wanting to ask, to blurt out the truth. That we know each other.

Beyond just the words we spoke last night and the touches we shared.

I can't explain it, but I *know* Sonia Hill. In my bones. As if somehow our souls recognize one another.

What the fuck? Soulmates don't exist and neither does true love.

Argh. My brain is just trying to make me feel better about being a horndog.

"How about you give Sonia a tour, and you two can get to know each other a bit? When you're done, just drop her off at her office, and then I'll go through the day-to-day with her."

I give Farley a curt nod. "After you, Ms..."

Sonia eyes me.

If I didn't know her before, I'd know her now. That sassy little stare is going to live rent-free in my head for years to come.

"*Sonia*. Or should I start calling you Mr. Lyons again?"

If I engage in witty banter with her, I'll have her bent over my desk before the tour is even over.

No, remain polite, professional.

And no flirting allowed whatsoever.

I nod. "After you, *Sonia.*"

As I hold the door open for our new operations manager, who happens to be the most beautiful woman I have ever laid eyes on, I get a whiff of her as she walks by.

The delicious verve of vanilla sets my blood boiling. Makes her even more scrumptious than before.

"I'll meet you at the top of the stairs." I tip my chin toward the end of the hallway that opens up to the bright light of the chandelier. "I'd like to have a word with Mr. Axford, first."

Sonia nods and floats away.

I have to tear my eyes away from her plump ass as it sways back and forth, back and forth, back and–

"So, first impressions, boss?" Farley crossed his arms over his chest, and a mischievous smile plays on his lips.

It's almost as if he hired Sonia just to fuck with me, to make sure I don't get any work done. To stage some sort of horny coup.

I check to make sure Sonia is out of earshot, then narrow my eyes at him. "If I didn't know you were gay, I'd swear you were thinking with your dick when you hired her."

Farley gapes at me, then laughs. "Oh, come on, Edwin. I don't know if you know this, but it's the twenty-first century. And believe it or not, beautiful women work. In fact, they can be very, very capable in their positions."

"I know that." And yet, my mind flies to all the positions I'd like to have Sonia twisted in. I'm a disgusting man.

"I mean, you wouldn't say Abigail doesn't deserve to be hired just because she's a pretty girl, would you?"

"That's not at all what I was saying..." Of course, an

attractive woman can be capable at her job. I never suggested otherwise. It's just Farley should know better than to hire *a distraction*.

It's not Sonia's fault, of course. It's this institution's. And mine. Because I'm as distractible as they come when I've got a pretty woman to watch instead of my work.

"Are you saying I should rescind the offer? You've barely even spoken to her."

I scoff. "I would never suggest such a thing."

"Then what's this about?"

I slide my hand into my pocket and clench it into a fist. "Forget it."

"Alright. Then don't keep Ms. Hill waiting. She's a more than qualified candidate, and I'm sure many other institutions would snatch her up if given the opportunity." Farley looks at me, then twiddles his fingers in my direction. "Now shoo."

I huff, then slam the door as I leave.

I can do this. I'm Edwin Lyons, after all. This is my club, my place. I am in complete and utter control.

I look down the hallway and take in Sonia's silhouette as she waits for me.

The dress she's chosen frames her curves as if they are a work of art. Though it's simple, sleek, and black, she'd stand out in any room above anyone else.

I just know it.

Goddammit. I'm doomed.

6

─────

SONIA

IF THERE'S ONE THING I'M PROUD OF, IT'S MY POKER face. And I've never needed it more than now.

The second he walked into the room, I recognized him. My Phoenix from last night.

Tall, broad, dark...even better without the mask. Although the real tell was the trim of his beard. The sideburns shaped to perfection, a few gray hairs mixed in the dark ones.

Not to mention, the silver at his temples.

Yep, my Phoenix alright.

That would have been bad enough if he were just any man, but *no*. The man I met last night is none other than Edwin Lyons.

AKA my boss.

But worse than that. My ex-boyfriend's *dad*.

I knew I'd have to meet Nate's father by working here. He's the owner of this place, the whole reason Nate ran away so as not to be looped up in the family business.

However, I didn't expect Nate's father to be *so fucking hot.*

Nate's attractive, but he's a surfer boy, with blonde wavy hair and the friendly smile of a golden retriever. I expected his father to be much older, scragglier, and nowhere near as buff.

Oh, how I wish he was all those things.

The fucked-up feeling is threefold.

For one, the most obvious, he's my ex's father.

If I were a lesser woman, I'd be all over the opportunity to give Nate a big fuck you by fucking his dad. But that's not who I am. I don't need to get entangled with another Lyons, regardless of their value differences.

For another, Edwin is now my boss. It was bad enough last night when I was too worried to fuck him because he might be a club member. Now, it's even worse because he's my superior.

I've been with people I've worked with before. Especially when I first entered the hospitality industry, and I was doing grunt work at the front desk of a luxury hotel.

I made the mistake of fucking around with management once, and that didn't end well, I'll just say that. Too messy to justify doing it again.

So, I will *not* be fucking around where I work. Not now. Not ever again.

The *final* reason that it feels so fucked up to be attracted to Edwin Lyons is what I know about him.

Nate nurses wounds about his father. He didn't give me all the details. And Nate wasn't the most guarded guy. He was all peace and love, vulnerability, and emotions. But when it came to his dad, he was rather mute.

I know those hurts run deep.

I'm not carrying a torch for Nate. I don't need to carry his hurts with me. But I do need to protect myself.

And if Edwin is a cruel man, I don't want to get caught up in it.

All my coherent thoughts fly out the window when Edwin steps out of Farley's office.

Dear god, why does he have to look like that?

He tucks his hand on the inside of his jacket and pulls it across his belly as if that will somehow hide the glorious muscles I can just tell lay beneath his business professional attire.

His eyes meet mine.

"Sorry to keep you waiting, Sonia."

I can't tell yet if he's recognized me or if he's just standoffish.

When he walked into the office, it seemed he wanted to be anywhere but there.

It would be for the best if he didn't recognize me. However, my heart falls at the thought that I'm not memorable enough. Especially after what happened between us last night.

I've known how thoughtless men can be, though. And given Edwin's incredible...everything, I'm sure he's no stranger to women falling at his feet. I mean, he's the dictionary definition of Daddy if I ever...

Stop. Now.

"Let's start with the entryway, shall we?" Edwin says, blowing past me and heading down the stairs.

What follows is the driest tour I've ever been on, and I don't just mean my panties.

Edwin says only what he needs to about each location.

I take mental notes of things I want to ask Farley about further. I don't want to trouble Edwin by wasting his precious time, nor do I want to elongate this "tour". At least for the sake of my horny addled brain.

My heart skids as we step onto the dance floor.

Edwin stops and glances back at me. "I've been wanting to replace the current dance floor with a water feature."

"You'd...get rid of the dance floor?" I ask.

He shakes his head. "No, just...plexiglass, lighting, water. Thoughts?"

I cross toward him, heels clipping across the floor.

The club is so quiet compared to last night. And yet, it feels the same. Like we are the only people in the whole world.

"That sounds like the upkeep would be a pain." I cross my arms over my chest.

Edwin smiles.

Score.

"Are you going to be a thorn in my side, Sonia?"

If that means you keep thinking about me, so be it.

"I guess it's Farley's call, but my two cents is that it's going to be too expensive for not a lot of payoff."

Edwin takes a few steps back from me, sizing me up. His eyes travel down the length of my body, and just like that, I'm naked. Or at least, I wish I was.

"What's your background, Sonia?"

I cock my eyebrow, for some reason not understanding quite what he means. "Sorry?"

Edwin turns on his heel and strides in the direction of the staircase.

I try to keep up without teetering over on these heels. I bought them when I was far younger and didn't mind the pain stilettos brought on.

Now, though, my pinkie toes are undergoing pure torture.

Of course, all of that is secondary to staring at Edwin's tight little ass and wishing I could bite it like a peach.

Christ, Sonia, are you for real right now?!

I can't help it! I'm a recently single gal, and last night, I met a handsome stranger who turned out to be my boss. It's like whiplash.

"People don't just earn a job at Lyons by accident," he calls out over his shoulder.

My heart drops into my stomach.

Oh god. He knows.

Not that I'm the girl from last night. That I'm Nate's ex.

Farley promised he wouldn't tell. But why would he have allegiance to me compared to his employer?

"You must be very accomplished in your line of work," he adds as we enter the hallway.

I breathe a sigh of relief. "Yes, well. I started working in hotels when I was in college and earned a degree in hospitality. So, it was just natural to–"

"You're familiar with our clientele, then?"

"What do you mean by that?"

Edwin bypasses the bathrooms and then stops. Right in front of the dark enclave where he and I almost kissed last night. Where he demanded my name, demanded to see my face.

Now he knows all of it. And I'm not sure he even knows it's me.

"High-end clientele. This isn't just another Comfort Inn."

What the... "I'm sorry if I wasn't clear, Edwin. I've been working at luxury establishments since the very beginning. In fact, I was salaried by the Ritz Carlton up until I came to work for you."

Edwin takes no offense to my tone, thank god. Sometimes I can't control a little bit of a bite.

He looks me in the eye and nods. "Very good. I'm sure

Farley vetted you well, I just need to be completely sure you're a correct fit for my establishment before we move on to the next leg of our tour."

I give a tight nod. "Of course, sir. I understand."

Edwin stops. Adam's apple bobs.

I wonder if he liked it when I called him sir like that.

"I'm sure Farley told you that we are more than just Lyons Pride?"

I nod.

"Good. The Lyons Club isn't an average club."

"He mentioned..." Although he was rather cagey about it.

"And all your paperwork is signed, including the NDAs?"

I nod again.

Edwin's dark eyes size me up.

Mmm, yes, please, thank you.

"If you don't think you can handle what I'm about to show you, then we will have to part ways. Is that understood?"

My heart pounds. "Is this where you keep the bodies?" I ask in a loud whisper, keeping a smile on my face.

"You think I'm joking, do you?" His voice is void of all traces of humor.

I retreat. Not my best move. "Um, no, sorry. Bad joke."

I lift my head high and tuck my hair behind my ear. Of course, my hair is tied back in a bun, so it's just a nervous motion, which must look stupid to Edwin.

I'm about to turn thirty and sometimes I feel like a kid.

"I think you'll find I'm a pretty tough cookie, Edwin. Not much can scare me off."

My heart soars when he cracks a smile. "I like that answer."

Edwin leads me down the stairs. With each step, I get the feeling I'm walking closer to my doom. His hand lands on the door handle, but before he opens it, he gives me one last look. I wait for him to say something, but he remains silent.

And just like that, I know. I can just tell.

He recognized me. He knows that last night he had me pressed up against a wall.

I mean, Edwin Lyons can be any number of things, but he is *not* an idiot. And he might be privileged, but that doesn't make someone ignorant.

"After you, Sonia," he says in a near growl, opening the door for me.

I have to force my feet to move as I pass by him, into this next space.

Somehow, it's even more luxurious than the nightclub. There are groups of leather chairs and couches surrounding the oblong room. It looks as if it's been ripped out of the pages of an interior design magazine. Green, damask wallpaper, burgeoning ferns and monsteras in every nook and cranny. Gorgeous faux skylights give the impression the room has access to the sky. A portion of the wall is made of glass, showing several conference rooms and offices.

What I assume is a member is sitting at a desk right now, talking on the phone.

When he sees Edwin and me, he gives us a nod.

"This is *our* place. The Lyons Club. Open twenty-four seven, with all the amenities our members might need. The place you will be managing."

I smile. "So, the Lyons Pride is what? A front?" I ask.

Edwin nods, a glint in his eye. "Good girl. You catch on fast."

Good girl. Why does that make me hot all over? "So, what is the Lyons Club?"

"Ever since my ancestors established it in the sixteen hundreds, the Lyons Club has been the place to be for the movers and shakers in America. It's an exclusive member's only club, currently with about a hundred members, but with a waiting list where people have been waiting for years."

"So, why not just let them join?"

"If we let everyone in, it loses that exclusive feel, doesn't it?" He smirks for a second, but his face goes right back to serious.

"I guess. So, what does it take to be a member? Besides money, that is."

"Money is not the main aspect, though it does factor in. Membership used to be by birthright alone, but now also includes invitation, and each applicant is thoroughly vetted by a committee. We need to be very particular when we choose our members because billion-dollar business deals are celebrated every day within these walls."

"Wow. I had no idea."

"Which is exactly the point. The club has been here for centuries, but only those in the know are aware of it. We like it that way, and that's how we want to keep things."

"And once you get in, that's it? Does anyone ever get out? Or is this like the mafia?" I jest a bit, but I'm so curious about this new and secret world that Lyons Club seems to be.

His lips twitch again, but he doesn't let the smile form. Damn.

"Once you get in, you never want to leave. Why would you? We cater to your every need. But membership can be revoked under extreme circumstances, though it has been a while since we had to throw anyone out."

I have to keep from chuckling. I wonder what those *extreme circumstances* might be for rich people. "So, you can be expelled like a misbehaved student. Got it. Note to self, don't misbehave."

His eyes shine and his nostrils flare.

What's that about?

"Our members are not kids. They pay a hefty monthly fee which helps maintain the Club, pays the salaries of all our employees, and helps cater for the more... let's call them, unusual requests."

Unusual? I have so many questions...

"But that's not all. The remaining membership fee proceedings go to a charity of the members' choosing. They have a yearly list of twelve to choose from and the most voted for each month is the recipient until every charity on the list has been contemplated. Each year the list varies."

"That's amazing."

"Yes. It's not just about helping ourselves, it's also about making lives easier for those who are less fortunate."

"So, Lyons Pride is..."

"Just another part of the Lyons Club. The only part that is open to the public, though as you might already know, it is a high-end club, so even there we maintain the exclusive clientele vibe."

"How does that work? How do you stop people from entering the club proper? Or are there separate entrances?" I mean, all we did was get inside a door. And it wasn't even locked or anything.

"Our members can roam freely between the Lyons Pride and the members' club through the Pride's VIP area, which only the club members can access. There's also a separate entryway for when they just want to access the club and not the nightclub."

This is mind-boggling. Who knew when I applied that a whole other world would be here?

Edwin takes long steps down the side of the massive room, pointing at each door as we pass. "This is for the pool, sauna, and workout areas, this is for the business center where they can do any sort of printing, copying, faxing–" Edwin measures me up and down with his eyes. "I hope you know how to deal with a paper jam."

"Absolutely," I say, voice cracking.

He continues, circling the room. There are the private offices, the hospitality wing where people can nap, or stay, or, um...handle *personal* affairs, then the media center including a library with an extensive classics collection and a private movie theatre for screenings.

Edwin stops at the final door. "And this...This is The Underground." He looks at me again, mouth parted, his lower lip moist, even more cherry and delicious than usual. "Well, I think I should let it speak for itself."

I look at the door, and my mind flies to a world of possibilities. A VR room where presidents meet to win or lose wars, a teleport room that some rich guy created that can bring people in from all over the world, an indoor heliport that opens James Bond style, a series of hidden tunnels that lets these people go all over town in secret.

It is just a door, nothing special or different about it, but it can be hiding anything.

And with how he is acting, I'm dying to know what.

He opens the door for me, and I step through, feeling like Alice moving through the looking glass, afraid and yet tantalized to know what exists on the other side.

My jaw drops. I wasn't even close.

I couldn't have guessed what secrets lay beyond this door in my wildest dreams.

Well. Maybe my wildest.

I have stepped inside what can only be described as BDSM heaven. A wonderland.

In the center of the room is a platform with several poles. The ceiling is made up of bars and from some of the bars hang chains and cuffs. Leather couches line the central platform as do several other doors that I'm sure are smaller versions of what I see here. More private enclosures for whatever devious delights members of the Lyons Club might like to get up to.

Edwin walks past me into the room. "It's very tame right now. We don't have too many members indulging here in the morning."

As I look around, he steps up onto the stage and holds his hands out, spinning around.

"Welcome to The Underground."

A dungeon. A frickin' BDSM dungeon! "The Underground...that's a good name for it." It *is* a good name. And... it conjures up all sorts of deep, dark desires.

"So, how does it work?"

Edwin leans up against one of the poles and looks down at me. "At any given point there are Doms and subs available for the unattached members. However, we also have members who simply like to play and experiment with each other." He stares me down. Hard.

And just like that my panties are ready to be trashed. Soaked to the point of dripping.

"We sometimes have performances down here. Last night, we had a burlesque troupe. Later this week, we're having a shibari rope performance. Sometimes we hire the performers, sometimes the members do public scenes."

Jeez, I guess I'm going to have to brush up on my understanding of what I'm getting into ASAP.

"Above all, it's imperative that we keep The Underground running smoothly. It requires a separate cleaning crew. They are always available on-site and make sure everything is fully sanitized and that any used disposable toys are replaced with new ones after every room or area has been vacated.

I shudder to think of the lengths the cleaners have to go to or what equipment they have to use to clean up The Underground.

His voice is deep when it reaches me. "Take a look around, if you like."

"Thanks, I will…"

I walk slowly through the room, taking it all in.

And Edwin…he takes *me* in. Watches every step I take.

I don't mind one bit.

I stop at one of the rooms. It has…windows. The blinds are drawn right now.

I put my hand on the door, needing to know *why*.

"All the rooms are different." His heat scorches my back as his breath almost caresses my neck.

I stop.

He's gotten closer. I hadn't even noticed.

"Some of them are for private play. Others are to fulfill certain desires. Like the room you're standing in front of. That's our voyeur room."

I brace myself and push the door open.

It looks rather normal-looking. In the corner, there is a chair, I'm imagining where someone can sit and watch.

"The windows probably told you that."

The windows told me nothing. My overstimulation has taken away my capacity for thinking.

"Some people use it to have an audience, others for cuckolding..." Edwin is drawing closer to me.

I'm too afraid to move. Something about his voice is so delicious that it's grounded me to the floor.

I want to know what it feels like to have that voice in my ear as his hands play with my breasts, and he fucks me however he pleases.

It's like my hands are tied to the bedposts. God, how I'd love that fantasy to play out. I want to be a good girl for him so badly.

"My favorite feature, though, is on the inside." He leans up against the doorframe.

"Oh?"

Edwin tips his head forward. "Go on."

I obey without thought, my muscles trembling. I'm afraid my legs might give out.

Edwin closes the door behind me, and for a split second, I'm afraid he might lock me in here, keep me as his little plaything.

Don't be ridiculous, Sonia. For one, people know you're here. For another, who would want to do that with you?

Edwin Lyons might be the answer to that question.

"Do you see that little knob at the center of the door?"

My eyes flick to a metal knob about eye level with me in the door. It's attached to an inlaid square cutout.

His voice commands me. "Open it."

The knob is cool metal, but the sensation is almost burning.

Shit.

I push up on the knob and find myself looking through a window right at Edwin. I gasp. "What the..."

"People who like exhibitionism love this room. They

can invite people to watch, heightening their pleasure by knowing others are enjoying the show."

"That's...great?" My breath fogs up the tiny window.

Edwin purses his lips, maybe he is trying to abstain from chuckling.

We stare at each other for far too long.

I can only imagine him popping by to watch me. Except I wouldn't want him to see me with another man. I'd only want it to be him pleasing me.

But touching myself...enjoying myself. Yeah...I think I'd like that.

"Well, that's nice." I slam the shudder shut and reach for the door handle, but the door flies open before I can. I jerk back in surprise, falling back against the wall.

Edwin corners me placing his hands on either side of my head. He's so tall, he looms over me. But his body isn't pressing against mine as I'd like. His distance is taunting me.

It takes all my concentration to draw my eyes up to his and, when I do, I don't think I could ever look away.

Edwin licks his lower lip. "Do you recognize me, Swan?"

I don't know whether to sigh in relief or shrink in fear at the confirmation that he remembers me. "I do."

His eyes flick across my face. "Good."

My chest heaves with breath.

Kiss me, please kiss me.

His smell is intoxicating. Rich oak and tobacco. Like a *man.*

Dear god, I don't feel like I've ever been with a man.

Guess I shouldn't start. Not with Edwin. My ex-boyfriend's dad, my boss, all that.

Edwin drops his hands and straightens back up. He

runs one hand through his hair—oh, how I wish that were my hand—before heading out of the room, not bothering to check if I'm following.

"Go ahead and get acquainted with the place. I've got to get back to work." He stops and looks back at me once more, staggering intensity in his eyes. "Looking forward to working with you, Sonia."

I remain glued to the wall long after Edwin abandons me in The Underground.

7

EDWIN

Having to work every day in the presence of Sonia Hill has been difficult. To say the least.

It doesn't matter where she is in the building. I can feel her presence. Of course, we've been in meetings together and crossed paths throughout the day.

However, it doesn't matter. My body has some sort of radar for her. I can feel when she gets closer and when she goes away.

It's impossible to get any work done knowing she's near.

Thank god, today is Friday. I don't have to work on the weekends, even if I often choose to.

However, Sonia's presence at the club might be as good a reason as any to take the weekend off.

Or...go in and see how she's doing with the place.

That's a problem for future Edwin to deal with. This evening, though, is special.

Jack and Abigail are coming over for our monthly "family" dinner. Although I'm not sure "family" encapsulates the fucked-up dynamic between a father and his two love children from different mothers.

No matter, though. I need the reminder that Sonia is completely off-limits. She could be one of my children.

I took a peek at her file when Farley was out of his office. Twenty-nine years old. Same age as Nate. That was humbling to learn.

But just as much as it was humbling, it was also stirring.

I know I look mature, but I look good for my age. I don't think I've read any of her body language wrong.

She's just as stirred by me as I am by her.

That just adds to my growing attraction to her.

Anyway, I can only hope dinner with my kids tonight gets my mind far, far, far away from Sonia.

Because Abigail told me she was able to convince Nate to come over.

I've tried to call him a couple of times this week to no avail. So, to be afforded a meeting with him in person is the biggest win I could get.

"Dad?" Jack's voice cries out from the front hall.

"In the kitchen." I dump out my final cup of coffee for the night. It's not my best habit, but caffeine barely impacts me anymore. I'm just maintaining my addiction at this point.

Jack waltzes in, although I'm not sure if Jack ever waltzes. The only way people know we're related is our same serious disposition. He's a carbon copy of his mother from his tan skin to his thick dark waves of hair.

I met Mari just a year after Nate was born. Clarissa and I weren't together. Didn't even try to maintain a romantic relationship, so I was still a freewheeling twenty-something. I was vacationing in Hawaii, and she was a local girl. After a two-week whirlwind, I brought her back to New York.

I should have known that it would be doomed from the beginning, but at the time, I was still a romantic.

We moved in together, got pregnant, had Jack, and then...

I went off the deep end.

It wasn't fair to Mari, and I've apologized since.

At the time, my father was grooming me to take on the Lyons Club. I was working all the time, feeling overwhelmed, so I needed an escape valve, not crying kids.

God, I was such a selfish asshole.

I regret it now. I do. But what's done is done.

Mari remarried when Jack was twelve and popped out three more kids in succession. That was my boon because Jack didn't want anything to do with the newborns and spent lots more time here with me.

I eye my son's button-down and prim slacks. "Looks like you just walked off Wall Street."

Jack rolls his eyes. "Your dad jokes aren't even jokes."

"Oh, come on, you love it." I grin. "Beer?"

Jack sits at the counter with a heavy sigh. "Please."

Jack works every day at the New York Stock Exchange.

I know it's eating him from the inside out, how much work it is. I'm just glad he makes time for me, though, even when I haven't been the best dad I can be.

I open a bottle of beer and slide it down the counter to my son before opening one for myself. "Was thinking pizza tonight."

Jack sighs. "Fine."

"Oh, come on, you love pizza."

"Yeah, but I'm watching my macros. Trying to bulk up." He holds his arm up to his side, flexing his well-developed biceps. "Pizza and beer? Recipe for disaster."

I smile at my son.

Another thing he inherited from his mother is her inability to gain weight no matter what she ate. He's tall and gangly, and I know he's always felt like he has to measure up to Nate's physique. "Girls like skinny guys, Jack."

"I'm not just doing it for *girls*, Dad." He swigs his beer. "I'm doing it for me."

Sure, kid, keep telling yourself that. "One night of pizza and beer won't kill you."

The front door opens, and my heart tries to fly out of my chest. "Unless there's something you haven't told me about your cholesterol," I add as I head out to the front hall to greet Abigail and Nate.

"It's *your* cholesterol I should be worried about, old man!"

I laugh.

When I enter the front hall, I have the wind knocked out of me by my daughter rushing into my arms and giving me a bear hug. "Hi, Daddy!"

"Hi, sugar." I kiss the side of Abigail's head, her auburn hair tickling my lips.

Abigail is the one I tried to do right by, at least compared to Nate and Jack.

Didn't make it out of my twenties before I knocked up another woman. But this was my forever girl, Grainne.

Irish girl, hold the Catholic. Didn't believe in marriage or settling down.

When she came to me with the positive pregnancy test, I was desperate to marry her.

Grainne wouldn't budge. She was committed to her wildness.

And I loved that about her.

I stayed longer than I had with Clarissa or Mari. Abigail was seven by the time we split up.

I just didn't feel like we even had anything to give each other.

In hindsight, her denial of marriage hurt more than I knew how to express.

I thought I had everything together. Was running Lyons Club all on my own by the time Abigail was born. Other than the fact we did things out of order, Grainne should have wanted me to marry her.

And she didn't.

That made it way too easy for me to walk away.

When I put Abigail down, I take a step forward only to find the front hall is empty, aside from us. "Where's..."

Abigail grabs my arm.

Fuck.

"He changed his mind, Daddy. I'm sorry."

My jaw ticks. I can count on one hand the number of times I've cried as an adult man, but Nate is close to bringing me to my breaking point.

"He knows I want to make amends, right?"

"I've told him, Daddy." Abigail shrugs. "He'll come to you when he's ready." She heads into the kitchen where she greets Jack.

I stare into the empty hall. My whole body sags.

I wish I could crawl into a hole and never come out again.

Everyone just pushes me away. I've believed for so long that I deserve it. But isn't it possible for people to change?

Can't I show myself to be worthy of love again?

Jack pokes his head out of the kitchen. "Dad, I'm hungry, can we order?"

I clap my hands together.

Though my kids are adults, I still have to put on a happy face for them. I'm their dad. Dads are strong.

And I know the more I throw myself into giving them attention, the more Nate will drift into the background.

He'll never fade away, though.

Just like Sonia, I can feel Nate's presence. He's in New York. And I just wish he'd make himself known to me. Give me one chance to prove to him that I'm ready to be the dad I should have always been and hear him out.

"Okay! Who wants anchovies?!"

My children's collective groan is music to my ears.

8

—————

SONIA

I RUN MY FINGERS ALONG THE FERN'S LEAF, ADMIRING its vivid green color as it drinks up all the water from my watering can.

It's a pleasant Thursday afternoon in the club. That's when traffic starts to pick up for the weekend.

Monday through Wednesday, things tend to be quiet. But as the Lyons Pride comes to life up above for Thirsty Thursday, so does Lyons Club. And with it, The Underground.

At least, that's what I've picked up from my first three weeks at the club.

While my job involves a lot of heavy lifting when it comes to making sure all the wings of the club are working as they should, I quite enjoy it. It keeps me busy.

My only catch is that I don't get to see Edwin that often. Or almost at all. And I hate myself for being disappointed about it.

Whenever I *do* see him, he's engaged in serious talks with members or off to enjoy a swim.

His jaw is set so tight at all times, his obsidian gaze so

hardened that I find it impossible to ever interrupt to even say hello.

The only time we ever really interact is our twice-weekly staff meetings in the nightclub where everyone gets together for upcoming events, problems we're having, or new employees.

I keep my eyes off him as much as possible, but it's hard not to stare when I know how he made me feel without even kissing me.

And I swear sometimes I can feel his eyes on me.

Might be just wishful thinking, though.

Once the fern has drunk all the water up, I head back toward my office; one of the glass-windowed offices is all mine, placed just right so I can always keep an eye on things.

However, a sob has me turning to find Hazel, one of our littles, stumbling through The Underground door. Tears are running down her face, adding to the innocence of her lace baby doll negligée, knee-high socks, and pigtails.

"Hazel, what's wrong?" I close the space between us. I don't know her headspace right now, and if she is in little space, she needs an adult to help her deal with her feelings.

"He-he-he's drunk."

My stomach drops.

"Who is, honey?"

"Master Ollie."

Shit. This has been a recent yet recurring problem with one of the club's longstanding members, Oliver Worthington.

Just his name gives me the heebie jeebies.

"Are you okay? Did he hurt you?"

From what I understand, Oliver's wife left him last year for a much younger man and sucked him dry during the divorce. To cope, he's turned to drinking and lots of visits to The Underground.

However, drinking and scening don't mix. Ever.

The maximum allowed to be able to scene at The Underground is one drink. Anyone who surpasses that limit is not allowed to play for at least six hours.

Hazel's hands twist as she starts nodding but then shakes her head.

I don't know how the subs do it. I mean...I'm curious as to how they know their limits. All the sex I've had has been fairly vanilla, even with Nate.

"Where's Ruby?" My eyes fly to the Dungeon Master's post, visible through the open door, but she is nowhere to be found.

She should have stopped Oliver from scening.

"I don't know." Hazel is shaking in my arms as I do what I can to calm her down.

I try not to let my frustration show.

All the Doms have to take turns as Dungeon Masters or Mistresses. It is both a safety measure for them and a way to make sure everyone is having a good time and no one is abusing their power, which I learned goes for both Doms and subs.

Huh! Who knew subs had power too? I sure didn't.

If Ruby has stepped away from her post and left the dungeon unattended, she's broken the rules, and she won't like the consequences.

Some of the members here are watching us and whispering. I give a polite, assured smile to the room. "Come, let's get you—"

She stomps her foot. "He should be in time out. He was mean to me and made me cry. And then he wouldn't stop." She starts sobbing again.

I hold her closer. This is not good.

"He doesn't want a little, he wants a doll to do whatever he pleases with. A toy. And I'm not a toy."

"I'm so sorry. It's going to be okay, honey."

"Why was he mean?" Her teary eyes turn to me. "I wanna go home. Please."

She's trembling in my arms.

"What happened in there, honey?"

She looks away from me. "I... He... I said broccoli. I said *broccoli*. But he just..." Sobs wrack her, and any words she might be saying are drowned by the anguish in her tears.

Broccoli is her safe word. It should have stopped everything immediately. If the Dom didn't respect the safe word, it was the Dungeon Master's job to step in.

Damnit, Ruby? Where are you?

"I'm so sorry. That shouldn't have happened." I hold her close to me, knowing she needs the reassurance and the touch. "You can go home, okay?"

Hazel nods. "Thank you."

I send her off to the staff quarters with one of our other subs, then look to The Underground door that's hanging open, taunting me with what I have to face now.

I lean my mouth down to my collar com and press the button to talk. "Security to The Underground, please."

As I head inside, my earpiece blares with the voice of our head security agent, Lourdes. "On our way."

The Underground is too quiet, with only the sound of rattling metal chains wafting back and forth.

"Ruby?" I call out.

Nothing.

"Oliver?"

Again, nothing.

I take out my tablet to access the room reservations. I scan the list and find Oliver's name. Room five.

I turn to the rooms.

All doors before me are closed, and the place is empty since it is still early.

You're the boss around here, Sonia. No need to be scared.

I walk with as much purpose as I can to room five with my anxiety at a level ten. However, when I open the door, Oliver's nowhere to be seen.

What the hell? If he changed rooms, that's another rule broken.

Footsteps sound from behind me, and I breathe a sigh of relief. "Lourdes, thank god you're –"

It's not security. It's Oliver. Completely clothed, thank god. And he's smiling at me in a way I can only describe as grotesque, his whole body moving as if he's standing on the deck of a boat in stormy seas.

"Looking for me, Sonia?"

My eyes fall to his hand. A flogger hangs between his fingers, a waterfall of leathery strips.

I look at his glossy eyes. "Where did you come from?"

"Around."

He might be a creep, but I feel sorry for him. He probably doesn't even know where he was a minute ago.

I straighten up. I just need to keep my cool until security arrives. Won't be long, surely. "We need to talk about what happened with Hazel."

Oliver's smile twists into a grimace. "She wouldn't obey me. I'm the master, not her. Brat."

"You know the rules. No one can be down here if they had more than one drink." I glance at the flogger. "Besides, I know that Hazel has everything other than hand and paddle as hard limits."

He rolls his eyes. "I can show you what happened." Oliver goes to one of the other doors, not the room assigned to him, and opens it. He waves me closer. "Come on."

I swallow. The last time I was in one of these rooms, I was just as terrified.

Except I was with Edwin, and I knew he wasn't going to hurt me. I was in a place of want, not true fear. Oliver Worthington, though, is a loose cannon.

Security will be here soon.

I take a few steps forward.

"Look." He gestures into the room.

I peek inside but see nothing out of the ordinary. Well, not for this kind of room.

In this case, the examination room, for fantasies of any sort of doctor roleplay you can imagine. Some scrubs hanging on the wall and restraints dangle from the table in the middle.

"I just needed to perform her check-up," Oliver says. His breath on my neck is so potent the odor curls into my nose. Whisky. Cheap. "I didn't do anything wrong, Sonia..."

His hand lands against my ass, sliding down the curve.

I gasp and try to draw away, but he corners me up against the door frame. I struggle as he presses his crotch to mine. "Oliver, let me–"

"I just want what I'm entitled to, Sonia." He looks so innocent for someone in the middle of an assault. "If not Hazel, you'll do just fine."

His mouth descends to mine, and I jerk my head away, a narrow miss as his lips land against my cheek instead.

This is so wrong. Not what BDSM is for. Not what The Underground is for.

And certainly not what *I'm* for. "Oliver, stop it!"

As his mouth is descending over mine again, Oliver is

ripped from over me and is no longer there, cold air bathing my face, and I stumble away and try to catch my breath.

Security's timing couldn't have been better. "Thank god you're here."

"What the hell is wrong with you, Worthington?!"

I look up in shock when the voice talking is not from one of Lourdes' security team.

Edwin.

He has Oliver pinned up against the wall by his shoulders. His strength is uncompromising and the look in his eye is downright murderous.

"Edwin, you're hurting me!" The other man struggles.

"That's the least you deserve." Edwin shoves Oliver hard against the wall again. "Do you not know the meaning of *stop*?"

"I can't breathe–" Oliver is panting. The flogger falls from his hand to the ground.

Thank god, Lourdes and one of her team members arrive.

Lourdes yanks Edwin off of Oliver. She's probably the only person in the world capable of doing that and making it look effortless. "Jesus, Edwin, you want a lawsuit?"

"He was about to hurt Sonia." He glares at Oliver. If looks could kill, the man would be lying on the floor in a pile of dust already.

"I wasn't going to *hurt* her." Oliver's voice is so pathetic it almost breaks my heart. *Almost.*

I'm not ever going to forget what he did. I'll have nightmares about what he might have done if Edwin hadn't come when he did.

"We'll take care of *him*," Lourdes says and then nods in my direction. "Check on her, eh? She looks like she can barely stand up."

I hadn't even noticed how weak my body had gotten as I stood here. The absolute shock of it all is just starting to hit me. "I think I need to...need to–"

Edwin rushes to my side and slides one hand onto my lower back, grabbing my other hand for support. "*Careful.*"

His touch makes me stronger. I don't know how to explain it. But it just *does*. Infuses me with comfort and steadiness.

All the same, I allow him to guide me to one of the sofas surrounding the center stage. I glance over at Lourdes who is pushing Oliver out of The Underground.

My boss helps me sit down. "Don't look at him."

I snap my attention back to Edwin.

He gets to his knees before me. "Just look at me."

Now that I'm looking at him, it would be impossible to look away.

"It's all okay now, alright?" He holds his hands out to me.

Is Edwin asking me to touch him when we know what kind of fire that can ignite?

However, I'd be denying myself so much if I refused. I need his steadiness. Something to hold onto. What better than his hands...

As soon as I set my palms in his, my heart starts to race once again. But this time, it's because of the warmth-in-your-chest feeling that overwhelms me.

He looks me over. "Are you hurt?"

I shake my head. "No."

"What...what happened?"

I hesitate.

"You don't have to tell me yet if you–"

"No, no, it's..." I keep my eyes glued to our hands. If I look up at the beautiful edges of his face, I might lose all ability to speak. "Hazel was sobbing after leaving a scene with Oliver–"

Edwin's grip tightens. "What did he do?"

"He wouldn't yield to the safe word."

"*Bastard.*"

"I let Hazel go home and went to find Oliver, but he– he–"

Edwin scans The Underground. "Why the hell didn't Ruby do something?"

I shake my head. "Don't know where she is."

"That's unacceptable."

I nod.

We are both quiet. From outside The Underground, an argument is escalating.

"Is he going to be expelled from the club?"

"We'll have a trial with the disciplinary council, but... this is serious. He can't be harassing or hurting anyone here."

"Of course." I wouldn't want anyone who works under me to be in jeopardy because this man can't get his act together. And yet, I still feel bad for him.

Edwin's eyes soften as he looks into mine. "We'll get him help, though. He needs serious rehabilitation for that drinking."

I remain silent. This is all too much for a Thursday afternoon.

"You should go home."

"I'm fine."

"No, that's an order, Sonia."

Heat rushes over me.

I don't mind Edwin ordering me around. I'd just rather it be in different circumstances.

"I never want you to feel like you have to put yourself in danger for the sake of money. Do you understand?"

I pull my eyes up to Edwin's, willing them to stay there for at least a few moments. "That's my job."

"I know it is. And you're too damn good at it for your own good."

Bashful, I laugh, turning away.

Edwin reaches up, fingers catching a piece of hair that's tumbled out of my slicked-back bun in all the chaos. "I mean it. I know it's only been a few weeks, but I..." He shakes his head and tucks my hair behind my ear. "We can't afford to lose you."

Was that what he was going to say? *I can't afford to lose you?*

Quit your daydreaming, Sonia. It's never going to happen. Can never happen.

Edwin places his hands on his knees to push to standing. He lets out a heavy breath, and for some reason, thinking about how he is older than me makes my stomach flip. In a fantastic way.

He stands before me for a second. "I'm going to go deal with this. Alright? I'll let everyone know you're gone for the day. And take tomorrow off too. Reset."

I can't manage to reply because if I tried, I'd probably just beg him to stay. My body seems to go limp as his footsteps get farther and farther away.

I try so hard, but I can't keep it in anymore. "You're good at that."

Why did you have to say that out loud?

"At what?"

I look up, thinking I could just slap myself, but I have to answer him anyway. "Comforting. You made me feel a lot better."

Edwin smiles. Not one full of mischief or knowingness I can't comprehend. A real smile. "Thank you."

The moment aches and aches. If only one of us would give up on being good at our jobs.

He clears his throat. Smile disappears. "I just couldn't help but imagine my daughter in your shoes, and..."

Is he fucking serious? Comparing me to his daughter?

He turns and starts walking away again. "Go home. Get some rest," he orders before he disappears out the door.

I lean back on the sofa and sink until I'm lying down with just my head upright. "What the fuck was that?" I'm more confused than I've ever been.

Not only was I in a situation I couldn't control with one of our members, but Edwin Lyons defended me. Made me feel safe. Held my hands and touched my hair.

Then basically put me on the same level as his daughter.

This is so fucked.

I need to get the hell over all of this, starting now.

But the feelings in my chest don't go away.

Okay. Now. I'm starting n*ow.*

Dammit. It's not going to be that easy, is it?

9

———

EDWIN

A MONTH OF SONIA. AND I'VE SOMEHOW MANAGED TO keep myself from going feral on her. I would say that's an accomplishment considering how my blood simmers any time she's near.

That's why I stay away, for the most part.

However, since the incident with Oliver Worthington, I have been on high alert. I'll be damned if anyone is going to fuck with Sonia.

She's the best manager we've ever had.

And also, she's *mine*.

I know I can't have her, but she makes all my instincts flare. I can't look at her without the word "mine" blaring at me.

That knowing feeling that we belong to each other is so rooted inside me that I have a hard time fighting it twenty-four-seven.

Even if I much prefer to spend my Saturdays out of the fray, I have to come in today because it was the only available time I had to meet a prospective new member who might fill Oliver Worthington's spot.

We've already gone through the vetting and interviewing with him; he seems to be a perfect candidate. Now, he just has to come in and tour the facilities, and according to tradition, that's up to me. And since I grew up breathing this place, who better to do the honors than the owner himself?

I find Marty Villanueva in front of the member's-only entrance.

He is squinting his eyes at the door, trying to figure it out.

I hold back a laugh. "Villanueva!"

"Ah! Lyons!"

We shake hands.

His smile is open and honest. "Thanks for meeting me today."

"Of course. I see you're trying to figure out our door, huh?" I ask.

Villanueva laughs. "I am. No handle, no lock–"

"No *obvious* lock." I wave my smartwatch over a hidden indent on the wall. After a clicking sound, the door slides open. "Every member gets access via their phone or smartwatch."

"That's very James Bond of you!" Villanueva laughs.

"Indeed." I chuckle. "Come on in, let me show you around."

Marty and I enter the club, chatting away.

He's an affable guy, been on the waitlist for membership for about five years.

Since he first signed up, he's gained about thirty pounds and expanded his manufacturing business across the Atlantic Ocean. Impressive stuff, making him a great candidate for the Lyons Club.

I can tell he's impressed from the way he appraises each of the facilities, smile growing larger and larger.

We get to the wine cellar, and his eyes light up. "My wife will like this."

"Do you have any children? They'll be grandfathered in once they're of age."

"Well, the twins are three right now, so–"

"Ah! You've got some time, then."

Marty grins. "Do you have children?"

"Three. Two boys and a girl. Grown."

My heart swells.

I didn't always get this feeling when talking about my kids. Honestly, there was a time when they were a distraction to me. I regret ever feeling that way and I'd never, ever admit it. What kind of father thinks that about their children?

"Grown? You don't look a day over forty!" Marty slaps me on the back.

It's unusual for men in my position to have children as young as I did. Most of them wait until they're in their forties, marry a twenty-something, and call it a day. I've never been one to follow trends, though. "Add another ten, and you're right on the money."

"What?! No."

"The gray didn't give it away?" I brush my fingers through my sideburns.

"Makes you look sophisticated, not old."

We continue our small talk through the rest of the tour, though the conversation about our children has me feeling bruised.

Any time my mind crosses Nate for just a moment, even if he's not brought up by name, creates a fog around me that I can't see past.

Still no word from my son.

Jack and Abigail are trying their best. So are Mason and Seth. Haven't managed to get through to him, though.

I'd love to speak to him before three years turns into four.

"Well, I've got to hand it to you, Lyons. This place is fucking incredible."

Fuck yes. I know this place is incredible, but it never loses its luster hearing other people think it's amazing too. "Can I welcome you to the club yet?"

"Let's not get ahead of ourselves, Lyons." Villanueva holds up his hands. "I want to get a handle on how your staff feels about this place."

I raise an eyebrow. "Sorry?"

"Look, the facilities are all well and good, but...I'm not going to be participating in a club that takes advantage of the little people. You understand?"

It takes a bit of effort, but I keep up my friendly, understanding smile.

On the one hand, I take offense that he'd think I might do that. That's not what Lyons Club is about. At all.

But on the other hand, I wouldn't want him anywhere near us if the coin were flipped.

"Of course. Well..." I glance around. "Let me give you audience with our sommelier since you mentioned your wife loves wine. And–" Sonia pops into my head.

Oh, yeah. She'll do just fine.

"I'll get our operations manager for you. She manages the day-to-day, and she'll be able to give it to you straight about how it is behind the scenes here."

"Fantastic, that works for me."

"Excellent." I look over to the wall of windows.

Sonia isn't at her desk. She could be anywhere.

Fuck.

I wave our sommelier over.

He has just delivered a round of wine to a group of members hosting an impromptu chess tournament, so he should be free for a couple of minutes. He wafts over to us.

I introduce the two of them and he engages Villanueva in a conversation about a specific provincial Italian grape.

I don't have time for this. I need to find Sonia and clinch the deal.

Touching the sommelier's arm, I keep glancing around, hoping to spot my operations manager. "Have you seen Sonia, by the way?"

He squints, thinking way too hard about this question. "I think she was working on a complaint about the sauna."

"Great, thanks." I leave them to their dry wine talk—no pun intended—and head through the door to the exercise wing.

Chlorine hits my nose as I walk down the long hall to the open dome of the pool where some members are doing laps and others are enjoying the hot tub.

However, my eyes gravitate toward the sauna door that is halfway propped open.

I stride over and poke my head in.

The sauna is not even close to as hot as it should be.

But Sonia is inside, bent over the stones, no doubt examining why they're not heating as they should.

I swallow. I know I should make my presence known, but the way she's bent over, moving back and forth, ass rocking side to side. God, I can't stop watching. It's hypnotic.

She stands up, resting her hands on her hips with a heavy sigh. "Stupid fucking thing…"

Okay, Edwin, stop your daydreaming. "Ehem."

Sonia whips around. "What?"

Her body jolts.

My eyes flick to the floor where her heel has gotten stuck between the wood-paneled floor.

Sonia throws her hands in the air and starts to tumble forward.

And I'm *right* in the way.

I try to brace myself for impact and make to grab onto the doorframe, but my hand misses, and I fall backward onto the tile floor of the pool deck.

Thank god, I manage to keep my head from hitting the ground, but my back screams out in pain.

"Oh, my god!" Sonia cries out from on top of me. "Are you okay, are you–"

I groan. "I'm alive if that's what you're asking."

"Did you–" She runs her fingers through my hair to the back of my head. "Did you hit your–"

"No, not my head."

But my fucking back.

Although... maybe I should just lie and say that my head is aching so she keeps touching me. Her fingernails against my scalp are divine.

Sonia drops her forehead to my chest. "Thank god, oh my god. Why'd you sneak up on me like that?"

I'm gritting my teeth. Holding on to my control tooth and nail. "It was an accident."

I'm trying my best not to get hard, but that's impossible given the proximity of our pelvises. I've dreamed of feeling her this way, pressed up to my front.

I just imagined it would be in private, both of us naked. I guess this will do.

She lifts her head and looks into my eyes, her cheeks bright red. "Um...can I help you with something?"

I know I have a big cock, but it's not hard enough to be noticeable yet, is it?

She cocks her head when I remain silent. "You were looking for me?"

I shut my eyes for a second. Refocus.

If only we could be having this conversation when she's not laying on top of me.

What am I supposed to do with my hands when all I can think about is having them sliding down her back to grip the perfect mounds of her ass? I settle for clenching them into fists. "Yes, I have a potential member who I want you to meet."

"Me?"

"Yes, you."

Sonia's lips twist into a smile. As if she's been told she's special. Which she is, beyond a shadow of a doubt.

"Uh, so, what's wrong with the sauna?"

"It's not hot."

I'm a fucking idiot.

She looks back at the rocks, then back at me. "I need to call a repairman."

"Makes sense."

A male throat clears somewhere nearby. "Everything alright here?"

I jolt upward, shoving Sonia off of me, when I recognize Farley's voice. "Yep, just...fell."

Wow, good save, idiot.

He's standing at the edge of the pool, hands tucked behind his back. "Need some help getting up?" There's a tone in his voice I don't like. Not one bit. It's...*suggestive.*

Sonia scrambles to her feet. "Here, let me help." She holds out a hand for me to grab.

I look from her hand to the hem of her skirt, which is at my eye level, and then up to her golden eyes.

"Thanks." I accept her hand, though I don't let her do any of the work, pushing myself to stand. I brush off the front of my slacks with a disgruntled sigh.

Farley grins, his eyes shining as if he is holding his laughter in. "I was sent to find you by a man named...Marty Villanueva?"

"Yeah, yeah. Sonia, you go with Farley, I'll make the call to the repairman."

Sonia nods, a placid smile on her lips I'd like to make disappear under mine. She goes with Farley, and the two of them leave the pool deck and disappear.

I stand there for far too long with my brow furrowed and hands in my pocket until someone kicks a little too hard during their freestyle stroke and splashes me with pool water, snapping me out of my funk.

Sooner or later, something has to break between Sonia and me, right? We either have to learn to hate each other or give into our instincts or...

My anger flares, thinking about her being taken by another man. It's not fair of me. But I can't help it.

She's young and beautiful. She should date someone Nate's age. Not me.

However, no amount of logic can contain my want.

After calling the sauna repairman, I retreat to my office and rub out this hard-on she's given me.

Releasing into my hand, though, is pathetic compared to the real thing.

10

SONIA

"I know it's small…"

Bridget looks around my tiny studio apartment and smiles. It's a real smile, not a fake one of politeness.

Still, though, I can't help being embarrassed inviting a woman who comes from so much money into my humble little apartment that is probably half the size of her closet.

"It's cute. I like it."

Cute, no doubt, is code for small.

"I'd say sit anywhere you'd like, but there's only one possible choice," and it's the couch against the wall that faces the rest of the apartment so I can look over my *domain.*

Smoothing out her skirt, Bridget sits on the couch with grace and care that don't lend themselves to the Facebook marketplace sofa. "And it's in Queens. I never make it out to Queens."

"Thanks for making the trek up here, I would have happily come to you if–"

"*Please*, Sonia, you work way harder than me. It's the least I can do."

I roll my eyes. "I don't work harder. It's just different. I can't imagine doing what you do."

"That reminds me, after you crack open the wine, I have some new sketches to show you." Bridget grins, pulling her portfolio out of her bag.

Since meeting at the Lyons masquerade, Bridget and I have become fast friends. I kept her at a distance at first, not wanting to mix business with pleasure further than I had already, but she made it clear that she wanted to be my friend, and if I'm being honest, I can use all the friends I can get in New York.

Other than the club, I don't have a network. And given how much I work right now, I don't have the time to join any extracurricular activities. So, I'm grateful for Bridget's persistence in our budding friendship.

"Oooh, what are you working on?" I grin as I take the two steps that take me into the kitchen and crack open the wine.

"Well, I've been really inspired by that new exhibit at the Met. You know, the Vivienne Westwood retrospective. And I want to do something inspired by that but with lingerie."

I pretend to gasp. "Scandal!"

"I know, who would have thought?!"

Certainly not me. When Bridget told me she was a designer working on starting her own line, I would never have guessed that her focus is in lingerie.

I pour the wine, relishing the sound of it glugging into the glasses. "Well, I can't wait to see."

Bridget looks out the window at the street below. "How long does it take you to get to Lyons?"

"A while. Do you want ice?"

She looks at me as if I've just told her I murdered her cat. "*Ice?!*"

"Uh, yeah?" What is so weird about that?

"It's already chilled."

I shrug and grab the ice tray from the freezer. "Yeah, but it could be chillier."

"Sonia, you don't put ice in *wine.*"

"Says who?" I scoff.

Bridget gapes. "Everyone?!"

"Okay. Well, I'm putting ice in my wine." Who gives a fuck about decorum, especially in my own home?

I head over to the couch.

Bridget watches the two cubes bob in my glass, close to throwing up.

I hand her the iceless glass. "Here's your could-be-chillier wine."

Bridget takes it and sips. "It's perfect. Unlike your soon-to-be watered-down wine."

I roll my eyes.

"You take the subway?" She looks at me with a tiny grimace, shifting the conversation back to the previous subject.

I laugh. "Are you judging me for doing something most New Yorkers do?"

Bridget blushes. "Not judging, no. Never. Just..."

With a playful glare, I sip my wine.

Ah...perfectly chilly.

She eyes her glass, twirling the liquid around for a second or two. "I swear, it's not judgment, it's just...dirty, right?"

I scoff. "You're terrible. Have you ever even been on the subway?"

"Yes! At least twice."

I can't help laughing. "Wow, *twice?* How did you make it?"

Bridget pouts. "Listen! I would never judge someone for taking the subway, it's just not for *me.*"

The wine hits us fast. We chat and chat and chat as the light through the window ebbs to darkness.

Bridget shows me her sketches, very tasteful Vivienne Westwood inspired punk designs. She asks me to model for her collection when the time comes, and I balk at the idea.

Me? A model? Fat chance.

Time flies when you're having fun, and hanging out with Bridget is *definitely* fun.

"So, have things been weird since the masquerade?" she asks.

My heart pounds. "Uh, what do you mean?"

Bridget laughs. "Come on, I'm not an idiot. The guy you were dancing with at the masquerade..."

I remain silent.

"Edwin Lyons isn't easy to ignore."

I grab her arm. "Lower your voice."

"It's just us! In your apartment! In *Queens!*"

I burst into laughter even though I'm deeply mortified she knows it was Edwin I was dancing with that night. The wine really hit me, ice and all. "It was an accident."

"An accident?!"

"I didn't know he was my boss," I admit. "But don't worry, we haven't done anything. We've remained extremely professional."

That's not quite the truth, is it, Sonia?

Bridget shrugs. "I mean, I'd never...you know, with my boss, but I wouldn't blame you if you did."

"*Bridget!*"

"Oh, come on, I could tell you guys were into it."

"You can be into anything while you're drinking." I finish off the last of my third glass of wine.

Bridget shakes her head. "No, y'all were about to fuck on the dance floor."

"We were *not*."

"You're really telling me nothing has happened since then?"

I hesitate. "Nothing."

"Nothing?"

"*Nothing*. And nothing ever can or will."

Bridget sighs. "Well, I guess you're both professionals. Edwin might get around, but I don't think he's ever put the club at risk for a lay."

I'm more jealous than I'd like to admit at the thought of Edwin being a playboy. I guess he doesn't want me enough to risk it all.

God, what am I thinking? "It's more complicated than that."

Her brow creases. "What do you mean?"

I'm about to respond when there's a banging on the door. "Sonia?!"

Fuck.

Speak of the fucking devil.

"Nate?" Bridget says.

I smash my hand against her mouth. "Okay, now *seriously*, lower your voice."

Of course, she would recognize him just by the sound of his voice. I'm sure they grew up together. After all, Solomon and Edwin are best fucking friends.

"Your lights are on. I know you're home."

But how did he find my address?

I look at Bridget, a silent plea for her to play along. "We'll just wait for him to go."

A moment. Silence outside.

Did he give up already?

His deep voice sounds from the other side of my door. "I'm happy to wait here as long as I have to."

Dammit. Wishful thinking.

This relationship is done. Over. Finished. There's nothing left to talk about, at least as far as I'm concerned.

I've been dodging Nate's calls for a whole month since I've been in New York. It's clear he still has something he feels he needs to say.

And just because I want nothing to do with him and can't stand to be around him doesn't mean I don't still care about him. We just ran our course, that's all.

He has another thing coming if he thinks we will *ever* be getting back together. Not in a million years. Because I'm not in love with him anymore. The illusion is gone, the pink lenses of love crashed, and all I see when I look at him is the painful memories of those last few months. Of all he did.

Fuck it.

I shoot up off the couch and grab Bridget's shoes. I try to be as quiet as I can. "You need to go."

"How do you know Nate? He never comes to the club!"

I drop the shoes in front of her. "I knew him before I started working at the club. Now, there's a window in the kitchen that can get you onto the fire escape–"

"*How* did you know him before the club? Is that how you got the job?"

"No." I push the sticking window with all my might. It groans only an inch at a time.

More banging on the door. "Sonia. *Please.*"

A sigh unleashes the heaviness on my chest as the window gives. "Great. Come on."

Bridget stands up from the couch, all ready to go, but

she makes no move to come closer. "I'm not leaving until you tell me how you know Nate Lyons."

"*Lower your voice*," I hiss.

"Then just tell–"

I can't believe I have to do this. I can't believe I really have to fucking tell Bridget who Nate is to me in order to get her out of my apartment. "Nate is my ex-boyfriend."

Bridget gapes at me. "He's your–"

"Shhhh! I told you what you wanted to hear, now climb out this window right this fucking second!"

Nate's voice is loud and clear through the door. "Are you talking to someone?"

Bridget finally comes to her senses and rushes over to me. "What do you mean, he's your ex-boyfriend?!"

"Is English not your first language?" I growl. "Here, up on the counter."

I help Bridget up so she can reach the open window.

"But you and Edwin!"

"Now you know why, on top of being his employee, 'me and Edwin' isn't a thing, Bridget! It can never be." I push her to get her out faster. "Now go!"

She glances out the window at the fire escape and then back at me. "You owe me a way better explanation."

"Fine."

"You bring the wine next time. No ice cubes. And god help me, but I'm not coming back to Queens."

"Sonia, please..." Nate's voice is no more than a whimper.

I begin to bid Bridget to leave again, but she's already ahead of the game. "Going, going!"

And in the blink of an eye, she scrambles out of sight, maneuvering the fire escape, the clanging of her feet growing more and more distant with each passing second.

Leaping across the apartment, I make it to the door.

When my hand lands on the handle, though, I pause. Take a deep breath.

I was so concerned with Bridget being here that I didn't even consider how seeing Nate would make me feel. It's like worms are crawling along my skin, my gut churns. Uneasy, nauseous.

Better get it over with.

When I open the door, Nate is leaning against the doorframe, his forehead resting on the back of his wrist.

I'd swoon if I still wanted him. But I don't.

His clear blue eyes are overcome by the gray ring around his irises. And though the corners of his eyes are drooping, he smiles.

Goddamn, he's got a beautiful smile. Big, wide, bright, dimples in his cheeks.

My stomach drops. I know where I've seen those dimples before.

Edwin.

I'm so disgusted. Or maybe I'm just disgusting.

"Sonia."

"You sound surprised. Like you weren't just pounding on my door crying out my name like a psycho."

He blushes, runs a hand through his dirty blond hair. He needs to get it cut; it's starting to touch his shoulders.

"Can I come in?"

"I guess."

Nate walks into my apartment, glancing around. "Nice place."

It doesn't compare to the apartment we shared.

Even when he didn't have access to his dad's money, Nate wasn't broke.

We had a beautiful beachfront condo together so he

could have direct access to the beach even though my commute to work was a pain. "How did you find out my address?"

He avoids looking at me. "Just some research."

I roll my eyes. "Research? That's what you call it?"

Nate is quiet. His eyes land on the open window.

Shit, I forgot to close it. I rush past him. "Just burned something. Was trying to air out the apartment."

As I work the window closed, I kick myself for that shitty fucking lie. You can't even smell anything burnt in here.

When I manage to get the window closed again, I turn around, and my heartbeat rages.

Nate is right in front of me, cornering me in the kitchen. "It's good to see you." He reaches out and touches my arm. "I've missed you."

I rip my arm away from his hand. Knee-jerk reaction. Ever since the altercation with Oliver Worthington, I've been very jittery.

Not to mention I don't want Nate to touch me again. Ever. "What do you want, Nate?"

"I just wanted to see you." He looks wounded.

That's how he roped me in so many times during our relationship. Those puppy dog eyes.

And fine, I know Nate would never hurt me like that.

He shoves his hands into his pockets. "I've missed you so much. You... You won't talk to me, what am I supposed to do?"

I stare at him. "We're broken up."

"I know, but I'm here in New York, aren't I? I came out here to...to..."

Eve though he doesn't say it, I can still hear it. *To get you back.*

His eyes are so intent on mine. "You know how much I hate New York."

I can't do this. Can't let him think there's a chance when I *know* we will never be together again. I need him to understand it once and for all.

I cross my arms over my chest. "Yeah, well, I love it."

Nate shakes his head. "It's... Sure, it's a great city. But you know, my family is here and..." He sighs. "I came out here despite how I feel about all of that shit. For you."

A throbbing starts at the base of my sternum.

So many emotions want to bubble out, emotions I've been able to pack away because I haven't needed to interact with Nate. Emotions I've been able to utilize for other things. Like pining for Nate's Dad.

Now that I know Edwin... I'm not sure how much I trust Nate's version of events.

Edwin may be brooding and standoffish and, sure, maybe not the best dad.

But a villain? Hardly.

"Nate, I always respected you needing distance from your family. In fact, I loved what a free spirit you were and how you didn't feel indebted to anyone or anything." I look Nate hard in the eye. "But then you took my family from me. The only family I had."

Nate's puppyish eyes slowly turn as the cogs work in his brain. They darken with confusion, and then... "That's not fair."

I lift my chin. "I think it is."

His lips I once thought were so beautiful and pillowy coil. "You can't blame me for your–"

"Don't you dare." I'm mesmerized by how cool I am.

While Nate's anger brews, I only seem to get calmer. And colder.

Nate shakes his head. "I love you. I wanted to be your family."

"You ruined too much for that."

"I didn't mean–"

"I don't care. It's done."

Nate takes a step back from me, appraising me from head to toe. His eyes give away his bewilderment.

Because I'm not the woman he knew in California. I've changed beyond recognition. I'm getting a grip on reality, fixing my problems. Becoming a boss.

Falling for his dad.

Yeah, I'm different.

As if the universe is playing a trick on me, a flash of Edwin comes out in Nate's expression.

I almost smile. Because I know Edwin would protect me from this. He's already done a much better job than Nate at taking care of me in the one month I've known him.

"You'll never be happy if you blame everybody else for the bad things that happen to you, Sonia." Nate's surfer boy exterior falls away for the angry bull inside.

Nate might be the go-with-the-flow kind of guy, but I'm not. I believe shit happens for a reason.

And Nate is my reason. So, I'm done.

"I don't think we have anything else to say to each other."

"You think I got your dad into something just by–"

My anger flares, calmness exchanged for ire. "I said, *don't talk about him.*"

"I won't take blame for something I had no control over, Sonia."

It all comes out at once, a terrible scream from the back of my throat.

I reach for something, anything, and my hands land on a

metal pot on the counter. I don't want to hurt him. I just want him gone. I whip the pot to the floor, past his feet.

It clatters, striking my eardrums.

Nate jumps away from me.

"GET OUT!"

If he says anything else, I don't hear it around the blood pounding in my ears.

As I calm down a bit, moments later, I'm alone.

I drop to the floor, tears cascading down my face.

I've lost so much in the past few years. And I have to work so hard to recover the damage.

And Nate... It's all his fault. I stand by that.

When the tears abate, I lift my chin as a resolve strikes me.

Nate took everything from me. My family, my life, my freedom to do as I please. How is it fair that he takes this as well? I'm done feeling bad about feeling attracted to Edwin on Nate's account.

Edwin is someone I never counted on. Someone I never knew I needed in my life. And I want Edwin Lyons. I want him so bad.

Taking Nate out of the equation means one of the tall walls preventing me from having my boss just collapsed. And I'm not sure the other wall is strong enough to hold by itself much longer.

11

———

EDWIN

Farley takes a measuring tape to the wall, spanning it from one wine rack to the other. Before he can get to where he needs to, the tape snaps back on him. He huffs.

I scoff. "You know, I can help." I look askance at the designer we've hired who is admiring the ceiling rather than helping with the measurements *he* asked for.

Farley laughs, an undercurrent of frustration in his voice. "No, no, I can do this. It's just a tape measure, for god's sake."

He tries again. Before the tape measure can snap back, I grab it and hold it up, giving the COO a knowing look.

Farley rolls his eyes. "Sometimes I feel like you're my dad."

After looking at the tape, Farley calls out to the designer. "Eight feet and change."

"Can I have an exact measurement?" His nasal voice echoes off my eardrum in a particularly grating way.

Farley sighs, looking at the tape again. "Eight feet and three inches."

"Thank you." The designer makes a note on his clipboard. I release the tape, chuckling at the yelp it elicits out of Farley when it snaps back into place.

Marty Villanueva was so impressed with the club after speaking with Sonia that he not only signed on for membership but also donated the money to have a whisky room built off of the wine cellar. "That way, my wife can keep an eye on me," he explained.

I don't know what Sonia did to make him so generous, but I'm not surprised. Everyone at the club loves Sonia, employees and members alike. She pours everything into her job and doesn't cut corners. She always wears a smile, looks her best, and manages to straddle the line between authority and friend with everyone that I've never seemed to manage.

I think she'll get a raise at her quarterly review. Seems only fair considering how much she's brought to the Lyons Club already.

Not to mention how much she's brought to me.

Farley huffs. "The construction will be a nightmare."

I can't help but agree as we watch the designer pace back and forth across the floor. "We'll leave that for the professionals to figure out."

Farley scoffs. "They'll have to dig out a whole new room! Surely that will make it nightmarish to be in the club."

"You know we will spare no expense to make sure the construction is soundproof and well ventilated." I pause. "And if we have to shut things down for a day here and there, then so be it. We can't look a gift horse in the mouth."

With a pout, Farley responds with a simple, "Neigh."

I shake my head. "You're impossible."

"I don't know how I feel about all of this. We can't just

spring this on Sonia, she just started. And you know how our members can get when things change on them."

Yes, they can get...difficult.

The designer points to a corner. "Can we get a measurement over here?"

Farley sighs. I pat him on the back. "Look, you keep measuring without killing yourself, and I'll get Sonia to get her opinion, alright?"

The mere mention of Sonia's name gets hot around the collar. I avoid saying it myself to avoid going up in flames.

If all it takes is her name to make my blood boil, seeing her sends me into a whole new stratosphere. Which is why I try my best to stay away.

Who am I kidding? I'm not trying my best at all. Not by a long shot. I offered to get her, didn't I?

"Sounds fair." Farley's attention goes to a bottle of red on one of the racks. "Oooh, a nineteen-seventy-five Yellerman pinot noir?"

I narrow my eyes at him. "And no sampling the merchandise.

I head back into the main atrium of the club, greeting members as I go, fielding complaints, concerns, and a compliment from Trudy Heller, who hasn't stopped hitting on me since I was twenty-three.

"Oh, Trudy, you're too much." I manage to avoid her grasp, *just*, as I go toward Sonia's office.

The blinds are drawn, which is unusual for her. When Sonia's in her office, she's the open-door type. Anyone can stop in to ask a question or say hello. So, her needing privacy is...different.

However, when I approach the door, I can tell it hasn't been shut all the way. Probably an oversight.

Inside, she is talking to someone with an urgency in her voice I had never heard before. Something is wrong.

"I gave you double last month because I could, not because that's going to be the norm." Her voice trembles.

I peek in through the crack in the door and spot her at the desk, her head resting in her hand, office phone pressed to her ear. Her crisp, slicked-back bun has tumbled completely out of control, reminding me of the night I met her. Long ribbons of dark hair. Gorgeous.

"Well, I can't get you that much this month. I just can't... I know the interest is accruing, I'm well aware."

My heart sinks. So, she's got some debts to pay. I wonder what for.

"You're going to have to be happy with what I already wired you. That's all there is this month."

From the sounds of it, this isn't normal debt. Sounds like she's dealing with something much seedier than that.

Debt collectors can annoy you with phone calls and by mail. But unregulated debt...who knows what lengths these people are willing to go to get her to pay up.

"Fine. Fine..." She scribbles something on a notepad. "Yes. I got it all down. Mhm." Her voice pitches higher and higher. "Thank you for–" She stops short, pulls the phone away from her ear, and looks at the receiver. With a heavy sigh, she hangs up the phone and droops over herself.

Seconds later, she's crying.

I feel like a creep watching her, just like I always seem to do. But I can't just let her sit there and cry.

She must feel so alone.

And I can't stand the thought of that. Not when she's such a wonderful human.

I rap on the door.

Sonia's head shoots up, tears staining her cheeks, and

when our eyes meet, she flushes even harder. "Oh, my god, Edwin–"

"Sorry, I don't mean to interrupt." *Yeah, right.* "Are you alright?"

Sonia looks at the phone, then back at me. She tries to speak, but all that comes out is a sob.

I go to her without thinking, get to my knees, wrap my arms around her, and pull her down into my chest as tight as I can.

Sonia cries into my neck.

All her emotions quake through my body. "Shhh...it's alright. Everything will be alright."

I might not know the details of her circumstances. But I know it will all be alright. Because as long as I'm around, I'll never let anything bad happen to Sonia. It's something coded into the back of my brain ever since I saw her at the masquerade ball. Before I even knew her name.

I must keep her safe. I must keep her from harm.

Because even if I never have her, whether it be in my bed or somewhere deeper and more intimate, Sonia will always be mine in some way.

I can't explain why. I just know.

"How much–" She hiccups. "How much did you hear?"

I push away a tear that escapes her eye, racing to reach her chin at a breakneck speed. "Just the tail end there."

Sonia shuts her eyes tight.

It kills me to have her closing away from me. "Don't be embarrassed."

"I shouldn't have been making a personal call at work, I'm sorry."

I shake my head. "Sonia, please don't apologize. You have nothing..." I cup the sides of her face to make sure she looks at me and the message gets across. "You have nothing to apologize for."

Sonia's eyes tremble in mine. She swallows. Hard.

I wonder if she's feeling what I'm feeling now. The brutal, almost irresistible urge to have my lips on hers. But I resist. It wouldn't be professional. I'd be taking advantage of her in a time of vulnerability.

Still, though, I won't let that take me away from her.

"You have debt."

Sonia nods. Her hands grip at my suit jacket, fingers digging into my sides. Almost like she needs me. "I do."

"Let me take care of them."

"*No.*" Her hands grip tighter.

"I want to."

Sonia is silent, shaking her head nonstop. Her brow bends. She's...considering it. But then she stops. "It's my responsibility. I can't let you. Then I'd feel indebted to you and–"

I slide one hand to the nape of her neck. "You would never owe me anything, Sonia. I promise."

We are both quiet, the thrumming of a heartbeat punctuating the silence. Mine? Hers?

"I just..." I can't manage my surly exterior much longer. It's something I've postured for my entire life. But beneath it all, I am soft. I just want to be loved.

And I want it to be Sonia. "I want to take care of you."

It's Sonia who tips forward first. I'm close to a hundred percent sure. I have to be in order not to feel like I've somehow taken advantage of this closeness.

But when her mouth touches mine, my body lights up like fireworks on New Year's Eve.

Her lips are poised and controlled.

Someone has to be. Because all I want to do is rip our

clothes off and do what has needed to be done since the very first night we met.

My hands wander down to her back, pressing her full body into me as our lips caress one another's.

The tension we have been building has been exquisite, but I am so ready for it all to end, right here, right now.

I will take her. With the door open. Where everyone can hear how good I can make her feel.

Sonia rips her lips away from mine before I can carry out my plan. Maybe for the best. Would have been unprofessional.

But holy hell, how my insides curdle without her mouth on mine.

"I'm sorry." Her whisper is so soft.

I want to tell her how *not* sorry she has to be. However, all that comes out is a mere, "It's alright."

It sounds like I'm accepting her apology, but what I mean is that it was more than alright for her to kiss me. In fact, I'd like her to do it again.

"I just got–" She falls back onto her heels, leaving my embrace—a painful, cold feeling—and laughs despite herself. "I just got carried away and you're so kind and–"

"It's alright, Sonia," I repeat, hoping the way I say her name will make it all clear.

I've never been the best at words. Never been the best at actions either. Perhaps I'm not meant for anything if I can't accomplish one or the other.

She wipes away the sticky tracks of tears with the back of her hand. "I really hope this won't change–"

"I don't see you any differently." Which is true. I see her just as I did before. Someone I want with a primal need I can't seem to tame. "I'm sorry if I...made you uncomfortable."

Sonia shakes her head. "No, no, not at all. I feel…"

I suck in a breath. The pause in her answer almost kills me with anticipation. Her answer means the world to me.

"Safe around you, Edwin. Seriously."

Safe. I make her feel *safe*.

On the one hand, that's a good thing. On the other, makes me feel a bit like I'm her dad. And that's a great reminder that she's the same age as my eldest son. She works under me, and I need to be a leader for her. Not someone kissing her when she cries and thinking about fucking her on the floor of her office without any sense of decorum.

She pushes herself back up into her chair. "Don't worry about me."

I follow suit, getting to my feet. I don't want to look like I'm begging for her on my knees.

Unless she'd like that…

"I will, but I will try not to." I smile and give her a curt nod.

Sonia smiles back. Delicious, closed lips I could kiss again and again and again if circumstances weren't what they are.

"Thank you, Edwin."

I leave her office, making sure the door stays closed behind me, and then skid to a stop.

Shit. I was supposed to bring her with me. Can't go back now, though, that'd be too awkward.

I walk away from Sonia's office with my head ducked while I try and come up with a fib about why she's not with me to tell Farley.

All the way back, my lips are still vibrating from her kiss.

12

SONIA

I don't spend much time in the nightclub, but Farley, Hazel, and a few others invited me to stay for a drink after my shift. It's been weeks since I've done anything social, which is my fault for being a workaholic, so I thought, what the hell? Nothing is more convenient than having a drink at my workplace. Especially in the VIP lounge area.

Hazel looks at all of us and the corner of her mouth upturns. "I had a guy proposition me."

I blink. "You're not supposed to talk about what happens in scenes, Hazel."

She laughs. "That's just it! It wasn't in a scene. It wasn't even in the club. That's why it is so funny. He asked me if I needed a Daddy."

My chin almost hits the floor. "You're serious? Who was he?"

"I'm very serious. Picture this." She leans forward, and we all lean in too. "I'm at the supermarket, and I'm wearing an outfit I sometimes wear at home when I'm feeling little."

She shakes her head as she smirks. "Before you ask, you

know I'm only comfortable showing that side of me here, so I have no idea what I was thinking."

"You were thinking you wanted to feel good about yourself, so nothing wrong with that. You do you, boo," Farley says.

"Yass, girl." Gina snaps her fingers and laughs, so we all join in.

"What happened next?" I'm so curious.

I don't think I could ever be brave enough to do what they do, either here or anywhere else, though I am more than a little curious about some parts of the lifestyle.

Hazel takes a sip of her drink. "I said yes and asked if he was offering."

Farley shakes his head as he empties his glass. "Girl, you are a menace."

With his hand, he signals the bartender to get us another round.

My glass is still half-full, so I drink some of it from the straw. "Why would you do that?"

She works here as a sub, so wouldn't that be something a lover might frown upon?

"Because..." Her cheeks turn red, and her eyes go to her glass.

Gina starts chanting, "Ohmygod, ohmygod, ohmygod."

"WHAT?" Farley and I shout together.

Gina looks at us and, points her finger at Hazel. "You guys, she likes him. She likes the Daddy guy." Facing Hazel, she adds, "Don't you?"

Taking a draw from her straw, she nods, and her cheeks go even redder.

"What did he say?" Farley is almost on top of the table now. "Was he serious or just trying to start up a conversation?"

"He was serious," she whispers. "He said if the position is open, he'd very much like to apply and that he always dreamed of having a little princess like me."

Her smile is huge now, and Farley and Gina are jumping in their seats.

As I lean down to catch the straw of my gin and tonic between my lips, all my thoughts are about my life and how I wish the universe would throw me a bone too.

As I sip, I survey the room, trying to avoid the joy at the table. I'm really happy for Hazel. I just feel bad for myself as well. Why can't I be propositioned by someone too?

And I know just the someone I'd love would do the propositioning.

My eyes fall on something that has me doing a double-take.

A sight I'd rather not see.

It's Edwin. And he's not alone. There's a woman draped in the tiniest bit of scarlet fabric glomming onto his arm. The two of them are talking very close up against the back wall.

She grabs his arm, hoisting herself up toward his ear.

As I watch, a smile spreads across his face.

I think I'm going to be sick.

Since our kiss last week, my body has been in overdrive with want for Edwin.

I knew the wall between employer and employee was growing weaker, I just didn't expect it to start crumbling so soon after I decided Nate wasn't enough of a deterrent.

That's why I pushed Edwin away. I knew that if I didn't stop it, all would be lost and we'd be...

Well, who knows. It's easier to be heartbroken over one kiss rather than going all the way with someone only to be destroyed at the end.

I would much rather have called it quits then than sleep with Edwin only for him to turn around and say, "That was great but can never happen again."

That doesn't mean I don't still want him. Or that I don't have regrets.

And watching him with this blonde model on his arm just proves the fact even more that I want him so badly I might explode.

To add insult to injury, Edwin reaches down, grabs her hand, and pulls her in the direction of the hallway where the bathrooms are. And beyond that...access to the Lyons Club.

I have no reason to even guess at where they might be going. But my mind has no trouble jumping to one thing and one thing only.

He's taking her to The Underground. He's going to do nasty things with her.

And she's going to become the new object of his affection because she isn't off-limits like I am.

"What about you, Sonia, any news on the love front?" Farley's voice snaps my attention back to the table.

"Have you met me? When would I even have the time? What about you, Farley? Roundabout is fair play."

"Yeah, right. Because I'm here less time than you?" Farley sasses.

I laugh, though my heart isn't in it. I just saw Edwin disappear down a hall just like he did with me all those weeks ago at the masquerade.

It should be me he takes down there. Not *her*. Whoever she is.

Maybe it's the anger, or maybe it's the gin, but I'm not going to sit here and let him have all the fun. I sit up on my stool and look down the long bar at all the patrons. I scan each face. No...no...no...

My eyes land on a guy toward the end of the bar who is chatting with the bartender a bit as he receives his drink. Looks like whisky neat.

Cute enough dude. Sexy drink. Easy enough.

Farley cocks an eyebrow. "What are you looking at?"

"My prey for the evening."

Gina, Hazel, and Farley laugh. They must think I'm joking. But I'm not.

"Which one is it?"

I knock back the rest of my gin and tonic. "Light brown hair, whisky, great eyebrows."

Farley does a double-take. "Uh, you sure you want to do that?"

"Yeah, why not? He's hot."

"He's—"

Hazel grabs Farley's arm. "Let her, she's a big girl."

More than that. I'm a grown ass woman. I'm almost thirty. And I can take what I want.

I abandon my stool and saunter down to the other end of the bar, letting my hair down in the process. I undo another button on my blouse to give just a sneak peek at the goods and then nestle in next to the guy, leaning on the bar to pretend like I'm getting the bartender's attention. Instead, though, I glance over my shoulder at the guy and smile. "Hey."

He smiles back. One cheek dimple. "Hey."

"It's like impossible to get service around here." I sigh.

"It's a busy night."

"You come here often?"

He shrugs. "Somewhat. You?"

"Oh, all the time."

"You do look a little familiar…"

I roll my eyes. "I bet you say that to all the girls."

"No, not usually. Now, what do you want to drink?"

I shrug. "Surprise me."

The guy laughs, a big guffaw. "Oh, you're going to regret that." He puts his fingers in his mouth and whistles so loud the bartender whips around at once.

I duck my face away so he doesn't recognize me right off.

With a point in my direction, the man says, "Sex on the Beach!"

"Oh my god, you're terrible."

With a playful waggle of his eyebrows, he brings his whisky to his lips. "You asked for it."

My drink comes, and the two of us continue shooting the shit, a veiled flirtation in every comment.

This guy is *hot*. Smoking hot. Not Edwin hot, but right now, I don't care.

He seems like a player, which is just fine. I'm not looking for a husband here tonight. Just something to distract me. "This drink is going to give me a headache, and it's going to be your fault."

The guy slides his hand onto my waist and pulls his lips toward my ear. "Maybe I can take your mind off the headache with something else, then, hm?"

"*Ehem.*"

Fuck. My eyes shut. What is *he* doing here?

Edwin's voice is deep and too close. "Seth, I didn't know you were back from your trip."

The guy I've been flirting with turns to face Edwin, however, I can't bring myself to do it.

It's not like I was doing something I shouldn't. Just because I feel some weird attachment to him doesn't mean we are in a relationship or that we can't be with other people. Which he just was.

So what if I was jealous? Doesn't mean he feels the same.

But at the same time, I don't want him to feel like I've forgotten about him. Because then maybe he'll feel even more inclined to forget about me.

Wait a second...

Seth...

Seth?

No way. This is Bridget's stepbrother, Seth Vance. Now, this is fucking rich.

The one time I try and have a little fun, I end up stepping into another situation that's off-limits.

"Yep, got back just last night. Thought I'd see how things are around here." Seth looks in my direction. "They're looking good."

"Yes, I see you've met our new operations manager, Sonia Hill."

Seth's suave expression melts into a crinkly frown. "*That's* how I know you. You were at the masquerade, weren't you? You were dancing with–" Seth stops and looks at Edwin. "Ah..."

"Fucking great," I mutter to myself, putting my hand over my eyes and leaning on the bar.

"You mind if I talk with Sonia privately for a moment, Seth?"

What now? It's not like I'm the only one who is fooling around with customers. Or those I thought were customers. Yeesh.

And why do I feel like I've done him wrong when he was just getting busy with someone?

God, sometimes, I hate myself.

"No problem. In fact, why don't you take my seat?" Seth touches my arm. "Nice to meet you, Sonia."

"You too." I can't bring myself to look at him.

I keep my eyes in the pool of swirly orange red Sex on the Beach as Edwin settles into the stool beside me. That headache is coming on faster than I expected.

"Flirting with Solomon's son, are we?"

"I had no idea he was Solomon's son." My eyes stay glued to the glass.

"He's been on a business trip the past month. Expanding his company."

I drink my cocktail and lick my lips. "Good for him."

Edwin leans toward me. Closer and closer. And I hate myself for noticing.

I hold my breath.

"It's very unprofessional to flirt with customers, let alone members, Sonia."

"You're one to talk."

Edwin chuckles in my ear, a dark rumble I wish I could feel pressed up against my inner thigh. "What are you talking about?"

I snap my attention at him, causing Edwin to straighten up too. "I just saw you go downstairs with—"

Now you've done it, Sonia. You've proven you're the jealous type. And you don't even have a valid reason. He isn't yours.

"Ah, so you saw me with another woman, and you got jealous."

"No!" Okay, that sounded way more defensive than it needed to. "I'm just saying if you're going to expect us to be professional, you should lead by example."

Edwin lifts his chin, just a slight tilt, giving me a good view of his sharp jawline.

I want to feel his stubble scraping up against my face again, want to feel how raw it will make my thighs, want him to have my essence left behind on his beard so he can smell me all day.

God, this is so bad.

"You're right. Good thing I wasn't flirting with her."

I scoff. "I saw you."

Edwin grins. "You were watching me?"

The hole I've dug myself is so deep there's no way I'm climbing out. "She was hanging on you, and you were smiling and whispering and–"

Edwin grabs my knee.

I gasp, marveling at the spot where his hand has connected with my skin.

Thank god the lip of the bar casts our lower bodies in shadow and the lights in the VIP lounge are too distracting for anyone to care about a man touching a woman's knee.

"Sonia."

I lift my head and stare into his onyx eyes.

His smile has faded, turned into something more serious. "Do you think that's how I flirt, Sonia?"

"I...I don't know." His grip is making it hard to even think.

He glances over his shoulder before sliding his hand further up, to my thigh, bending back the hem of my skirt to get what he wants. "Well, I can assure you, my flirting isn't nearly so trite as touching and giggling."

I open and close my mouth, trying to say something in return. But I can't. Edwin's hand is so far under my skirt I know he has only one mission. I start to panic, looking around to see if anyone can see us.

"Don't look at them, *look at me.*"

Holy hell. His demand is mine to fulfill. Our eyes lock

again just in time for his fingers to brush up against my panties. My whole pussy tightens, clit throbbing with want.

"No one is looking. And even if they were, you shouldn't care. Because *this* is how I flirt, Sonia."

I swallow.

"Give me permission to touch you." His demand comes in that panties-melting tone.

I nod slowly.

Edwin's fingers thread through my underwear, brushing up against my labia. He smiles. "Wet. For me?"

I nod again. God, I'm turning into a sex-starved bobblehead.

He laughs lowly and pets my pussy gently. He slings his arm over the back of my stool shielding us from prying eyes even further.

But I couldn't give a fuck at this point who sees. His fingers in my pussy are a dangerous combination.

"Listen to me, Sonia Hill. I have no need to pick up women at my club and take them downstairs to have my way with them. I could if I wanted. In fact, I have. Many women, over the years, have become my playthings. And I've enjoyed them however I wanted."

I seal my lips together when his fingers start to circle my clit, shoulders rising. I want to undulate my hips against his hand so damn hard, but that would be a recipe for disaster.

"I have no interest in that anymore, though. Because..."

His finger presses my clit like it's a button.

I gasp, turning my face toward him, realizing his mouth is only an inch away.

I could have him. Here and now. We could say fuck all and just *take* each other. It's obvious we both want it.

"...now, my mind is on someone else entirely."

Me? The way his gaze is intent on me, it has to be. *Right?*

Before we can go any further, Edwin removes his hand from my underwear.

I let out a sigh of frustration, gripping the edge of the bar.

Edwin takes out his pocket square, unraveling it into a handkerchief, and wipes off the tips of his fingers that were just inside me.

I watch all of his movements with rapt attention.

"Anyway, I'll let Seth know that you are once again available since our conversation is over."

What? Who?

How *dare* he do this to me? Leave me mindless with lust and then throw me into another man's arms.

"No need. I'm going home. Headache." I gesture to the half-finished drink. "Sex on the Beach."

Edwin doesn't respond, just licks his lower lip, eyes falling to the place where I've unbuttoned my shirt enough to give a glimpse into the behind-the-scenes of Sonia Hill. "Then have a good night, Sonia."

He strides off before I can utter another word.

13

EDWIN

When I'm not thinking about Sonia, I'm thinking about Nate.

It's become clear that Nate will not be coming to see me on his own accord and that Abigail and Jack are making it close to impossible for me to get to him.

So, I had to go about contacting my son another way. I hired the foremost PI in New York City to track down my son's whereabouts. I should have done it sooner because he had Nate's location for me in less than a day.

"He's got an apartment in Queens right by the Rockaways."

"Queens?" That had been quite the shock.

"Only legal surfing spot in the city," the PI explained.

"Surfing?" The hits just kept on coming, showing me how much of my son I am unfamiliar with.

But now, here I am, on the Rockaway Peninsula, staring at a group of surfers who are all waxing their boards on the beach.

I can spot him from a mile away. My boy. His blond windswept hair is crinkled as it dries in the sun. And his smile gleams, just like his mother's. That's what brought me under her spell all those years ago. Although he got the dimples from me, a perfect combination of his parentage.

I stand there for far too long to look like I have all my sanity. But I can't help it. I'm stuck in this spot. It's not easy to see your son for the first time in years. Everything feels so important to say that I can't pick out just one thing.

A coward. That's what I am. In every realm of my life.

I pulled away from Sonia just the other day at the bar when I should have taken things all the way. I pushed my son away and forced everyone else to bring him to me rather than demanding to see him, making it my main priority to track him down and find him.

That streak of cowardice ends today.

I head down the beach, not paying much mind to my expensive Italian leather shoes sinking into the sand. There are far more important things than Italian leather in life. It's taken me far too many years to realize that.

The sea breeze whips through my air, sending my perfect coif askew.

Shit. I know he's my son and not a woman I'm trying to impress, but I wanted to show up looking my best. Wanted to show him just how serious I am about this.

When I'm halfway down the beach, close enough I can catch most of the conversation between the surfers, Nate alerts. His eyes whip toward me. And that fantastic smile drops. "Give me a second," I read on his lips as he shoulders past a few of the surfers and comes in my direction.

Well, at least he's not running for the hills.

I smile at him as he comes closer, but that doesn't seem to help anything.

Nate stops a few feet away, crosses his arms over his chest, and plants his feet in a wide stance. Trying to intimidate his old man. He only has an inch of height on me, and he's all lank. Although, his arms and legs are muscled in a way I've never seen before, made even more obvious through his wet suit.

"What are you doing here?"

"Good to see you too."

Nate's stoic countenance doesn't break.

"You..." Shit, I don't know what to say. "You surf."

Nice going, Captain Obvious.

"Uh..." Nate glances back at the group of surfers who are all looking over at him with concern, shielding their whispers from our ears. Nate turns back, tugs on his ear lobe, and shakes his head to the side. Water caught in his ear maybe? "Yeah, I surf."

"Picked that up in California?"

"Dad–"

That warms my heart more than it should. He's still calling me dad, that's a start.

"Seriously, what the fuck are you doing here?"

"I came to see you. Since you won't come to see me."

Nate snorts. "Why in the world would I want to see you?"

"Because I'm your old man?"

"As if you've ever acted like it."

"Hey–" I stop myself. He has every right to be upset with me. I wasn't around. There're no excuses to make.

Nate juts his chin forward. "Hey what?"

"Hey nothing." My hand goes to my hair. "I know I've never been the most...present."

"That's an understatement."

I sigh. "Your mom was always very protective."

"Seriously? You're going to blame my mom?"

Maybe a little?

"That's really low, even for you," Nate says. "She fucking stepped up because she had to. Because you left her–"

"You and your mom never wanted for anything, did you?"

Nate purses his lips and looks off into the ocean. Something tells me he's much more comfortable out there than on land. Too bad he can't become a fish person or something and swim away from me.

"Not in the way *you* would define want."

I understand what he means. There's something of a numbing effect when you have access to so much money. You think you can use it to patch up just about anything.

I've done that my whole life. Ever since Clarissa told me she was pregnant. Just throw money at the problem to make sure everything's okay, keep myself from having to, you know, face the way I feel.

Maybe if I'd started expressing my feelings earlier, my son might understand where I'm coming from just a bit more. "What are *you* doing here?" I confess I'm curious. "In New York."

Nate's jaw tenses, a clear indication that I won't get the truth from him. At least not yet. "I wanted to be close to Mom. That's all."

I smile and nod. I know that's not true.

Clarissa is as bad now as I was then. She chases after rich men to fund her next exhibitions. I know Nate wants no part in that.

"I'm sure she'll appreciate that."

"Yep."

"I do too, for the record."

"Well, I didn't do it for you."

"Not even a little?"

Nate narrows his eyes. "Not. Even. A little."

Damn. He knows how to cut deep. Wonder where he got that from. "So, have you...reconsidered things?"

Nate scoffs. "I *knew* it. I knew you wouldn't be able to have just one conversation with me without bringing up the club."

"Technically, I didn't."

"Okay, then." Nate raises an eyebrow. "What things are you asking if I've reconsidered?"

I hold my hands up. "Okay, you got me."

"Wow. Shocking."

"I just have to ask. The way we left things, I thought I might never..." I control the tremble at the back of my throat. "I thought I might not see you again."

Nate won't look at me. If he did, he might realize I'm a person with feelings, not the monster who gave him that ultimatum three years ago. I've changed a lot. I've had to. Abigail and Jack can attest.

"I know it hasn't always been easy having me as a father–"

"Whatever this new tactic you're using is, it's fucking manipulative, okay? So, cut this shit out."

I furrow my brow. "What?"

"This whole, 'Oh, I'm a good guy, I've just made mistakes' thing. You're not going to make me feel bad for you."

"It's not a tactic. It's...it's how I feel."

Nate's laugh is cold. "Yeah, okay. I'll believe that when pigs fly. Everything is a tactic to you, Dad. You do whatever you can to get what you want. Always."

I'm a shrewd businessman. That would be a compliment coming from anyone else but one of my own children. "Nate, I'm really trying here."

"You fucking stalked me to the beach and want to talk to me about the club. That's not trying. It's fucking sadistic."

Frustration and rage war inside me.

I've been trying so hard to maintain an even temper, but how am I supposed to do that when he's insulting me at every turn? I want to fix things, but I'm only human. I'm still me. And he's pushing my buttons. "You can't speak to me like that."

"Of course, I can."

"I'm your *father*."

"And I'm a grown fucking man!" Nate seethes, blue eyes wild. "If you cared to pay attention, you'd know that. I am trying to live my life, not yours. And you couldn't *stand* that. So, I left. And you couldn't stand that either, and now I'm back and you can't stand *that*, so–"

"I love that you're back, I just want you to let me in!"

Nate makes a noise of disgust. "As if you've earned that."

"I shouldn't have to earn it, I'm–"

"Stop using the fact you're my dad to justify *anything*. All you did was fuck someone without a condom."

"Don't–" I bite my tongue again. What's the use? No matter how I try to defend myself, he'll find a way to discredit me and my feelings. "Nate, I just want to fix things."

My son stares at me. So much anger in his lithe frame. "I have spent my whole life trying to figure out how to be a man that loves anything. I never had that. Never had a dad who gave a shit–"

"That's not true."

"Never had a male father figure at all–"

"I was. I tried, I–" I did what my father did. That was

my version of a father figure. It's all I knew. Nate and I are more similar than he'd like to believe.

"But I fucking learned. I found things and people I love and–" His anger breaks for a second, and there's a flash of pain in his eyes.

*Sweet Nate...*Once he got to be a certain age, he stopped wanting hugs, would push me away if I tried to give him a pat on the back. The anger has been building for a while.

Still, though, all I want to do right now is hug my son. I want to make him feel better any way I can.

Even if I'm the cause of all his hurt.

"And yet, you want me to be like you."

I shouldn't ask. But I need to know. "And what would that mean? Being like me?"

"Cold and unfeeling." He puts his hand to his chest, rubbing like it's a muscle that aches. "I don't want that."

I don't either, I think, but can't say it aloud. If I tried to speak, it probably would come out all garbled with pain.

Nate's eyes fall to the ground in front of my feet. "There's nothing for me to reconsider."

He turns on his heel and heads back to the group of guys, calling something out to which his friends laugh.

I doubt he said anything bad about me. In fact, I doubt he said anything about me at all.

That's almost worse.

I have to get out of here before I break down. It seldom happens, so when it does, I need to be prepared for the worst.

I rush back to my Range Rover, lock myself inside, and grip the wheel so tight for a second I fear my knuckles might break.

With a loud, unending roar, I allow the boiling, painful fury out of my body.

And then I cry.

I don't like crying. It hurts me. Not just my soul. My body, my heart. Reveals tensions in my neck and jaw I didn't know existed from grinning and bearing it in my day-to-day life.

Maybe I'm not capable of changing. Maybe Nate is right to keep his distance.

How can I trade forty-nine years of coldness for warmth in the blink of an eye?

14

___

SONIA

There's something wrong with Edwin.

When I first got to know him, I thought he was quite unreadable. This is just further proof I've spent too much time watching him, thinking about him, pining for him.

Because now I can pinpoint every micro-expression of tension in his ever-present stern expression. The way he holds his jaw, in the pinch of his forehead.

I should be going through the procedure documents for our upcoming construction on the wine cellar.

The club might have to close for a day or two here and there to avoid members having to deal with the noise and the dust. This will be unprecedented for most of them, so I need to make sure the dissemination of information is clear and far-reaching.

However, it's hard to be focused on work when Edwin is roving the lobby, talking with our newest member Marty Villanueva.

Whenever I've seen the two together, Edwin is a laugh a minute. Right now, though, he's got his lips forced into a perpetual smile. I'm not even sure he's listening.

Something is troubling him. And as much as I shouldn't, I still want to try and fix this. Need to. If I can alleviate his burden, then I will.

And herein lies the problem. It's not just that my body aches for him, that I thirst for him, that he's starting to appear in my dreams.

It's that I want to be there for him in ways that would bring us too close together for a boss and an employee. Let alone a father and his son's ex-girlfriend.

I push Nate from my mind and get to my feet before I can question what I'm about to do. I open my office door and lean my head out, hoping to catch Edwin's attention.

And I do. At once. He feels me just as much as I feel him. He raises his eyebrows in question.

"I'm sorry to interrupt. Can we talk?" I point over my shoulder into my office. "About the construction."

Marty grins and smacks Edwin on the arm. "Oh, please, go right ahead. Wouldn't dream of getting in the way of that."

I'm grateful the new whisky-tasting room was Marty's idea. Makes it easy to snatch Edwin away without any balking.

He nods at Marty before striding toward me, head held high. He's always striding as if the earth is rising to meet his feet. Like he owns the place. Which he does. But there's something completely intoxicating about it.

I retreat into my office and close the blinds. I'm intent on finding out what's wrong with him, and if that means breaking him down a little, so be it.

However, I know Edwin is a prideful man. I don't want people ogling us through the window.

Edwin closes the door behind him and stops to watch

the blinds fall. "Is there something about your question that needs to be so...secretive?"

I blush and shake my head. "I have a confession to make."

He raises an eyebrow. "Oh?"

"I don't really have a question about the cellar construction." My mouth grows hot.

What on earth is wrong with you? What are you doing?

Edwin and I don't have any kind of personal relationship outside a few heated encounters that never went anywhere. But boy, did they scorch me.

Although, I guess that's not quite true. He's been there for me, served me at bended knee when I was in peril. Twice. After that awful incident with Oliver Worthington. And when he found me crying over that phone call with the debt collector.

Edwin has shown a want to be there for me.

And I want to show it back to him.

"Well, first of all..." I fold my hands in front of me. "I'm sorry to interrupt your conversation with Mr. Villanueva."

Edwin rubs his chin. The soft rasping of his stubble against his hand reminds me how good it felt as our lips twined together, leaving my skin raw in the most delicious way.

"No apology necessary. He was talking my ear off; I needed an out anyway."

I chuckle, trying to ignore the intensity of his obsidian eyes on me. It almost feels like he's devouring me, sizing up each part of me. That might just be wishful thinking, though.

"I wanted to ask you if you were alright."

Edwin's face softens. All the tension he was carrying in

his jaw seems to melt. And his lips part just so. It seems I've taken him off-guard.

"Because I..." I clear my throat. This is kind of awkward. "I just noticed that you seem a little tense today and–"

"You were watching me?"

I hold my breath. *I'm always watching you.* "I can't help but notice you when you're here. I want to make sure that everything is to your liking around here. That's my job, after all."

Edwin tips his chin up.

"Anyway..." I tighten my hands together. I can feel my pulse in my palms. "It seems like you have something on your mind and, well, it's none of my business. I'm not trying to pry, but if you needed someone to talk to–"

Edwin grabs my wrist, swings me around so my back is pressed up against my office door, and kisses me. Hard. His body is flush against mine as his kiss sinks deeper into my body, down to the pit of my stomach.

I try to fight it at first. Not because I don't want it. Because I want it too much. I already feel a throbbing between my legs and a wet patch growing in my underwear.

Edwin locks his hands around my wrists, holding them up above my head. His teeth sink into my lower lip as he pulls back to whisper, "I can't do this anymore."

What? Oh my god, what is he talking about? Is this about the kiss? Because I wouldn't mind a repeat—

Any other thoughts fly out the window when he kisses me again. His hips rut against me, his erection pressing into my belly.

Holy...fucking...

Edwin tears his lips from mine and grazes his teeth along my ear lobe. "Feel me?" His voice is but a mere breath. His hips idle forward harder as he grows. So big. And long. And everything I could have ever dreamed of.

"Yes..."

Edwin drags his lips down to my neck, bestowing a line of kisses down the sensitive skin. His teeth sink in just enough to stings but not bruise. After all, I still have to walk out of my office like I wasn't just being devoured by my boss. "Sonia...I've wanted you since the night we met."

That much was clear for both of us.

"I've needed you ever since."

The second his grip lets up the tiniest bit on my wrists, I lunge for him, engulfing his face in my hands and yanking him into a desperate kiss.

Our open mouths collide, tongues clashing at first before settling into a languid motion.

I drag my fingers through his hair, messing up his perfect coif.

Edwin moans into my mouth as I tug on his hair, then pulls on the doorknob to keep me pressed against the door. "You're a bit of a brat, aren't you?" He tries to catch his breath.

My heart leaps. I don't know what he is talking about but it sounds good. "A brat? What do you mean?"

Edwin's mouth twitches to the side. "You're the type that likes to challenge me. So that I can put you in your place."

My mind flashes to The Underground, to all the ways that Edwin could "put me in my place."

I've never been flogged or spanked or tied down, never had a vibrator used against me to be overstimulated to high heaven, have never had to kneel before someone and say, "Yes, Daddy" and be punished if I didn't follow the rules.

But just because I've never done it before, doesn't mean I don't know I want it.

"I could tame you, you know?"

I let out a sigh that turns into a groan, coming from some deep place inside me that's just been unlocked. "I never knew I needed to be tamed."

Edwin chuckles and nips a kiss from my lips. "You've never been with someone who knew how to handle you, then."

He presses his erection harder against me.

I tip my head back against the door, trying to keep my breath steady as his eyes lock into mine. Edwin terrifies me in the best way possible. In the way that makes me want to keep watching a scary movie or in the way that drives me to keep exploring a dark room for its secrets.

He is like the buried treasure I've been scouring the earth for, that's been eluding me all this time.

"I want you so bad." The words are a pathetic whimper, squeezed out from my lungs.

Edwin pinches my chin between his forefinger and thumb, considering me for a long moment. "Then you're going to have to learn to be a good girl for me."

Oh fuck.

"Can you do that?"

I'm nodding before I can even find the words. "Y-yes, I can do that."

"We're off to a good start, then."

To my chagrin, Edwin backs away from me. He tugs on his suit jacket, resetting any wrinkles, and then runs his fingers back through his hair, managing to somehow get it all back into place without much effort.

I watch, hypnotized, as he runs his finger along his

lower lips, rubbing off the trace of lipstick left behind by my kiss. He looks at his finger and smiles to himself.

I think I'm going to combust.

"You'll need to clean yourself up before you leave your office, Sonia."

I spring myself up off the door and try to straighten myself out too. However, I don't seem to have the same dexterity to bring me back to a reality before Edwin all but fucked me against my office door.

Edwin laughs through closed lips, his eyes crisping at the sides.

I've never seen this look from him, the kind that is... endeared to something. That something being me.

"Clean yourself up..." He runs a hand down the side of my head, catching a few fly-aways in his fingers.

Then, he slides past me and opens the door.

I start to gasp, stepping backward, further into the office. What the hell is he doing?

"I want to remodel room eleven." His voice is stronger than it needs to be as he looks at me over his shoulder. "Finish up what you're doing, and I'll show you what I mean."

I watch him go, saying his hellos to members as he walks through the main member area toward The Underground door.

Oh. *Oh.*

"Sounds good," I say as calmly as I can.

Edwin smiles at me over his shoulder and then disappears into The Underground.

I gulp and sit back down at my computer. I don't know how long I should wait to make this look like a natural meet-up between boss and employee. Just two people discussing a room in the BDSM dungeon. Nothing at all unsavory about that.

I click around on the spreadsheet I was looking at before, but my eyes aren't seeing anything, and my brain certainly isn't thinking anything but *Edwin*.

Edwin's lips on my lips. His hands on my body. His body pressed to mine.

Am I about to fuck Edwin Lyons? My boss?

My ex-boyfriend's dad?

Does any of that even matter at this point?

Yes. No.

I know what I want, and I know he needs me just as much as I need him, so we can have this today. Right?

Besides, there are worse things I could do. I could commit arson. Or worse, murder. Having sex with someone because my body can't cope without it is not a bad thing. Let's call it self-care.

After only two minutes, I stand up from my desk, glancing at myself in the reflection of the window for a single moment to make sure I'm tuned up and not looking suspicious. Then, I walk through the club to The Underground.

As I go, I can't focus on anything but the bubbling warmth between my thighs. Though Edwin isn't pressed up against me, hard and wanting, I am still throbbing as if he is.

Soon, Sonia.

However, as I open the door to The Underground, I realize I don't know what to expect. This isn't just a moment of passion that will culminate in fucking.

Edwin called me a brat. He said he had to tame me.

I shiver. I never imagined the thought of being tamed would get me so hot. But here we are.

Maybe Edwin is right. Maybe he is the first man who

might know how to handle me.

I say hello to Morgan who is serving a shift as dungeon master and then Hazel who I cross paths with as I cross the main area.

She regards me with a slight, sneaking smile.

"Edwin and I are checking out room eleven. Considering a remodel."

"Of course." She nods.

Something tells me she doesn't believe that for a second. But if there's anyone in the club I'm alright being suspicious about my "professional" relationship with Edwin, it would be the Doms and subs. They are required to keep confidentiality for everyone's sake. I know she won't cross me.

I make my way down to room eleven.

The door is closed.

I put my hand on the knob and take a breath. I rack my brain to remember what room eleven looks like, but I can't. Even when I shut my eyes and try to paint the picture, it's impossible.

Breathe. He won't hurt you.

I force myself to open the door. And though I saw Edwin only a few minutes ago, I can't help but swoon.

He's taken off his jacket and tie, tossed them over a chair in the corner. He's rolling up the sleeves of his white button-down. "That was quick." He doesn't look at me.

I swallow.

Against one wall is a padded leather 'x' with restraints attached to it. I've been told this is called a St. Andrew's cross. It scares the hell out of me.

Steering clear of it, I obey when Edwin demands I sit at the end of a chair in the middle of the room that looks like it has stirrups attached to the end of it.

Edwin comes toward me and presses the door closed,

lingering over me, only inches away. A smile crosses his lips before he cups the side of my face.

I poise my lips to be kissed, but he speaks instead.

"Have you ever been with a Dom, Sonia?"

I shake my head. I've had guys who prefer to be on top, like to be in charge. But somehow, I think this is so much more than that.

"Alright, then let me explain the rules to you. While we are inside this room, I am in control at all times. In control of your body. Of your pleasure. Of how and how often you get to come." His thumb grazes my lower lip. "If you get to come at all."

"What–"

A grin broadens his lips. "Did I give you permission to speak, pet?"

Pet? Oh god. Why do I like that nickname so much?

I shake my head. "But—"

He kisses me silent.

I resist puddling at his feet. Each kiss weakens my muscles. It won't be hard to be under his complete control, that's for sure.

"This is about you giving me control over you. Even if for just this session."

"I don't know how this all is supposed to work. With all the..." I look over at the wall where rows and rows of toys hang from hooks.

Edwin guides my face back toward his. "We will keep it simple today. We never have to touch any of that if you don't want to."

He skims his hand up and down my arm. It's unlike any image of domination I've ever had. He is in control of me without having to yell or grab or press. It is just *inherent* in the way he speaks.

"Today, I will touch you. I will tease you." He pauses. "I will *fuck* you."

I gasp.

"And if it is ever too much, you just have to—"

"A safe word."

He chuckles. "Yes, my swan, a safe word."

I warm at the reminder of that first night. The way he knew me at the very beginning.

"Green means everything is good, and we are good to continue. Yellow means you are unsure about something, which is kind of like hitting a pause button. We stop for a bit and talk about it so that together we decide if we do something or not. Red means stop. No questions asked. You so much as whisper it, and everything stops. I check on you, we get dressed, and leave this room."

"Just like that?" It can't be that easy.

"Just like that." He is so calm, so firm about what he is saying. "Here is the thing most people don't understand about the lifestyle, swan. Though the Dom is in control at all times, the power is all in the hands of the sub. In this case, you."

What is he talking about? If he is the one doing the tying up, the spanking, the controlling, or whatever this is about, how is the power mine?

"Your confusion is so cute." His finger skims over the center of my forehead. "The ultimate power lies in the safe word."

Is he serious?

"BDSM is about trust, respect, and open communication. You talk, with your mouth or your body, and I listen and provide. Whether that is pleasure through pleasure, pleasure through pain, a simple cuddle, or space and time, distance."

This is blowing my mind. I thought this was about spanking and pain and being depraved or something like that.

"Before any session, a contract is signed or agreed upon where each partner makes his limits known. You need to trust me to respect your limits, and I need to trust you to let me know if I missed a cue and went too far." His hand goes to my face. "Safewording is not about being weak, it's about knowing how far you can go, how much you can take, and when too much is too much."

His finger caresses my bottom lip.

"I need to trust that you'll safeword, and you need to trust that I won't be mad because you did. But you also need to understand that I'll be devastated if you need to safeword but don't. Does that make sense?"

"Wow. It's just..."

"Not what you expected, huh?"

"Not even a little."

He chuckles. "Since I won't be using any hard toys on you, and you know your color-coded safe words, we should talk about testing. I get tested regularly."

"I'm clean. I had a physical right before I took on my new job and had the testing lumped in."

He nods. "And–" He clears his throat. "Protection?"

"I have an IUD." Just makes things easier.

Edwin's Adam's apple jumps. "I'd love to be inside you raw if you'd let me."

I can't resist a grin. "Yes. Please." To feel his cock without any barrier sounds like heaven.

He kisses me. "I would usually sit down and talk about every possible thing, but I..." His fingers slip in between two buttons on my blouse, skin slipping against mine.

I suck in a breath.

He brings his face as close to mine as possible without kissing me. "I need you now."

I kiss him, a soft press of the lips.

"Then, let's begin."

I'm not scared. For some reason, I trust him. I think I've trusted him this whole time.

He could have easily used his power over me to take advantage. He could have told me at every turn to be more professional, to not cry at my desk, to have handled Oliver Worthington, to be something I'm not.

Edwin has taken care of me in so many ways already.

I'm ready for him to take care of this.

"It's my job to tell you when we begin." The darkness in his voice sends shivers down my spine. "Sit." He points to the chair.

My insides flare with excitement I never knew existed inside me. I sit on the end of the chair.

Edwin circles to the back of the chair, grabs my hips from behind, and pulls me so I'm flush against the seatback.

"Much better." His hand ensnares my throat gently, tipping my chin back to look into his eyes.

My neck strains in his hand.

"Take off your shirt." He releases me and circles back to the front of the chair where my legs are now straddling the cushion.

I tremble as I work button after button.

"Are you trying to tease me, swan?"

"No, I'm going as fast as I can."

"Did I give you permission to speak, pet?" Edwin leans onto the chair, over me, face only an inch from mine as a sharp sting hits my thigh.

Holy... Heat spreads from the thigh he just spanked to my clit.

I love this. Love the loss of control. "No, but–"

Pain and heat sting my other thigh, his hands caressing the sting away on both sides.

"Next time you talk back," he growls as his hands go higher on my waist and he pulls down my skirt, throws it to the ground, leaving me only in my panties and half-done shirt, "I might want to find something to occupy that pretty little mouth."

God, I'm close to coming already just from this alone. I want to push him so bad, to test him, to make him lose control, like he does me.

I smile, eyes falling to the crotch of his pants that are about to burst at the seams with his erection. "Did anyone see you were hard?"

"Looks like the brat is out to play and needs some taming. Very well." He grabs the collar of my shirt and rips it the rest of the way off me, buttons popping off.

I don't even have the wherewithal to be worried about what I'll wear later. Who knew what a feral beast Edwin was?

Edwin has me stand and runs his hands up my torso, cupping my breasts through my bra. "Goddammit, how is a man supposed to think when he knows what you're hiding under these clothes?"

He kisses the swell of one of my breasts before biting at the skin.

I yelp as a pulse of electricity spins down to my pussy.

Edwin pauses. "Color."

"Green."

"Good."

Bites and nips across my breasts and chest.

I wrap my body around him, giggling at the building ecstasy between us.

Edwin doesn't take kindly to being grabbed. He takes me by the hand and has me lie down on the bed where he grabs my wrists and forces them back against the headrest. There is a wild look in his eye.

"Who is in charge here?"

I smile. "You are."

"Then act like it, or I'll tie you up." He pauses. "Color?"

I can't ignore the way my heart quickens. "Green…"

A smile peels across his face. "You've never been tied up before." Not a question. He can see it in my eyes.

I still shake my head.

Edwin leans down and kisses the hollow of my neck. "We'll start slow. Just the wrists."

He retreats to a chest in the corner, rifling through what I can only imagine is a menagerie of toys and implements. As I wait, I let my eyes dance across the wall. There is a wide, wooden paddle, a stick with a flurry of feathers on the end, a simple leather belt. A whip.

My body flushes when my eyes land on the riding crop. The triangulated piece of leather at the end of a taut handle. Something about it is…erotic. The soft inside of the leather, the finished outside. The way it taunts me from above.

"Here we are," Edwin says.

I'm expecting fuzzy handcuffs with bright pink marabou feathers, but instead, Edwin lifts a silken rope from the chest.

Returning to me, I remain quiet as he hooks the rope to the headboard designed for bondage.

"You're being very good."

I laugh, a raw sound. "Do you want me to be bad?"

Edwin takes one of my wrists, guides it to the rope,

teasing the fabric along the inside of my arm. "I want you to be *you*."

With careful but sure movements, he restrains both my wrists, assuring they're not too tight.

His hands contour and massage my arms as they leave my hands and go all the way to my shoulders. "Remember, you can change your mind at any time. Just say yellow if you need a pause or red if you want me to stop at any time."

I let out a long sigh, realizing my back has tensed. *Breathe...* I attempt to move my wrists, the rope giving me only a couple of inches and then pulling back on me. This is a new feeling, but the lack of control makes me relax even more. Whatever happens now, I don't have to feel guilty about it. It's out of my control. And that is so liberating.

I smile. "Green."

Edwin cups my jaw. Obsidian eyes sparking with fire like a blacksmith's forge. His thumb drifts back and forth across my skin. We are suspended in time, an animation that feels like it may go on and on forever.

"You look beautiful like this, my pet." A finger feathers my skin.

My pet. The space between my thighs grows wetter.

"Mine to observe. Mine to control. Mine to devour."

Oh lord, belonging to Edwin is an aphrodisiac.

My eyes drift and then skitter to the crop.

He looks over his shoulder at the wall and then smiles. "You're curious..."

I nod.

"Use your words." He lifts his hand from my jaw.

"Yes, sir."

"Good girl." He goes to the wall. "Tell me when."

Edwin ghosts his hands over the instruments of torturous pleasure. The paddle, the feathered bow, the belt—

"There." My entire body jumps as his hand touches the crop like it's somehow an extension of me.

His fingers trail down the leather. "You like this?"

A knot of pleasure builds in my belly. I nod.

"Words, swan."

"Yes."

"You want to feel it."

"Yes." The word is a mere breath.

Edwin chuckles. "Well, you've been so good, I don't see why I shouldn't reward you."

He unhooks it from the wall, the muscles on his forearm bristling as he works it into his grip. He's done this before. The movements are innate, choreography built into his muscles.

Circling to the side of the bed, he looks down at me with the intensity of a hawk. "We'll have to do some preparation, of course."

I've never been one to take it slow in the bedroom. Sex is messy and uncomfortable, and most men don't know or don't care enough to do better.

But here? Now? All I want is for Edwin to take his time with me. Have him tease me until I can't take it anymore.

I want him to break me down and build me back up.

Edwin's hand touches my thigh, running up my skin until it reaches my underwear.

Wanting no barriers between us, I lift my lower body the best I can, my hands clenching in their restraints.

He slides the tiny piece of fabric off me and then pushes it into his pocket. "For later."

"You're dirty."

Edwin's eyes narrow.

His hands caress my thighs, first one, then the other. His

hands are mapping my skin, and he is so close and yet so far from where I want his hands.

He just looks at me and massages my thighs for a while, until three sharp slaps hit each thigh in quick succession. All in different spots.

All the air in my body leaves me to be burned by the heat spreading from those scorching hits.

Then he just steps back. He admires my exposed body. His eyes fall to my blushing, gushing center, and he groans like he's some sort of sculptor who is taking in his finished work.

Suddenly, he engages the crop against my thigh, a tiny whisper of touch.

I gasp. A torturous, pleasurable churning starts in my belly.

"Leather is one of the most luxurious materials." He moves the crop back and forth against the inside of my thigh. "Expensive leather is soft and supple."

The crop slides further toward my center, teasing at my lips. I hold my breath.

"Which is why it's amazing how much power a tiny square of leather has."

He flicks the leather against my inner thigh. A teensy pinch.

I inhale sharply.

"Did you like that, my swan?"

"Yes."

He flicks the inside of my other thigh. "Yes, *what?*"

"Yes, *sir.*"

Edwin considers. "That will work. For now."

Gosh, what does he want me to call *him?*

Edwin stares at me for so long that I wonder if I've

somehow frozen time. Then he flicks the crop between my thighs with a quick flick of his wrist.

I gasp, pulling my body back with the leverage from my binding. It's reflexive, my nerves curling tight within me, a subconscious part of my brain saying, "Pain! Retreat!"

However, above all of that is the budding rose between my thighs. It aches for more. The dull pleasure zapped by the slaps, electric shocks of arousal straight to my bloodstream.

Fuck, it's like a drug.

"You're dripping..." Edwin licks his lips. "You like it, don't you?"

Before I can confirm, he thwacks the inside of my thigh again.

I whimper. It burns more. The same spot being abused again and again. Harder and harder. I can't wait to see the mark it makes.

"You were made to bear my marks. Beautiful. So responsive."

Edwin slides the crop up between the lips of my pussy, coating it in my juices. He extends it up over my mouth. "Lick."

I flick my tongue across the leather, getting a taste of my essence mixed with the musky material.

"How does it taste?"

I sigh. "Good."

Thwack-thwack. The insides of my thighs are vibrating from the snare of pain, tingling up to my center. My hips buck in response.

Edwin's forehead pinches at the center, his lips part. For a split second, there is a breach in the mask of his domination. It's clear how badly he wants me. How he wants to taste and feel me. Yet he is still fully clothed.

"I want to see you."

Something flashes in his eyes, and he resets into his domination. "I'm sure you do."

My heart thumps in my chest.

"But you don't always get everything you want, Swan." Edwin places his finger on my clit as the crop licks my thighs, over and over again.

"*I* get what I want. And what I want is to watch you come apart."

My breath quickens, the exquisite mix of pleasure and pain makes it hard to tell which is which. "Oh..."

"Will you come apart for me?"

I'm completely at his mercy. My hands can't claw for him, my legs can't wrap around him. And if he keeps it up, I'll be shredded to ribbons. "Oh god."

His finger stops, and the crop hits my clit. My back lifts off the bed, my wrists jerk in their restraints.

"Address me properly, Swan, as I address you."

"Yes, sir." My skin burns for more of the crop, for his touch. I lift my back, trying to find a connection point. "Please, sir. Please keep going, sir."

Edwin's obsidian eyes are bottomless pits. His nostrils flare.

"Please, sir, I need–" I thrust upward as best I can. "I need you, I want you, I–"

The crop falls to the ground. Edwin grabs my wrists, pinning his clothed hips to mine. I can feel his erection pressing against me. "You beg..." His voice trembles. "*So* nicely."

I tilt my chin up, trying to snatch a kiss. He moves just in time to avoid me, and I whine wordlessly.

"I want to take my time, but when you beg like that–"

"I *need you*, sir. Please, please, please..."

Edwin's brow splits like he he's in pain. With his eyes glued to mine, he undoes his belt, letting it clatter to the ground. Then, he undoes his pants the rest of the way.

My eyes grow wide at the sight of his cock bursting free from his underwear.

"Eyes up here."

I snap my gaze back to his.

Edwin's jaw tenses as I look at him. "Beautiful." His hand wraps around his cock. "You're fucking beautiful."

I smile, grateful that I please him.

Edwin positions himself between my legs.

I hold my breath, preparing to take him.

He presses his length into my dripping center, head of his cock pressing firmly against my clit.

I hold my breath.

"Say 'thank you', Swan."

"Thank you, Swan."

Something like anger mixed with amusement flashes in his eyes. It doesn't scare me. It turns me on. "Fucking *brat*."

And then he slides inside.

My back lifts off the bed as I stretch around him. I try to lift my arms to grab him, pull him all the way inside, but I can't. I wail in disappointment.

I've wanted this for so long, and he did such a beautiful job getting me wanting and panting, but now I can't show him how much I crave his closeness.

"My fucking god, you're tight."

He takes his time finding a rhythm, dipping inside me deeper and deeper.

"Eyes on mine, Swan."

"Yes, sir."

"*Good girl.*"

I burst with pride at his words, moving my hips against his, eager to feel him closer.

Edwin reaches down and his hands caress the marks left by the crop. The shock of the pleasurable pain sends pangs straight to my clit.

"I did this to you."

"You did this to me, sir."

"Fucking *hell*." His firm pecs ripple through his shirt.

I wish I could touch and tease, feel the hardness in my hands.

With my eyes locked in Edwin's, I get to watch his face descend into desperation as he fucks me harder and harder. His nostrils flare, his chin juts out, and his eyes are close to rolling back.

"So deep." My head dips back. I am at his mercy. Bound to him. Might as well give in.

Edwin laughs, retreating from me for only a moment before plunging back inside.

I howl, bending back, trying to crawl out of my own skin. I'm so hot, trembling, close to an orgasm.

"You'll wait to come with me," he grunts into my ear.

I can only hum. With his chest against mine, I try and rub my breasts back and forth against him, my nipples tingling.

"You will be a good girl for once, and you *will wait*."

"I can't, I–" My legs are shaking, hips jerking. How can he be in control of my body when I'm not?

Edwin grips my jaw. "*You will wait.*" A slap on my thigh adds to the heat.

Oh fuck.

And then he begins thrusting at an impossible speed. Harder and harder.

I hold onto my sanity for dear life, on the cusp of an

orgasm for far too long.

I am moaning and I am begging. I'm not strong enough. I can't make it.

Each time I'm near tethering, a new slap comes, and the build-up starts all over again. Until I'm half-delirious with pleasure and pain.

Until Edwin's lips part. "You ready?"

I ball my hands into fists, grabbing onto the strength I need out of thin air not to completely burst into a million pieces. "Yes, god yes."

"Now!" With one final thrust, Edwin releases inside me, a primal grunt stuttering from his lips.

The moment his cock unfurls, I do too, feeling euphoria I have never *ever* felt in my life. The orgasm threatens to snap me in two and lasts for far longer than I know what to do with.

I try to catch my breath as the glow settles over me, but Edwin steals it with a final kiss.

His hands slide over the rope and into mine. Our fingers interlock. We trade the same breath back and forth.

The warmth of him coming inside me brands me. I will carry it with me for the rest of the day.

"How are you?" His voice is tender. Soft.

I smile against his mouth. "So good."

My insides, however, are starting to run cold. Because I have to go out there and pretend like none of this happened. Like I didn't just let my boss fuck me into oblivion, let him use me as a plaything, break a boundary I swore I wouldn't with him.

Now I have to swear to myself I'll never do it again. But how is it possible when Edwin Lyons calls me his swan?

How is it possible when all I want is to be his good girl? His.

15

EDWIN

Sᴏᴍᴇ

She won't look at me.

I'm a mere foot from her, and she won't look at me.

Granted, our attention should be on the architect who is currently explaining to us and any interested members what the process is going to be like to move forward in the building of our new whisky-tasting room.

But to not even get a look from her?

That's just not right. That's downright bratty. Except I don't think I can chalk it up to that.

Sonia is new to the whole concept. She'd at least bear a look in my direction. At least a small smile.

And yet, here she is, staring straight ahead, listening to what is being said, a hard hat encasing her head just like we've all been required to wear for the inaugural day of construction.

The walls of the wine cellar are barren, all the wine having been relocated to our temporary wine bar in the main member area.

"This project requires a good deal of engineering ingenuity." I've heard the designer's speech before. And it is miraculous. However, how am I supposed to focus when an absolute goddess is standing beside me? One I happened to be inside of just yesterday?

I shuffle one of my feet in her direction, closing the gap between us only an inch as we listen.

And she responds by moving an inch away.

That is no coincidence.

My heart tightens and then falls into my stomach.

It's not just about wanting her body. It's about her soul. I may not know her very well beyond her work ethic and her wit, but I want to know her in every way possible. Fuck this distance and this wall we've had to keep between us because of our positions.

I'm willing to throw it all away. All that professionalism, all of that levelheadedness.

I want her with every fiber of my being. I thought maybe having her once would sate that desire.

It didn't. I just want more.

To me, that means it's not just about the sex. I can get sex by snapping my fingers. I can throw money at the problem. I can go through my little black book and pick out any name I'd like. It's not the sex that is drawing me to her. It's something deeper.

Something I need to know.

Sonia crosses her arms over her chest. She's chosen a looser fitting top than usual. Perhaps to hide herself from me.

Although, now that I know, I can't help picturing the gorgeous curves of her body, her jutting hip bones, her blushing, tender–

"Would you like to say anything, Edwin?" the designer asks, gesturing in my direction.

I hop to attention. "Um, no. I think you covered it."

Light laughter from the crowd.

"Then, would you do the honors?" He holds out a sledgehammer in my direction.

"Sure." I take it as I clear my throat.

The designer waves everyone away from the wall so I have a wide enough berth to swing the thing.

I undo the button on my suit jacket. "Never used one of these in my life," I say with a hapless laugh toward the audience.

"Would have never guessed, Edwin!" Marty chortles, followed by a laugh from the crowd.

I glance back at Sonia. She's finally looking at me but looks away when our eyes meet. *Fucking great.*

I eye the hammer.

Might as well get some anger out with this one.

I swing it back and slam it against the wall with all my might.

The sledgehammer bounces off the brick like it's made of plastic, almost tearing my arm out when it comes back, and I have to catch my balance.

Suave, Edwin. Very attractive.

What is it the kids say when they lose interest in someone? Getting the ick? Well, if Sonia didn't get it already, I'm sure she has it now.

I laugh at myself, pushing my hair back into place even though I'm embarrassed as all hell. "Well, I loosened it up for you." I smirk at the designer.

The crowd laughs again. I hand the hammer back to the professional and clap my hands. "Well, celebratory cocktails in the main lounge, hm?"

As people slither out of the cellar in order to allow construction to begin, I realize that Sonia has disappeared into the throng.

Shit. I wanted to grab her afterward to talk. About things. Relating to us, maybe, but also professional things.

Oh, who am I kidding? I can't play it cool with her. And that's the whole problem. I'm always able to play it cool. I'm aloof and hard to please. Women chase me, not the other way around.

With Sonia, though, I'm willing to sprint.

I finagle my way out of several conversations, including one with Marty that I feel extra bad about after abandoning him yesterday to spend time with Sonia.

And what a time we spent. But now is not the time. I have to find Sonia.

I check her office first. No dice. Then The Underground. She's been keeping a closer eye on the Dungeon Masters since the incident with Hazel, Ruby, and Oliver Worthington. But the Dungeon Master of the moment, River, tells me he hasn't seen her.

I check every single wing of the members club like a bloodhound trying to sniff out my catch, except I'm not even close to having as good of a nose. Would probably help me in this circumstance if I could catch a whiff of her perfume from as far away as possible.

My smartwatch beeps, and I look at it. Fuck. I'll have to try again later. I have a meeting in ten minutes.

I head back up to the executive floor and *that's* my boon.

Because who is standing outside of Farley's office but Miss Sonia Hill.

My swan.

She's leaning in the door, looking at her portfolio and scribbling something down. "I'm worried about putting a firm date on it. You know how construction never seems to be done on..." Her eyes land on me and widen. Her gaze darts back into the office. "You know, let's continue this later, I have a call I have to be on." The portfolio claps shut, and she rushes toward the front staircase.

My jaw hardens. She can't run from me forever. I could be patient and just wait for that inevitable moment.

But I'm not letting her get away with this. Not a chance.

I rush down the hall after her. Her heels clap against the stairs. "Sonia!"

She pretends like she doesn't hear me, though my voice echoes through the front hall.

"Sonia, wait." I scramble down the stairs. Thank god for my long legs. I catch up to her and latch my hand to her bicep just as she crosses the threshold into the nightclub.

Sonia turns, jerking her arm out of my hand. "What?!"

I recoil. I hope I haven't hurt her. I just wanted her to look at me. "Talk to me. Hell, just look at me for a second."

Sonia makes no effort to run away, thank god. "What do you want, Edwin?"

I have to restrain myself from staggering backward as if she's pushed me in the chest. "What do I want? I want…" *So many things.* "You're acting like yesterday never happened."

Her eyes fall to my feet. "Because I have to."

She starts to walk away again, but I follow at her heels.

"Why?" I'm pleading, but right now, I don't care. I hate this distance she is putting between us.

"Because I work for you."

"So?"

She gives me a perturbed look over her shoulder. "So, *I work for you,* and none of that should have happened."

We wind through the main floor of the club, which won't be open until later this afternoon. This won't do. I rush past her and cut her off at the end of the bar, leaning right in her way. "Stop walking away from me."

"Is that an order as my employer?" She frowns at me.

"No, it's..." I sigh. Doesn't she know how she's breaking my heart, avoiding me like this? "Sonia, I can't just forget about what happened yesterday."

Her throat bobs up and down. "You should try."

"Why?"

"Because it– it–"

"It was wrong?"

A flicker of pain crosses her eye, but it is gone the next second. "Exactly."

I shake my head. "That's where *you're* wrong."

"Edwin, I've been here before. I've fucked around with people I shouldn't have and got into trouble and–"

"Listen to me, Sonia–" I slide my hand through her hair, locking her gaze into mine.

I don't care if someone walks through. Don't care if someone sees us on the cameras. I don't care about anything but Sonia and me right now. "I wasn't just fucking around."

The tension on her face slackens. She doesn't draw away.

"I promise you, I wasn't just..." I don't know how I got here. I've never been flooded with thoughts of a single woman like this. It must mean that Sonia is special. That we are meant for one another in some way I can't explain. The harder I try to rationalize it, the more it eludes me. "It's not just your body that I want. You understand?"

Sonia blinks slowly, her mouth parting. "How can you possibly know that?"

I seal my lips together, searching the depths of her amber eyes. Caverns of secrets I am yet to learn. "Don't tell me you don't feel it too."

"Edwin..."

"Don't lie to yourself. To either of us."

Tilting her head away from my hand, she flushes.

"You'll get over me. Once the thrill is gone. The sneaking around, the—"

"Don't pretend to tell me who I am or what I'll do."

Sonia goes silent, a pained expression on her face.

"I *crave* you, Sonia." The thrumming in my blood is evidence enough. But so does the fact that she is my first and last thought every single day since the masquerade. "Not just your body, but your mind. I want to know everything about you. I want you in my bed. I want you in my arms. I want to be the one person in the world who knows you the best of anyone."

I take a step closer, my lips so close to hers I might die. "I want you to know me that way, too."

"Edwin..."

I can tell her strength is starting to fade. She won't be able to resist me forever.

Her gaze searches mine. "I need this job."

"It's yours. As long as you want it."

"But what if—"

"I don't talk about what ifs. I talk about what will." I frame her face in my hands, sliding my thumbs against her cheekbones. "And you *will* be mine, Sonia. It's a fact."

I expect more resistance, more arguments. But her resolve cracks faster than I could have anticipated.

She falls into my chest, her lips landing against mine, hands dragging down my waist and locking into place at my lower back.

My groin presses against her belly, sending my mind spinning. All the things I could do to her. All the things I *want* to do to her.

And yet, more important than all of them is being here with her right now. Letting her know that I'm not just going to use her up like I have all the rest of them.

I haven't ever been a good man. But I want to be one for Sonia.

Footsteps are the only thing that can break us apart, and as soon as they echo through the upper level, we draw apart from one another.

"Lipstick." She touches her lower lip.

I swipe my finger over mine, removing the evidence of our clandestine kiss.

"Is someone down there?" Solomon calls out.

I nod in the direction of the back hall, instructing Sonia to go. She rushes out of the club before Solomon can lean over the second-floor railing to spy me.

He peeks over the railing. "Oh, it's you? What are you doing down here?"

"I, um–" I adjust the knot of my tie. "Just checking that the bar is fully stocked."

Solomon folds his arms onto the railing, narrowing his eyes at me. "Since when have you–"

My watch gets another notification. Saved by the bell. "Do you mind?" I lift my wrist, pointing to the notification as if he can see.

"You're hiding something, Edwin. I don't like it."

Yes, I am hiding something.

And I do like it. I like it very, very much.

16

______

SONIA

Bridget's chin hits the floor. "You *what?!*"

"Not so loud." I grit my teeth as I look around us.

"You and Edwin–"

"*Bridget!*"

Bridget looks around the restaurant. "Oh relax, no one is listening."

"You don't know that for sure." I lean forward, wanting to keep this conversation as private as possible with Ms. Blabbermouth in front of me.

If we were in a restaurant in Queens or even the Lower East Side, I wouldn't be so on edge. But we're at a restaurant in SoHo where the plates are all upwards of forty dollars and with the kind of clientele that hangs every day at the club. Who knows who might be listening to us?

"Tell me more, tell me more." Bridget ignores my concern.

I shrug. "That's it. That's all."

"You mean, you two haven't slept together again?"

"Not so *loud!*"

"Oh my gosh, Sonia! If you were so worried about being

overheard, you shouldn't have told me about this affair with Edwin–"

"It's not an affair!"

"In a *restaurant*. Time and place!" My friend has on a minx-ish smile as she sips her wine.

I run my hand through my hair. It's oily. Needs a wash when I get home. I came here right from the club.

I hadn't anticipated on telling her about my encounter with Edwin yesterday or the way he chased me down today, but the second we were settled in and had our drinks, I burst at the seams and told her that Edwin and I...well, fucked doesn't even seem like the right way to put it. Because what happened between us was something spiritual.

I discovered so much about myself. What I like. And he took me there.

"Okay, so it's not an affair." She's sawing off a piece of the thickest asparagus I've ever seen. "Then what is it?"

My stomach flips. "I think it's more. Because...well, Edwin said as much."

"Edwin *Lyons* said he wants more?!"

I nod.

"That's...insane."

"Am I stupid for believing him?"

Bridget shakes her head. "No, I don't think so. Because I don't know if Edwin has ever been capable of saying something like that. Mind you, all I hear is through the grapevine from my dad and sometimes Seth, but..."

I wince at the mention of Seth.

Apparently, her stepbrother didn't tell her about our weird flirtation at the bar.

And that's something I will take to my grave. I don't need Bridget freaking out that I might take her stepbrother into The Underground and let him do wicked things to me.

"I'm not surprised it's you. I'm just surprised it's *anyone*."

We are both quiet, the buzz of the restaurant making up for our silence.

"How does that make you feel? That he might want more?" Her tone bears no judgment. Just a question.

I shake my head. "Confused."

"Understandable."

"Like an asshole."

"That's not fair to yourself."

"Bridget–"

"Sonia."

We glare at each other, and then we both smile.

We have a shared language already. Like we've known each other for years and years. That's how it is with kindred spirits, I guess.

"He's my boss."

Bridget shrugs. "I think we're kind of over that at this point. But maybe it's that other little problem. The surfing one?"

I close my eyes and tap my foot on the ground.

After Bridget had to sneak out of my apartment, we talked about the Nate thing. I told her the truth, that Nate is my ex-boyfriend, and I knew that the Lyons Club was his family's place, but I had no idea that when I danced with Edwin the night of the masquerade that Edwin was his *dad*. "You're the only person who knows about N-A-T-E."

"People can spell, Sonia. It's not like we're in a restaurant full of dogs."

I look over my shoulder again to make sure no one is

listening. "That's the problem. Edwin doesn't even know that Nate is my ex."

Bridget's eyes widen. "Ohhhh...."

"Yeah...."

"That is..."

"Mhm..."

"Conflict of interest. Just a little."

I smack my hand against my forehead and lean on the table. "Why oh why did I have to fall for my ex-boyfriend's *dad*?"

"Well, it's not like they talk." Bridget lowers her cutlery. "Like, you could probably go on like this for a while without Edwin even finding out."

I sigh. "Nate's still ignoring him?"

"Yeah, it's been...well, it's been intense."

I know that Nate has a lot of grudges against his father. But he never told me all the details. All I know is that it's messy, and he moved out to California to start anew.

Bridget told me that Edwin has been trying to get into contact with Nate, and Nate's been avoiding it. But I didn't think Nate would dog his own father forever. He's all peace and love on the inside, except for when he's angry.

And maybe that's just it. Maybe he and Edwin are more alike than either would like to admit. Nate's been ignoring that fire.

And Edwin...maybe Edwin's been ignoring the love.

If they could just see things from each other's shoes, they'd probably be able to fix everything.

However, I'd be cut out of the equation if father and son reunited. A common enemy.

"You should just tell Edwin."

"Are you crazy?"

"Why not?! He's obsessed with you. I don't think it would change anything."

I shake my head. "No, it would change *everything*. Because there'd be so many questions. He'd wonder if I planned this all and if I was just trying to get under Nate's skin and Nate–" I get a flash of Nate in my apartment.

Thank god, he's left me alone since, including phone calls.

I think we both made it very clear all we want to do is hurt each other right now.

Still. "I just can't."

"Okay, I won't push you too hard."

I stab my fork into the last asparagus spear. I've never eaten a more delicious vegetable in my life, even if I can't bear to believe this pile of asparagus is worth over forty dollars.

"Just listen to me, Sonia."

I lift my gaze to Bridget.

Her expression is serious. And I've never seen her be for-real *serious*. She's always smiling, always giggling, or looking at me with understanding eyes.

Now, I feel like she's about to lay down a truth I'm not sure I want to hear.

"Edwin is attractive. He's got money. And I'm really glad he seems to be trying to prove himself to you." Bridget folds her hands under her chin. "But you can't put all your eggs in that basket."

My shoulders tense.

"Because Edwin has never been known to put all his eggs in one basket either. He's a player. And I'm not saying people aren't capable of change but...well, why do you think he has three children from three different mothers?"

I've tried to ignore that part. Nate always talked about

that as one of his father's failings. How he loved his brother and sister, but always thought it was so pathetic that Edwin couldn't just lock it down with one of them or wrap up his dick to stop making the same mistake over and over.

"Now, this is the only time I'm going to get all 'be careful' on you, I promise." And just like that, her smile returns.

Relief spreads through my chest. "Okay, thank you. I appreciate it. Both the concern and the fact that you're going to put the concern away."

Bridget giggles, then flags down the waiter for another round of wine. As soon as he goes, she leans in. "So, tell me what happened in The Underground. I need to know."

"I don't kiss and tell."

"Sonia! Please! Let me live vicariously through you," Bridget groans. "Not all of us can be lucky and find a Dom at their workplace."

I laugh.

Bridget is full of surprises and her hints at being desperate to find a partner to play with are not subtle.

I glance around the restaurant. I almost feel like I'm a spy with all the looking around. The inner eye roll is well deserved. "Fine. But this is the only time I'm telling you. And you can't repeat it to a soul."

Bridget claps her hands. "Promise. Now, tell me *everything*."

17

EDWIN

"I need to see him, Sol. You understand."

Solomon crosses his legs and leans back in the chair across from my desk. "I don't know, Ed. You know Seth and me, it can be hard for me to convince him to do things."

Seth might be Solomon's stepson, but that doesn't mean there's much familial kinship on Seth's part. Though my friend loves him like a son, Seth always resented his mother remarrying, even if just a bit. I know Sol would love for them to be closer. And I know Seth has nothing against Solomon. It's just the principle of the thing for him, I guess.

But I still need my friend to try. "I need to see Nate. In private." That meeting at the beach wasn't enough. Five minutes of hurling insults at each other was the last thing I wanted.

No, I need an audience with Nate somewhere we can talk. Give each other hell. Maybe even find some common ground. "Jack has tried, Abigail has tried...Mason isn't an option here. So, I need Seth to work a little harder."

"Edwin, have you ever considered that you might just need to let Nate come to you?"

I scoff. "That will never happen."

"You wouldn't know unless you tried."

"And what would I have to do to allow that to happen?" I look at Sol like he's crazy.

Solomon smiles, ageless sadness in his eyes. "You'd have to let it go."

I push myself up from the windowsill where I've been leaning up talking to Solomon and head for my office door. "You know I can't do that."

"Is this your way of saying the conversation is over?"

"Yup." I open the door and start to step out to go deal with *anything* else.

"Edwin, wait."

I stop and turn back to face my friend.

Solomon pushes himself up out of the chair, the wood creaking, until he stands to his full height. He smiles and gives me a nod. "I'll try my best. Okay? I can't make promises, but I'll try. I know Seth still has very fond memories of his father. He might take kindly to your plight."

I can't explain it, but his agreement makes me want to cry. I know he'd do anything for me, anything in his power. However, it's the feeling that there is still a possibility in patching things up with Nate. This might be my last shot. "Thank you, Sol."

My friend shakes my hand and then kicks off down the hall to go answer emails.

Against my better judgment, my feet guide me to the member's club. It's never a bad idea to show face around there, field comments and concerns, or connect with members new and old. However, now it's always a risk that I'll run into Sonia.

Of course, running into Sonia is never a bad thing. Just difficult to stay focused on work when I lay eyes on her.

All I want to do is throw her over my shoulder, kicking and screaming, and take her into The Underground to give her a deserved spanking for forcing this distance between us. And then shower her with pleasures beyond her wildest dreams.

Other times, though, I see her and just want to feel engulfed by her arms, feel her breath on my neck.

I've considered telling her about the troubles with my son. I don't want to burden her with more, considering she seems to be having her own personal difficulties.

When she asked me if I was alright, though, that's when everything snapped open.

To my delight, Sonia is out of her office, talking with the sommelier at the makeshift wine bar. Our eyes connect for the briefest moment. I give her a small nod and a smile. "Sonia."

"Edwin."

I continue my trajectory into the member's area.

I'm giving Sonia time. To come to me. I know there was a tentative agreement between us that something is budding here. But I already chased her through the club, trying to get her to look at me. Now I have to wait for her move.

However, I am not good at playing coy. I'm good at being withholding, but staying away from what I want is a whole other ballgame.

I take a seat with some members just a bit off from the wine bar. And I tune my ears not to the conversation in front of me, since one can only chat about stocks so much, but to the one between Sonia and the sommelier.

"I'm running out of pantyhose." Sonia sighs.

"Oh, come on, that's what your stipend is for."

We give all our employees a rather substantial clothing stipend doled out in monthly increments.

"I already used all my stipend for the month." Her voice wavers just enough that I pick up on it, but not enough to be noticeable to everyone. "I used it for...something else."

Her debts, no doubt.

Shit. I can't have her feeling like she's falling apart at the seams, whether that means her life or her clothes.

"Between my rent and living expenses, I'm going to be wearing the same shoes until next summer." Sonia attempts a laugh. "They'll be flats by then, heels worn down to nubs."

The sommelier and Sonia both laugh. But my gut churns.

I can't have her sacrificing her beauty and comfort for her expenses. And if she won't let me take care of the debt, there is something else I know I *can* take care of.

I RAP ON HER OPEN OFFICE DOOR A BIT LATER. I'VE HAD to save face with the members who didn't take long to realize I wasn't paying attention to anything being said.

They forced me into a game of billiards that lasted far too long for my taste.

By the time I got back, Sonia was holed up in her office. However, the blinds are up, the door is open.

Must mean it's been a good day.

"Yes?" She lifts her head, smile growing tentative when she sees me.

"Something has come up. Requires your attention."

Her eyebrows jerk up. "Oh?"

"Can you make an emergency meeting after your shift is over?"

Sonia nods before she speaks. "What is this about?"

"Meet me in the front lobby at six."

Her eyes narrow. "Edwin... What kind of *meeting* is this?"

The emphasis she places on the word "meeting" gives me the distinct impression she thinks that I'm going to be having my way with her in The Underground tonight. Oh, if only.

However, once I'm through with her this evening, she'll be lucky if she sees a room outside The Underground for weeks to come. I'm sure of it.

"Sonia, may I remind you that I'm your employer?" I give her a careful smirk to make sure she can tell that I'm not trying to distance myself.

"Yes, sir."

Fuck. That shoots right to my cock. "And your presence at this meeting isn't a request. It's an order."

My turn to make her head spin. Her cheeks glow like she's been out in the sun far too long.

She touches the back of her neck. "Six in the lobby."

I smile, taking this as her agreement. "On the dot."

Sonia nods. "I'll see you there, then."

I stand in the doorway for a moment, letting my eyes take in every inch of her with abandon.

Sonia shifts in her seat, only a bit uncomfortable, before settling under the heft of my gaze.

"Have you been told how...nice you look today?"

Sonia's eyes fall. A sneaking smile on her lips. "Not yet."

"Well, you look very nice, Ms. Hill."

"Thank you, sir."

God, if she keeps doing that, I'm going to come right in my pants without a single touch. This will not do. "I think you'll look even better after our meeting tonight."

And with that, I leave the office, letting her gawk after me, no doubt wondering what sort of deviance awaits her tonight.

18

SONIA

When Edwin said I would look better after our meeting, a thousand thoughts crossed my mind, but I never even came close to this.

I thought that was some flirtation about how he was going to have his way with me and leave me all sweaty and sticky, more beautiful to his eye than anyone's.

But after hustling me into his private car, he made no move to tear me apart. Instead, he sat on his side and I sat on mine, both of us pretending our eyes wanted to be on anything but each other.

However, by the end of the ride, our hands were plastered onto the seat between us, pinkies touching. Once the car was parked, Edwin grabbed me by the hand and yanked me out onto the sidewalk right in front of Bergdorf's.

Edwin opens the door for me, and I step out and look around. "What are we doing here?"

"You'll see."

The second I step inside, I feel like I'm not even worthy of *looking* at anything. Past Birkin bags and jewels of mythic proportion, up an elevator to a floor where I am greeted by furs and couture gowns.

My eyes take everything in. "We have a...a 'meeting' here?"

"Yes, there's someone here I'd like you to meet. Therefore, it's a meeting, isn't it?"

Edwin guides me through the store, a delicate hand on my back.

I'm still so shell-shocked I'm not sure I'd be able to walk without his prompting.

We eventually make it to a private area where there's an older woman waiting with a rack of clothes.

"Rebecca." His tone shows fondness as he goes to the woman, kissing both her cheeks.

"Edwin, it's been a while, hasn't it?" She looks him up and down. "This suit is old, isn't it?"

He clears his throat. "Some would call it vintage?"

"Five years is not vintage yet, sweet pea. Now, who is this?" Rebecca's eyes, magnified through her dark, circular glasses, lock onto me.

My body warms all over when Edwin rests his hand on my shoulder. "This is Sonia. She's our operations manager at the club, and she's in need of some new pieces for her wardrobe."

I gasp. "Really, Edwin, that's not necessary, I–"

"Ah, yes, I see that. We're looking a little dusty."

I do a double-take. *Dusty?!*

"Well, I wouldn't say that, not at all."

Rebecca eyes Edwin. "Well, I would. Because that's my job. Now, come here, Sonia. Let's get started, shall we? I've already pulled some items here for you. I think we should start with this one." She pulls out a gray dress that has structured shoulders and geometric darts at the hips. The design is amazing.

And far too expensive.

I look over at Edwin with what I'm sure look like crazed eyes.

He's taking a seat on one of the leather couches.

It's all clicking into place that this is some *Pretty Woman* thing.

"Edwin, I can't afford even the air in this place." I try a small laugh, though I'm embarrassed to my core.

He cocks his head to the side, a look of confusion on his face. "Who said you'd be paying for anything?"

My heart flutters. This is every girl's dream. It seems too good to be true. "Edwin, I can't accept that." I go toward him.

"And why not?" He frowns.

"Because..." *Because I work for you. Because I'm keeping secrets from you. And therefore, I don't deserve any of this.*

Edwin takes one of my hands, and caresses the back of it with his thumb. His eyes entreat me not to look away. "Because I want you to feel as beautiful as you are to me. Is that a problem, Sonia?"

I could kiss him. Right here in front of Rebecca. Fuck it, I could even jump him right here and not care who saw. "No, that's not a problem."

Rebecca clears her throat.

He nods his head in the direction of the stylist. "Best not keep Rebecca waiting. She has a bit of a temper."

I scurry off to follow Rebecca into the changing room but stop before heading inside to look back at Edwin once more.

Edwin's eyes are already in his phone, dealing with

business. And there's something about the way he concentrates that pushes my body into overdrive.

"Edwin?"

He jumps, looking at me, his concentration melting into a look of...well, I'd have to call it adoration.

"Thank you"

Edwin smiles. "I should be thanking you. You're about to give me a show."

My heart leaps into my throat.

———

I'VE TRIED ON AT LEAST TEN DIFFERENT OUTFITS, varieties of dresses, skirts, blouses, and slacks, even a brand-new wool coat that Edwin insists I have for the depths of winter, explaining to me that Californians never know how to buy the right coats.

I listen to him. Not only because I want to make him happy, but also because this new side of him is so delicious and wonderful, I don't want it to go away.

This latest dress, a black Carolina Herrara with silvery embellishments across the collar, waist, and hips, has clearly caught Edwin's eye. He keeps circling me over and over, discussing with Rebecca how I look.

I already said I love it, and it's true, I do. It fits my body so well and shows off my legs. The dress is a little shorter than I wear to work, but if it pleases Edwin, it more than pleases me.

I never thought I'd be that type of woman.

Nate always wanted me to follow my heart, be a free spirit and do whatever I wanted to do. How I dressed, how I behaved, how I spoke was all fine in his book.

All that freedom is wonderful, but sometimes can also be a bit overwhelming.

To go from all of that freedom to considering a man's opinion of what I dress and how I act shouldn't be as arousing as it is.

I can't help it, though. Edwin has introduced me to a side of me I never knew existed. The one that wants to submit. To abandon control. To trust someone else to know what is best for me every once in a while.

For so long, I've had to take care of myself. But most of all, I've had to take care of those around me. My dad, Nate, a few friends from back home.

And it's not that I mind having people depend on me, but for the first time, I'm starting to understand how good it feels to be on the other side. To be taken care of. To just trust that someone will do what's right for you, what's best for you. Someone else takes the helm and you just go with the flow and trust they'll lead you to safe ports.

I always thought control was dangerous. In Edwin's hands, though, it is not about power and aggression. His dominance is loving. He just wants to take care of me. Wants me to feel wanted and beautiful.

And under his sharp gaze, I do. Always.

After circling for what feels like forever, Edwin stops in front of me. His focused expression seems much more suited for a boardroom than a dressing room. "Do you want it, Sonia?"

I hesitate. That would add at least another five k to the already growing receipt.

"Money is no object," he reminds me. "I just need to know if you like it."

Damn, it's like he's in my head.

He very well may be. Is that part of being my Dom?

Knowing what I'm thinking before I say it? As long as he doesn't use it against me, I'm alright with that.

I smile and nod. "Yes, I like it very much."

"Then, we'll take this one too."

Rebecca grins.

I glance over at the rack of clothing. We've worked our way through everything, which means my time as a doll has come to an end, much to my disappointment. However, I hope to look forward to more opportunities like this in the future.

Edwin hums. "Rebecca, do you think we can take a look at that green piece that's in the front window?"

"The Naeem Khan?"

I've never even heard the name, which makes me worry it's even more expensive than the things I've already tried on.

"Yes, with the beading. And the flowers." Edwin's eyes settle on me. "I can't help but think it was made for her."

Rebecca cocks her head to the side and takes me in as well. "I think you're right. Give me a few minutes, I'll be back with it."

Without another word, Rebecca hustles out of the room, leaving the two of us alone. At last.

"You didn't have to do all this." But I'm so grateful he did.

Edwin tucks his hands behind his back, standing tall. He's so handsome and distinguished at all times, never a hair out of place. And even if there *is* a hair out of place, it's not actually out of place. He's sculpted like an Adonis.

"I never do anything I have to, Sonia."

Meaning, he wants to do this. For me. I will remember that. For every one of Edwin's actions toward me, I will remember it's because he wants to.

In the silence, Edwin extends a hand toward me. "Let me show you something."

I take it, let him guide me off the pedestal I've been standing on to show off every outfit, and toward the big mirror that has served to reflect each and every outfit back toward me. He situates himself behind me, hands on my shoulders. "Do you see?"

I don't know what I'm supposed to be looking for.

He strokes my cheek with the back of his hand. I watch how his eyes fall to the reflection of my lips. "Do you see how beautiful you are, Sonia?"

Leaning into his touch, I shake my head. My skin looks sallow from a long day, bags under my eyes growing heavier. My hair needs a wash, yet again, and my makeup has all but crumbled off my face. "I don't see it quite the way you do, I think."

"Well, that's just a crime." He kisses my temple, his hands falling to my waist. "What about the men before me? They were never able to make you realize how beautiful you are?"

I get a lump in my throat. *The men before me...* Edwin doesn't want to know about the men before him, I guarantee it.

"Answer me, Swan."

His tone is a shock to my system in the best way. I've only known this Edwin in The Underground. Where he's in control of me. Taming me. "No, they never were."

"Pathetic. They didn't deserve you, then."

"And you do?" I know I'm flirting, and I know this is dangerous, but I don't think I can keep away from him any longer. The brat, as he calls this side of me, is ready to play again.

I expect to get a bit of angry, edgy Dom in return, but

instead, Edwin lifts his chin, meeting my eyes in the mirror. "No, I don't."

We stare at each other. And the longer I look, the more I see the hurt in his eyes.

Edwin Lyons hates parts of himself. The way he carries himself with so much confidence and untouchable poise seems to indicate otherwise.

However, I can see it all right there, tremoring in his irises.

He might be able to control me. What I wear. How I act. When I come.

But he cannot control the hate he has in his heart for himself.

Just as much as he wants to make me believe in my beauty, I want to find the pieces Edwin does not love and kiss them better.

I know he's a good man. At his core. He may have done bad things in his near-fifty years, but who hasn't?

Edwin slinks his arms around me, buries his face in my neck, and breathes in. "I will do everything with this chance. To have you, Sonia. To be with you."

His touch makes me melt. Every goddamn time.

Now that I know what he's capable of doing, I can't just turn off my brain.

I need him.

Now.

"Take off my panties."

Edwin lifts his head, gaze hardened on me in the mirror.

"And fuck me."

The corner of his mouth tilts up.

"Please, sir."

"That's better." He sounds near breathlessness.

Maybe I've taken him off-guard. Not as off-guard as I am, though.

His growl caresses me all over. "Hands on the mirror."

I do as commanded, not caring about leaving prints. "Yes, sir."

Edwin reaches down and grabs the inside of my thigh. "Spread your legs."

"Yes, sir." I follow his instructions.

His hand slides up the inside of my thigh to my pussy. He cups it through my panties and grins. "You're hot. And wet."

"Which is why I asked you to take them off." *Duh.*

"I should spank you for that."

"Yes. You should." It just comes out.

Fire blazes through Edwin's eyes, magma passing over ancient lava rock.

Not wasting a moment, he lifts the skirt, bearing my ass to the cool air, shirks my panties down just enough to get them out of his way, and slides his hand over one of my ass cheeks. Tender circles.

The anticipation builds in my belly.

He's loving this as much as I am. He's watching me watching him. A standoff.

When I've gotten comfortable with the warmth of his touch on my backside, he strikes, a loud slap cracking through the room. I gasp as a hot sting spreads out across my skin.

"Now, we don't have much time. You *have* to be good," he growls in my ear.

Oh, I want to be difficult and test his patience so badly, but he's right. Who knows how long it will take Rebecca to fetch the green beaded gown from the window.

If we're caught, it will only be shameful for me.

Edwin can get away with whatever he pleases, given his bank account.

But me? I can already picture the hot shame I'll feel for years to come.

Edwin pulls my panties down to my knees. The shuffling of his pants as he lets them slink around his hips loud as he frees himself just enough to slide his cock in between my thighs.

"Fuck..." He glides back and forth through the fortress of my groin, coating himself in my juice. "Look at me."

Our eyes lock in the mirror.

"I want to see your face change."

Edwin positions himself at my entrance and slides in, my jaw dropping as the stretch overcomes my entire body.

"Yes, fucking *yes*." His hands slide up my arms and align with my palms on the mirror. "I'm going to fuck you so good you won't be able to walk."

"Yes, please."

Edwin thrusts his cock deep into me and chuckles in my ear. "Remind me next time I want to hear you beg."

"I'll try." My one attempt at being obstinate.

Edwin thrusts his hips against mine so hard that my front presses up against the mirror, the beautiful dress suffocating.

The cold mirror touches my bare skin, making me shiver even harder than I already am with his cock sliding in and out of me.

"You think you're so clever, don't you?"

I twist my head over my shoulder, grabbing his lower lip with my teeth, begging for a kiss.

Edwin groans, but resists.

"Please kiss me." I'm nowhere near above begging.

"Aw, you want me to kiss you?"

"Uh-huh." I nod. "Before I—"

"You're not going to come already, are you?"

Not *already*, but soon. I moan.

One of Edwin's hands slides around my mouth, our eyes meeting. "You have to be quiet." His breath on my ear drives me wilder. "Otherwise..."

Wet heat builds in his palm, my eyes rolling back as he rocks me into the mirror. I do my best to buck in return, but I am at his mercy.

Just the way I like it.

Harder, faster, until I forget where I am, and I'm seeing double, catching reflections of us fucking in the mirror.

I try to hold on as long as I can until Edwin slides his hand down into my crotch, tweaks my clit between his forefinger and thumb, like a button releasing me.

My knees buckle as a wash of red bathes my insides. Sweet release.

"That's it. Draw me out. Squeeze me."

I clench around him as the orgasm waves through me.

Edwin sinks his teeth into my neck to keep from making a sound as he comes.

Warm heat coats my insides. What that seed could do if circumstances were different...

Makes me want to go again. And again.

I never, ever had a taste for breeding. Not with Nate or any of my partners before him.

But with Edwin... Well, let's just say I understand now how he managed to have three children with three different women. I wouldn't refuse him either, even if I didn't have protection from the IUD.

More than anything, I'd like to curl up into his arms and have him hold me. Aftercare is something I haven't been able to experience due to the constraint of time. Nothing more than a sweet kiss on the cheek, a firm squeeze of my hand.

And we don't have time for that now, either.

Edwin slips out of me, readjusts my underwear to their former position, and just in time manages to tuck himself away when Rebecca wafts back in with the long, green dress.

She announces her arrival. "It's a stunning piece."

I straighten myself up, hands tucked behind my back like I'm an innocent.

"Yes, exactly the one I had in mind." Edwin crosses to the dress and, with careful and measured movements, lifts the long skirt in his hands.

My insides quake again at just the tender way he handles the dress.

"I want to see you in this, Sonia."

Rebecca looks at me with a knowing smile.

We both know better than to refuse Edwin. Not that I ever would. In any universe.

When I emerge from the changing room in the green dress, Edwin doesn't speak. He holds out his hand to me, helps me up onto the pedestal and has me face the mirror.

"Beautiful."

And I can't help but agree. Though my cheeks are still blotchy and my underwear sullied, I feel like a goddess of springtime in this green dress.

Rebecca grins. "You'll take it, then?"

Edwin nods. "Absolutely."

I love myself in this piece, but this is too much. "I have nowhere to wear something like this."

"Not yet." He makes sure our eyes are locked in the mirror as he says the next part. "But you will. Soon."

I can already picture it. Me on Edwin's arm at a gala or

the opera or fucking Sunday dinner. The most beautiful couple in the room.

He wants to make me a part of his life. Regardless of these conflicts of interest.

Fuck it. I'm done holding myself back. Damn the debt, damn Nate, damn even my fucking job.

I want Edwin Lyons above anything else. I'm terrified to know what I'll give up to have him.

EDWIN

Sonia walks into the staff meeting at the top of next week in the very first dress she tried on, that gray number that makes her look like she's the captain of some futuristic spaceship in the sexiest way possible.

She strides to the front of the room with all the other managers, as is the way these meetings work.

I hang in the back with Solomon and the higher ups just to keep tabs on things, while the managers do their song and dance.

Today, she looks at me. Hard. Doesn't stray away from the feeling of my eyes on her. And she smiles.

God almighty, what that does to my heart is unparalleled to any feeling I've had before, even being inside her.

Just proves to me that Sonia Hill only gets better with time.

I've already watched several people approach her with compliments on her new dress. I can tell, because every time it happens, she looks down the front of her dress and touches it like it's a treasure.

I'm more than proud to have given her such a gift.

Solomon hums. "Sonia Hill…"

I shoot daggers at him through my eyes. "What about her?"

He looks at me like I'm crazy. "I just never really noticed her before."

"Never really noticed?!" That's the most preposterous thing I've ever heard in my life. She could turn heads a mile away.

Solomon shrugs. "I mean, you know, I've always preferred women my own age."

"And you never fail to brag about it." I smirk.

My friend shrugs. "What can I say? I'm not stunted, unlike the rest of you."

I tear my eyes back across the room to Sonia. Yes, she may be my son's age, but I don't see her as being young or immature. She's the one who can tame this wild heart.

Farley walks to the front of the room. "Happy Monday, folks!" Though he's not one of the managers people report to, Farley can never resist being the star of the show. "We've got lots of announcements for this week, so listen up."

Farley begins to talk about the shutdown that will occur next week in order to finish up the main construction on the whisky tasting room, which will make club attendance untenable, or at the very least, uncomfortable.

It's hard to remain attentive, though, as Sonia sits up there, her legs crossed, hands folded in her lap.

We keep stealing glances at each other, the smile apparent on her lips.

And on mine. I can't stop.

Someone is going to start asking about it.

Farley's voice registers for a second or two. "We have a few new security protocols in place as well, including the installation of call buttons in all spaces with safes. They will be placed clandestinely so as to alert the police ASAP."

I tune him out again and pull my phone out of my pocket, tipping the screen away from Solomon's prying eye in order to type out a message to Sonia.

I want to kiss every square inch of your body, starting with your beautiful ankles.

Send.

Only a moment later, Sonia alerts and pulls out her phone. Her face is blank as she reads, but her tell is that creeping redness in her cheeks.

She could play it off to anyone else that she's just fielding a text from an employee calling off. But she can't hide anything from me.

To my delight, she types something out, and a second later, her text appears on my screen.

> It's only fair then that I get to see you naked should I let you do that.

I almost laugh out loud.

It's true, I've been clothed during both of our encounters. Sonia is so perfect it feels almost embarrassing to try and measure up to her.

It's nice, though, to be wanted that way.

I type out another text.

> I don't know if you've been good enough for that.

I watch Sonia read, then look at me over the heads of all the employees.

It's almost as if we're the only two people here. Our eyes lock and burn into one another's.

She might have been right that it's a problem to mix business and pleasure.

However, I think that's a good problem to have.

Sonia only tears her gaze away to type something else out.

> I would be very good if I got to see you naked, sir.

I cough.

Solomon pats my back. "Are you alright?"

"Fine, I'm great." My smile must be coming off as maniac.

Before I can type out another text to Sonia, there's another notification on my phone. From Seth. I rush to open it.

It's been a few days since I asked Solomon to ask his stepson if he could set up a meeting between Nate and me. I assumed no news was bad news.

> Hey, Edwin. Dad asked me to help you get in touch with Nate. He's coming over for dinner tonight with Mason and me. I don't like tricking him, but I don't think you're going to get him to ever agree to a meeting with you. So, now is as good a time as ever.

I don't waste a single second texting back.

> What time?

I AM ON PINS AND NEEDLES THE WHOLE DAY KNOWING I'm going to see Nate tonight. So much so, that I remain in my office for most of the day.

I also left Sonia hanging mid sext. It's not because I don't want to talk to her. I just can't today. And this is where I have fallen short with every woman I've ever cared for. I always put myself first.

Today, though, I justify that I am putting Nate first. Sonia can understand that, right? Maybe that will make me even more wanted in her eyes.

As I ride the elevator up to Seth's apartment, I try to collect my thoughts. There's not a lot I can plan, though, considering how awry everything went at the beach.

I just want a clean slate. I want to offer an apology. I'd also like one in return, but I'll settle for a hug. Or a smile. Anything that will let me know that Nate will let me in just a bit more. The dream goal is to integrate back into his life completely.

Baby steps, though.

As Seth instructed me, the door to his apartment is open. I stand at the threshold for a long moment collecting myself.

Nathan's voice booms out. "Oh, no fucking way. No fucking way!" He laughs. "Fuck, I'm dead."

I smile to myself.

Mason's voice follows. "I'll revive you, hold on!"

They must be playing some sort of video game.

I didn't appreciate this enough when they were younger, listening to them play and laugh. Hell, I wasn't there for most of it. I've missed out on a lot.

That requires an apology in and of itself.

Nate groans. "Game over, man, dammit."

I'll take that as my cue and open the door, heading through the front hall and into Seth's living room.

The couch is facing away from me, all the boys

enchanted by the big screen television. Nate right in between Mason and Seth.

I breathe deep. It's now or never. "Having fun?"

Seth and Mason both turn, greeting me with tentative smiles.

Nate, on the other hand, sits up straighter, his back to me.

Seth nods at me. "Hey, Edwin."

"Hey."

Nate looks at both his friends. "What the hell is he doing here?" His voice is an ushered breath, but the silence is so oppressive we could even hear a pin dropping.

Seth chews on his lower lip, looking at Mason for some backup, and he doesn't let him down.

"Uh... We invited him, man."

Seth looks at me and back at my son. "You two should talk."

Nate keels over into his lap, rubbing his face. "What the fuck. How much did he pay you?"

"I didn't pay them, son."

"*Don't* call me son."

Seth and Mason exchange a look. "You wouldn't have seen him if we didn't set up something like this, Nate."

"Yeah, that's the point. I don't want to see him."

Nate hasn't even looked at me once.

"He's your dad." Seth's voice strains.

"Doesn't fucking matter. Not everybody likes their dad."

A few years ago, a barb like that would have meant nothing. I've grown softer, though. And it stings.

"I'm right here, Nate."

My son's gaze flies to mine, blond strands of hair

hanging in his face. "Yeah. That's the point. I want you to hear how much I–"

Seth jumps up from the couch. "Can I get you something to drink?" He comes toward me. "Sparkling water? Coffee?"

"Beer?" Mason adds.

"I'm fine, Seth, thank you. If you wouldn't mind just leaving the two of us alone for just a few minutes?"

Nate jumps up, turning to face me. "This is bullshit! You guys are supposed to be my friends, and you fucking trapped me into–"

"Nate, come on, man, you know it was only a matter of time before–"

"Before what? Before I *have* to talk to him? Before I *have* to start doing what he says?" Our eyes meet. "No fucking chance."

"Don't blame them, Nate. I asked them to do this."

He gives me a hollow smile. "Of course, you did. Because you can get everyone to bend to your wishes with a couple threats and–"

"I didn't *threaten* them, I asked them to help me. Because I love you. And you're my son."

"When has that ever mattered before, *Dad*?"

Silence falls over the room.

Mason jerks his thumb into the hall. "I think we're gonna give you those few minutes now."

Seth and Mason skitter out before Nate can hurl another angry rant in their direction. As it should be. They don't deserve them.

I'm the one at fault here, the one who has worked to corner my son so I can have him right where I want him. In the same fucking room as me.

Nate puts his hands on his hips. "This is getting ridiculous. Verging on stalker behavior."

"Oh, relax, I'm your dad, not a fucking criminal."

"That's what you say."

"Look, I came here with good intentions. The least you can do is hear me out."

Nate grips his hair and groans. "You don't get it, do you?! You're the one who disowned me for not doing what you wanted. Now you realize that was a little harsh and you think you can just *fix* things but still trying to force me to do things your way?!"

"Why did you come back to New York, Nate? The real reason."

His eyes flick to the side. "I told you already."

"No, I want the truth."

"I said, I told you."

"You told me before you left New York that you would never be back. Ever. And now, here you are, three years later. I can't help but wonder if it might have something to do with me."

My son laughs. "You wish."

I slide my hands into my pockets. "I was wrong to give you an ultimatum like I did."

Nate purses his lips.

"I...I never had a choice when it came to the club. You know this. I just got lucky that it was something I wanted to do. But..." A tremor creeps into my throat. "You're way more important to me than the club, Nate."

He has no idea what I've gone through since he left. What I've realized. And this shows on his face. His blatant disdain does not simply melt away. It hardens. "I don't believe you."

I cross the room to get closer to my son. "Nate, I'm

sorry." So fucking sorry. "I am sorry I wasn't a good father. I'm sorry I wasn't around. I'm sorry I put expectations on you that didn't align with the person you were because I... Because I didn't take the time to know you."

For each step I take to get to him, he takes one to distance himself.

"We can start again." My voice is no louder than a whisper.

Nate stares at me, and begins to shake his head. "No, Dad. We can't."

I've already been stabbed in the gut by his words. Now he's twisted the knife. "Can't we? Please?"

My son remains mute.

All of this is my fault. I pushed him so hard he ran across the country. Just because he's back in town doesn't mean I deserve a second chance. I don't. I have no right to it.

What I'm offering is too little too late.

I stumble backward; my legs are weak.

"I understand." I'm holding on to the last bit of composure I have. "I under..." Before I go, I swallow, take one last breath. One more word. Not that I deserve it. "My door is always open to you. Always. If you ever want to give me the chance I don't deserve to...to get to know you again."

Nate's forehead wrinkles.

"Anyway..." My vision is hazy as I rush out of Seth's apartment.

Seth and Mason call out after me, but I don't bother to acknowledge them.

I can't look them in the eye right now having been rejected by my own son. I'll lose it.

Once I'm out on the city street, I walk for a while without knowing where I'm going, my heart pumping, muscles burning, feet aching.

By the time I come back to reality, it's dark. And I'm alone, somewhere in the city I have never been.

Grown up here all my life and there are so many corners I've never explored. Even more so since I've been cordoned off by my wealth.

I need to get home.

But when I pull my phone out of my pocket, I don't call my driver.

"Edwin?" Sonia's voice is like coming home.

I don't know where she is, how far she is from me, but that doesn't matter. I have her on the phone. She answered.

"Sonia."

"What's wrong? You sound…"

"I need to see you." Not the way I've needed her before. I hope that's clear in the tenor of my voice. I need her in a new way. "Please, I need…"

"Where are you? Are you alright?"

"Yes, I'm fine. I'm–" *Pull it together, Edwin.* "I'll send a car to your residence. As soon as possible. Please."

I'm afraid she'll refuse me in the name of her brattish behavior. Or worse, refuse me because what right do I have to demand her time on a whim like this. That she'll think I'm some sort of controlling asshole rather than a man desperate for the comfort of the woman he—

"Of course. I'll be there as soon as I can."

My heart swells. "You have no idea what that means, you have…" I inhale. Deep. "I'll see you soon."

Knowing that Sonia is on my horizon, I could run the length of Manhattan if I needed to and not care about my aching body or my sadness. I would run around the world if I had to.

20

———

SONIA

When I walk in, Edwin is sitting in a highbacked easy chair, staring into an empty fireplace, a glass of whisky in his hand.

At first, he does not notice me, lost in thought. His teeth gnaw on his lower lip.

I knew something was wrong when he called me. The sound of his voice was desperate. I thought he might burst into tears. Now that I'm seeing him in the flesh, I'm even more worried.

His eyes are glazed over, trembling in the limited light in the room.

I'm afraid to interrupt him.

Whatever deep thoughts he's having are consuming him into oblivion. Almost like he's sleepwalking.

Are you supposed to wake a sleepwalker? Or leave them alone?

"Edwin."

He snaps to attention and shoots to his feet. "Oh, Sonia. I'm sorry, I didn't hear you come in."

"It's alright."

We stand facing one another for a long time. Quiet.

"What's wrong, Edwin?"

He tries to laugh, but his attempt at humor is betrayed by his rumpled shirt and loosened tie. His hair has never looked so messy, like he's been pulling at it. "I just...needed to see you."

I take a few steps toward him.

He can't lie to me. It's obvious on his face that he feels his world is breaking down around him.

However, I bet even if it was hidden beneath the surface, I'd be able to see through him. I've spent so much time watching him. Learning him.

"Edwin, tell me what's going on."

He seals his lips tight together.

I keep going toward him, his body bracing.

The room is wide and long, feels never-ending.

My footsteps echo against the marble floors. My eyes are fixed only on Edwin.

His eyes flick back and forth across my face. He's nervous. But he's also calling to me.

When I am close enough to touch him, I slide my arms around him and pull him into my chest. Edwin's body is tense in my arms.

"I'm here."

And then he melts, relaxing into me, resting his head on my shoulder as his hands clutch at my waist.

A few tears wet my collarbone. Just a few.

"I'm sorry."

"Why are you sorry?"

"I called you, I interrupted your night, I–"

"There's nowhere I'd rather be than here. With you." And I mean it.

Edwin sighs into my shoulder. "You are an angel,

Sonia."

I smile. I like being his angel. His good girl. I also like to be a bit bad, but not right now. Not when he needs me.

"What happened, Edwin?" I slide my hand through his hair. "Tell me."

Edwin lifts his head, pinching at his eyes maybe to keep from revealing the tears I already felt on my skin. He clears his throat. "We don't need to get into it."

"Edwin, please tell me. I want to know."

His eyes fall to the ground between us.

I won't release my grip on him. I won't let him get away. "I can tell something has been bothering you for weeks now."

"I don't want to burden you."

"It's not a burden if I want to know. I...I care for you, Edwin." I cup his cheek. "You've taken such good care of me. Please let me take care of you."

Edwin lifts his chin, almost like he's recoiling from my touch. However, his eyes flutter shut a moment later. He's not used to this.

I wonder, when was the last time someone took care of Edwin Lyons? Has it really been long enough that he doesn't know how to let someone care for him?

That makes me want to cry.

His next words freeze me to the bone. "It's my son."

It takes everything in me not to withdraw. "Your son?"

"Yes, Nathan."

Oh my god.

It was hard enough to walk through the front hall where pictures of Edwin's three children clutter the top of a credenza, including a huge portrait of the three of them when they must have been teenagers, Nate standing at the apex of the triangle with his usual, open grin.

Now we have to *talk* about him.

I don't know if I'm ready for this.

But Edwin needs me, so I'll try.

"What about him?"

"We haven't spoken in years. My fault."

My heart breaks for all the times I listened to Nate complain about his father and how his father wanted nothing to do with him, empathizing with my ex, secretly hating his father for what he'd done. Oh, how the tables have turned.

"Anyway, he was in California. Now he's back and he wants nothing to do with me."

I should tell him. I feel so guilty for not telling him so far. But I would just be making things worse.

Edwin is bereft. Not to mention, by telling him I'm Nate's ex, I'd almost certainly lose Edwin too.

"It's my fault. I was a bad father."

"No, Edwin."

"I was. It's a fact. I was so young and so selfish and–"

I caress his cheek. "We all make mistakes."

Edwin's eyes soften. Though the obsidian never loses its hard edge, there's something so comforting about the endless black of his eyes. "He's about your age. Probably more suited for you than I am."

My mouth grows hot.

Tell him, tell him, tell him. "I think you're perfectly suited for me."

His mouth spreads into a smile. Then, he leans down and kisses my forehead like I'm some dear, innocent thing.

But I'm not. I'm a liar.

His breath caresses my skin. "Thank you for coming."

"Thank you for calling. You can always call me."

What are we really doing here? Our little affair is

turning more romantic by the minute.

It seemed fine when we had our clandestine meeting in The Underground. Even when we fucked at Bergdorf's. But the emotions bubbling up are *not* fine.

The closer our lives get to becoming entangled, the closer I get to the whole thing combusting when he finds out the truth of who I really am.

Edwin kisses each of my cheeks, his eyelashes tickling my face.

I giggle before he plants an eager, soft kiss on my lips.

"Are you hungry?" He smooths his hand down the back of my head. "I've had my chef start on dinner."

"Your chef?"

"I'm not much of a cook." He shrugs.

Enjoy this. After everything you've both been through, you both deserve someone to take care of you tonight.

"I could eat."

Edwin grins.

I DON'T KNOW HOW WE'VE BEEN ABLE TO RESIST EACH other this long.

Through dinner and dessert, Edwin and I managed to keep our hands off each other. We talked about so many things upon which we haven't touched. Our taste in art and music, our opinions on politics and current events, stories from our past, even if I was skirting around the past three-ish years to keep him from getting any hints at who my ex-boyfriend is.

Now, we're in the den, which is a very simple word for the place where Edwin stores his collection of books and vinyl records.

He thumbs the vinyls lining one of the walls. "When I have time, *if* I have time..." He picks out our soundtrack for the evening. "I like to come in here, put on a record, and disappear into a really good book."

He chooses some classic easy jazz, heavy on upright bass.

At first, we sit at opposite ends of the couch, but eventually, we gravitate close enough that I can grab his hand and pull him into letting his head settle on my thigh.

I stroke the side of his face, letting my fingers explore the ridges of his eyebrows and the prickly sensation of his unshaven jaw. "So pretty." And it's true.

He's the sexiest example of a man I've ever seen, but he could also be in a museum, with how sculptural and chiseled he is.

Edwin's lips perk up. "Pretty? Not sure I've ever been described as pretty."

"Well, you are."

"Not nearly as pretty as you."

My insides flip flop.

Edwin reaches his hand down to my calf and strokes it gently. "You don't need to take care of me."

I can tell he's not totally convinced by his words.

"Want to." I shrug.

He looks up at me. "Why?"

I scoff. "Why?!"

"Yes, why? I'm...supposed to take care of you."

I capture his chin in my hand. "You might be my Dom, Edwin, but that doesn't mean you don't need to be cared for just like anyone else."

His eyes glimmer, warmth in his cheeks. "I'm your Dom?"

Shit. "Um, well–" I hesitate. "I mean, I thought you

were, but if I'm wrong–"

"Not wrong." He grabs one of my hands and brings it to his lips. He ghosts his blushing mouth across my knuckles, before whispering, "I've just never heard you say it. And it does things to me."

I smile. "What kinds of things?"

"You want to know?"

"I do."

"Mmm..." Edwin's hand slides up under my T-shirt dress and he twists over onto his stomach. With the notch of my groin revealed, he presses his face into my underwear and inhales. "Delicious."

My body locks up and then unwinds into the couch.

Edwin's fingers push the tiny piece of fabric out of the way.

He kisses my lower lips as if it's my mouth.

His fingers trace the peaks and valleys as he continues to bestow soft kisses.

It feels so nice. Though Edwin has always been aggressive in our previous encounters, I can still feel how eager he is, though there is slowness to his motions.

It feels like worship the way he pokes, prods, and tastes now and then.

"Edwin..." I moan. "Let me take care of you, let me—"

"No," he growls before snaring my clit between his lips. As he sucks on it, he savors it.

And that shuts me up. My head falls back onto the couch, and I let my body succumb to Edwin's touch.

As he circles my clit with his tongue, two of his fingers tease my opening before dipping inside.

I tangle my fingers through his hair, my body starting to grow taut as a plank of wood. "Edwin..."

He rips his mouth of my clit. "Tell me you need me."

It almost sounds like he's begging.

"I need you. I need you so bad. Please."

I don't just mean I need him to continue pleasuring me. I mean that my body and soul need him in a way I've never experienced. Like there's something so right about us. Beyond my control. Which makes my history with Nate feel even worse. Because I can't resist Edwin. It's been written in the stars from the moment we met.

Maybe even before that.

He pinches his lips around my clit, sending a spark of pleasure through me.

I groan.

Edwin rips his mouth from me, but his fingers remain inside, torturing, teasing, pleasuring, stretching me for what's to come. He slides his hand up my chest and to my neck, holding it. "I want to take care of you, Sonia."

"And I'd let you." My breathing is shallow. "But tonight, I need to take care of you."

I'm not sure if I muster an unprecedented strength or if I catch Edwin in a moment of weakness, but I'm able to take him off-guard and corner him against the arm of the sofa.

I rake my hands down his body, yanking his clothes off as I go.

At last, I get to see his beautiful, bare chest, run my hands along the curves of his pectorals.

As my thumbs brush his nipples, they grow hard.

Edwin swallows. "You're acting up, Sonia."

"Yes. And I'm going to continue to." I trail kisses from his collarbone, down his chest, his navel, and all the way to the waistband of his slacks.

I let my lips linger in the light trail of hair that leads into the precious safety of his pants, working the button open, then the zipper, and then...

"Jesus Christ..." He sighs as I take his cock into my mouth.

I lick and lap, exploring the terrain, indulging in the slight raise of his skin where a prominent vein runs across his cock. Popping my lips around the head. I hum.

"Sonia..." Edwin moans. "Take me like a good girl."

It's amazing that even though I'm in control of his body, he's still in control of me.

All I want to do is give him what he needs. Make him happy. Make him need me over and over and over again.

I don't know how long I'm down there, sucking him off, alternating tempo and pressure to keep him on his toes.

Edwin is enjoying every moment, whispering about what a good girl I am.

And for once, that's all I want to be. A good girl. Not a brat trying to get my way or have him wrangle me in.

I just want to submit to him. It's the only thing I know how to do in this moment.

"Slow down, or I'll–" Edwin's hips jerk before he grips my hair and yanks me off his cock.

I heave, still salivating for his cock. "Don't you want more?"

Edwin's eyes are wide. "You haven't come yet. You will always come first. Worst case scenario, you come with me."

"But I don't care about that." It's true. With him, I don't. It wouldn't feel like he's taking advantage of me. It would be my version of caring for him.

Edwin rocks his head from side to side. "That's not how this work, pet."

I smirk. "Pet."

He rubs a hand over his face. "God, you're going to be the death of me."

Before I can respond, Edwin grabs the front of my dress

and drags my chest to his.

Our lips lock in an intense kiss.

Then, he pushes me off. "Take your clothes off. Now."

As I strip, so does he, and when I return to him, he's naked, sitting up on the couch.

His nude form is beautiful, rippling with muscles, hair dusting his chest and thighs. Edwin is a man, through and through.

He extends his hands to me. "Get on top of me, baby."

I take his hand.

Edwin pulls. "I want you to ride me. Would that make you feel good?"

The idea of taking care of him and pleasing him, watching him writhe under me as he's squeezed between my thighs sounds like heaven.

"Yes, sir." I straddle him.

His hands cup my hips. "Good girl."

I sink down onto him, head dipping back as I let out a long moan.

For the first time, we can just let go. Be ourselves. Be free to express what we are feeling.

No one will walk in on us. No one can hear us.

It's just Edwin and me, our bodies communing together into something explosive.

"My god, you're beautiful." His eyes devour me as I thrust. "How are you so gorgeous?"

I still can't believe he sees me that way. How he honors my body with just a single look. I've never felt I'm special or stand out in any way. No more than any other girl. But Edwin makes me feel the truth in his words.

His mouth goes to my breasts, pinching my nipples between his teeth.

My body gallops with pleasure, spurring me to work

faster and harder. Though my muscles are starting to burn, I can't stop.

I need him to come.

Grabbing the back of the couch, I pull myself forward, harder and faster.

"Christ, Sonia."

"I want you to come. Please."

"Not before you."

I whimper into his hair. "Edwin, please."

"You come before me, Sonia."

"But I need you to come. I want to feel you filling me up. That will–that will–"

Fuck, just the thought of his warm seed inside me is bringing me closer to orgasm.

Edwin's hands grip my ass so hard it feels like he might leave imprints. "Sonia, *please.*" The raggedness of his voice tells me he's not long for this earth.

I just have to keep working.

"Can't...stop..." My body is in control in ways I can't even comprehend.

I take him as deep as I can, over and over.

Edwin's legs start to shake. "Fucking dammit!" He locks his arms around me, pulls my chest to his, and presses himself deep inside me, all the way.

I wail into his neck. Feels so good to be stretched by him.

And in an instant, he snaps, releasing his load inside. "Augh! God!"

Knowing I did this to him, I wrecked him this way, pushes me to my orgasm.

I clutch his shoulders, slick with sweat, as a warm stampede of pleasure thrums up from my belly.

The sounds I'm making are inhuman.

But Edwin holds me all the same, cooing to me to keep going, to feel everything, to enjoy it.

I don't care that I've been a little bad. Because I feel so goddamn good.

As we come down from our high, Edwin doesn't let go of me. He nuzzles my neck and the sides of my face, desperate huffs from between his lips, as if he can't get close enough.

I pull him closer, locking him in an embrace.

I'm not going anywhere.

"Stay tonight" It is not a demand. It is a plea. "I mean... would you?"

"Oh, Edwin..." I shouldn't. He's my boss. My ex's father. I've lied. I've threatened his trust, and he doesn't even know it yet.

But we are already in so deep. Our bodies have twined together several times. And our hearts...

It's too late for me to stop this.

And why would I want to?

"Of course, I'll stay."

Edwin lets out a sigh. "Good. Good, I...I don't want to be alone tonight."

He slides his hand to my chest, catching my heartbeat in his palm. And for a long time, he considers my face before whispering, "I don't deserve you."

I want to echo what he's said right back to him.

I don't deserve any of this when I've been so dishonest. But I can't stop.

"Don't be silly." I take his face in my hands. "Now, take me to your bed."

Edwin gets a second wind, throws me over his shoulder, and carries me through the beautiful penthouse to his bedroom.

21

———

EDWIN

It's her. "You wanted to see me?"

Her silhouette in the doorway of my office is enough to make me faint. The same one that I spied as she snuck out of my bedroom early this morning. The one I wanted to call out for but didn't have the courage to.

Though she didn't spend the night in her own bed, she looks as well rested as can be.

Skin glowing, hair shining, pinned back in its usual updo.

Oh, thank god, she's smiling. I wasn't sure if I had done something wrong when I woke up without her in bed beside me.

"Yes, I did." I clear my throat. "Close the door, would you?"

"I'd better not." She pops an eyebrow upward.

"Um. Alright." It's clear I shouldn't press the issue.

This is why I don't mix business and pleasure. The lines get blurred.

I wasn't able to help myself with Sonia. And I don't think I'm going to be able to help myself any time soon.

I keep my voice low. "You left. Why?"

Sonia glances over her shoulder before taking another step into my office. "I'm sorry. I had to make it home before work, and I'm all the way up in Queens, I–"

"I'm your employer. I would have had you call off."

She tightens her lips, shrinking them back to a mere line. "That wouldn't be very professional of us, would it?"

"We left professionalism behind a while ago." I rise to my feet.

Sonia's body is rigid. She's afraid of me. "I need this job, Edwin."

I frown. "No one is threatening to take it from you."

"Not yet."

Something else is going on, and I'm determined to find out what. I'll wait.

I'm a stranger to waiting to get what I want, but for Sonia, I will wait forever if need be.

"Last night..." I called her up here with the intention of saying something very specific, a monologue I crafted throughout the morning from the time I woke up to moment she walked into my office.

I should have written it down, though, because my face is hot, and I'm flustered, more so than I've ever been.

"Was wonderful." She smiles. But it's a sad smile. "But I work for you. And–"

"I don't care about that."

"It's not just that, it's "

"Listen to me, Sonia." I step out from behind the desk, feeling naked and so vulnerable. But I have to follow through. I have to.

My Swan.

"From the outside, I have everything a person could want. But I am a man with nothing."

Sonia's face slackens. "Edwin..."

I clutch my heart. "Listen to me, just listen."

She nods.

"I have been a terrible lover. And a terrible father. All I have is a business that doesn't really love me back. Not the way a person could."

Sonia's eyes crinkle. Lips lift.

"I know there is so much we would have to learn about each other. And so much we would have to overcome. But please give me one chance to show you how good of a man I know I can be for you."

These feelings have been burning up in my chest since the moment I met her.

I've wanted to become a better version of myself for too long now. I will never do that if I close myself off from love. Even if she works for me.

"Edwin, I'm not a perfect person either."

I take the moment to close the space between us, take her cheeks in both my hands, so thankful she doesn't draw away.

"You are to me."

"I'm not. I shouldn't be." She blinks, tears welling in her eyes.

"How can I prove to you how perfect you are? How good we could be for each other? Just say the word and I'll do anything." The words come so fast, they're stumbling from my mouth.

Sonia grips the lapels of my jacket, half-laughing. "The door, Edwin."

"I don't care who sees." And with that, I kiss her with everything I have in me.

A kiss through which I try to give her all of me.

I've never felt this way about anyone. Not even the

mothers of my children.

I'm about to be half a century old, and it's taken me way too long to figure out what's valuable in life. I won't lose this. Not again.

Not after all the people and love I've sacrificed in my life to stay the immature, cold businessman I've been my whole life.

Sonia's hands slip up my chest and hook around my neck, pulling me closer to her, her hips brushing up against me as our lips meet. She might be tentative, but her body is vibrating at the same frequency as mine.

A deep voice comes from the door. "What the hell?"

Sonia pushes me off, touching her mouth. "Oh, my god."

My eyes fly to the doorway of my office.

"Nathan."

He's wearing slacks and a dress shirt. He's even got his suit jacket slung over his shoulder.

My heart sings at the sight of him as it bleeds for his poor timing.

"It's so good to see you." I want to go toward him, embrace him, but knowing Nate, he'd run away before I could get even a foot away. "I'm sorry, you've walked in at such an...inopportune moment."

Nate stares at me. "What is *she* doing here?"

If I wasn't so stunned, I'd ask him to mind his manners.

"Um, Nathan, this is Sonia Hill." I gesture toward her. "She's our operations manager at the club.

They both just stare at each other.

"Alright, then." I try to laugh to cut the tension in the room, but it doesn't seem to do the trick. "I'm so glad you came, but what are you doing here?"

Nate is pale as a sheet, expression unreadable. "I was

thinking about what you said last night and I... Open door. Ha..." He runs his hand through his blond hair. "You've got a really strange sense of humor, Dad."

"What the hell are you talking about?"

"This is why you came to New York, huh?" Nate directs the question at Sonia.

"Please, I didn't mean–" Her voice tremors.

What the hell is going on?

"You came all the way here just to fuck my dad? Is this some twisted plan you're both in on to fuck up my whole life?"

My head swings back and forth as they volley words in a game I don't know. I'm not sure where to look or what to say. It's all going over my head.

Sonia puts her hands on her hips. "For fuck's sake, Nate, not everything is about you!"

"You're damn right it's about me!"

Wait... I introduced him as Nathan. She called him Nate. "You two know each other?"

Sonia's face falls, the tears that were threatening to fall earlier now gliding down her cheeks.

Our eyes meet for only a moment, but she looks away.

"*Know* each other?" Nate scoffs. "Sonia is my ex-girlfriend."

My heart stops.

22

SONIA

I want to die. Right now.

The news lingers in the air, falling heavy over all of us.

As if in slow motion, Edwin turns toward me, and I can't even bear to look at him. To see the betrayal in his eyes. Imagining it is hard enough.

"Ex-girlfriend?"

I shut my eyes. Can't I just wish this all away?

"Sonia?" He sounds mad.

He's never directed his anger at me.

And I am praying he doesn't start now.

"It's true." I keep my eyes averted. "I'm...Nate's ex-girlfriend."

Edwin is silent for a long moment. "I think I need to sit down." He retreats to the edge of his desk to lean.

Nate's eyes are growing wilder by the second, the same way he looked when he cornered me in my apartment. "Are you two really expecting me to believe that you didn't do this on purpose?"

Is he insane? "Why in the world would I sleep with your dad on purpose?"

"*Sleep* with?!" Nate gapes.

I throw my arms up. "You were the one just accusing me of it!"

Nate looks behind me at his father. "He didn't know, did he? You didn't tell him."

I still haven't looked back at Edwin. "I didn't know how."

"Disgusting."

My gaze is drawn back to Edwin.

His eyes are trained on the floor, hands gripping the side of his desk.

I did that. By lying to him by omission, I think I broke him.

Any other time, if circumstances were different, I would hope he'd speak up and defend me. He practically just declared his love for me, didn't he?

But I don't deserve it. I don't think I ever did.

I knew this would happen. I knew I should have stayed away.

"You knew he was my dad, and you still seduced him."

"I didn't seduce him. It was... We both–" Except, I'm starting to question everything.

Was I just trying to get back at Nate all this time? That doesn't account for the immediate attraction I felt for Edwin. Unless somehow my body just knew to seek him out?

God, I'm so screwed up in the head I don't even know which way is up anymore.

"You're so fucked up, Sonia. You went out of your way to get a job at my family's business in order to get to my dad and hurt me. Why?"

I shake my head. "No, that's...that's insane! I didn't

want to get to your dad, it just happened, I swear." I turn on my heel. "Edwin, I swear."

Edwin doesn't look up. My heart breaks further.

"So, you just accidentally applied to the Lyons Club? The club I told you I left behind? On purpose?" Nate presses harder, coming toward me.

"Stay away from me."

"I'm not doing anything, I'm just holding you fucking accountable since you've–"

"Sonia."

We both look over at Edwin. He looks so...sad. A curl of hair fallen over his forehead. "Yes, Edwin?"

"Is that true? That you knew when you applied for the job that..." His eyes find mine at last. The betrayal in his gaze reaches into my chest and grabs my heart, squeezing it until it might explode.

"Edwin, I–"

"Answer me. Please."

Fuck. More tears well in my eyes. "Yes, I knew. But I didn't come here trying to–"

"That's all I need to hear."

"I promise, Edwin, I–"

Nate turns to his father. "Don't act like you're better than her, Dad."

For once, I'm grateful he's interrupting me because I have no idea what I would have said.

But he doesn't have the same problem. "I'm sure if you had known Sonia was my ex, you would have hired her just to get in her pants."

Edwin stands, gripping his fists at his sides. "Get out."

"Funny how you've been begging me to come see you at the club, and now you're making me leave. I guess some things never change."

"I will not stand here and have you insult my character. I didn't know until this moment that you and Sonia–" Edwin huffs. "And if I had known, nothing ever would have happened."

I knew it. I knew he never would have touched me if he knew.

Nate snorts. "Likely story."

"Are you questioning me?!"

"What else is new?! You're just an old man who is clinging onto youth by fucking every and any pretty thing he sees! Sonia could have been anyone to you!"

I put my hands over my face. I can't keep from crying any longer. "Please stop..."

Edwin's voice is low. "You don't know me at all, Nate."

"I know that you have three children with three different women, all of whom hate your guts because you're a shitty excuse for a father and for a man!"

"GET OUT!"

Shit, was that me?

From the look on Nate and Edwin's faces, it really *was* me.

But he can't talk like that. Not about Edwin.

I don't care what he says about me, but he needs to watch his mouth when it comes to his father.

"If you hate us so much, if we're such bad people, why don't you just leave–" I push on Nate's shoulders, "–us–" again, "– alone!" I've pushed him all the way to the door.

Nate rubs his hands over the places I've pushed him as if I've burned him.

"You think I'm a terrible person for what happened to your dad. But you're just as bad as me, Sonia." His blue eyes rise to Edwin and then focus back on mine. "You two deserve each other. You're both—"

"If you insult her one more time, I'll be the one removing you from the room, and I won't be nearly as nice." Edwin's voice trembles with darkness.

Nate says nothing else. But the way he stares at each of us shakes me to my core.

And then he's gone. Just like that.

I don't bother to watch him go. I grab the doorframe for support and try and catch my breath.

"Sonia."

My heart falls. I still have Edwin to deal with. "What?"

"Look at me." The sound of his voice hurts.

I know what he's going to say. I know he's going to break my heart, take back all of the beautiful confessions he made before Nate came in and wreaked havoc between us.

That's not fair, though, to blame it on Nate.

Because it's my fault.

I ruined this from the very beginning. From before I even step foot into the Lyons Club. Way before that. When I was still in California. When I left Nate. When I applied for the job. Hell, when I even met Nate.

I've been misreading all the signs that my relationship with Edwin is some wondrous, cosmic thing.

The way it looks now, it's been cursed from before the night we met.

"I can't."

"Yes, you can."

Gripping the doorframe, I force myself to turn around and look at Edwin.

I still want him. So bad.

The lips that have kissed every inch of my body. The eyes that still grip my soul.

We are destroying each other.

"I'm sorry. Please don't...please, I need this job."

"I know you do." His tone is so... detached.

Why is that worse than anger or sorrow?

He shakes his head. "I'm not taking that from you."

I breathe a sigh of relief.

His eyes burn me. Wreck me. Shatter me. "But we can't–"

I wave my hand. "That's all I need to know. We don't need to...I don't need you to do the whole letting me down easy thing. I don't deserve that. Let's just– let's just–"

"Sonia, wait–"

Without me realizing, my feet have been taking me out the door, into the hall, farther and farther from Edwin. "I'm sorry." My voice doesn't come. Just a whisper. A breath.

"Sonia–" He rushes to the door.

"I'm sorry!" I run down the hall at top speed. I don't stop until I'm in my office, door locked, blinds drawn. I turn off the lights and try to breathe.

I don't know what happens next.

I'm not sure I want to.

23

EDWIN

If I felt like a shell last night after Nate castigated me, I don't think there's even a shell of me left now that I know the truth.

Sonia is my son's ex-girlfriend. And she didn't tell me.

I should be mad at the news. But I'm not. I'm sad. And hurt.

My insides feel like they're all over the floor of my office. A one-two punch combination of losing my son and the woman I care for in an instant.

I hate that Nate had to see that. I hate it even more that it happened when he was coming to me to make amends.

Things are ruined now. Destroyed. More than I ever thought possible.

I leave the club right after Sonia disappears. I can't be here. Need to take some time to sort things out.

I go for a walk on a park to try to lose myself. On the view, on the pace, on the mechanical movement of putting one foot in front of the other without care as to where it will take me.

But the longer and farther I go, the more I find that nothing can shake how much this hurts.

I can't blame Sonia for not having the confidence to tell me the truth. But she betrayed me and allowed me to fall for her.

What could have been an easy choice at the beginning between Sonia and Nate now feels impossible.

I know what I have to do, though.

If I'm trying to be the father I always should have been, I'll choose my son over Sonia.

I love Nate, want to give him the father he deserves, twenty-nine years too late.

And being with my son's ex-girlfriend would be a sure way to lose merit to one of those mugs that says "#1 Dad" on it.

However, every time my mind settles on the fact that I'm going to have to give Sonia up to appease Nate, my stomach sours. Can I really give Sonia up when she's melted the ice around my heart? Made me feel things I thought I was incapable of feeling.

This is an impossible choice.

As I contemplate going back to head home, my phone rings.

Abigail. Perfect timing. My daughter always makes me feel like I'm not a total shithead of a father.

As I answer, before I can even say "Hello", I know something's wrong.

"Daddy." Abigail's voice warbles.

I brace my hand on the nearest tree, ready to run in any direction she tells me to. "What's wrong?"

"It's Nate. There's been an accident."

"He's lucky to be alive."

I let my eyes linger over my son's body.

He's breathing through some sort of ventilator, one of his arms in a cast, and a plastic brace encircles his neck.

The doctor clicks his pen off and puts it in his pocket. "He's had significant damage to his spinal cord."

"How did that happen?" From what I gathered from Abigail through her heaving sobs, Nate was thrown from his board while surfing, which isn't unusual in and of itself, until he didn't come up for air and several of his mates had to go retrieve him from the sea spray.

"Until he wakes up and tells us, we can't know for sure. Surfing at the Rockaways is definitely not something I'd recommend to someone who doesn't want to risk some danger."

I swallow.

Nate must have gone straight there from my office.

I can't imagine surfing under the influence of anger is a smart thing to do.

"So, his spinal cord. What's that mean?" I know the meaning of the words and I know them in that order. But what that means for my son...

The doctor clears his throat. "Well, for now, it means we wait. I think his prognosis is good. He'll walk again. But it will take a lot of time and work."

I sigh. "Well, good, that's...good." As good as it can be, I suppose.

Although, I don't just want my son to be able to walk. I want him to be able to surf too. Do all the things his heart wishes. I might not be familiar with his passion for surfing quite yet, but I can just imagine the look on his face if he's told he can't do it.

That might kill me.

I look back at Abigail who is sitting in a chair beside the bed with Nate's hand in hers. Her face is sticky from trails of tears.

"For now, he just needs to rest. We have nurses on rotation, and they'll be checking in on him from time to time."

"Good, alright, well...good." I have no idea what else I can say.

We bid the doctor goodbye. I shuffle over to Nate's bedside and again let my eyes cross over him.

"You know, the only time your brother's been in a hospital was when he was born?" I manage a small smile.

I remember the day with a very strange fondness.

Clarissa had wanted me there and, though at first I resisted, my father pushed me. It was my duty as the child's father. And so, I was with her throughout her labor.

And thank goodness I was. I might have been a shitty dad the past twenty-nine years, but no one can take away the absolute full-body love that overcame me at the sound of my son's first cry or the first time I held him and felt that life was worth a lot more than the silly club or the Lyons family name.

Instead of running toward that feeling, though, I ran away from it. Pushed it away. Told myself that I wasn't made for fatherhood. I was made for business.

Besides, the way I decided I could support Nate, and then Jack, and then Abigail, was with my money. Why would they want *me* when they had their mothers and could have my money?

I can't believe how wrong I've been all this time.

My eyes settle on my daughter again. "Honey."

Abigail lifts her green eyes.

"Could you...um..."

I don't want to cry in front of her. It's a stupid point of

pride, but one I hang onto, nonetheless. "I'll take over for a bit. Why don't you go take a walk? Grab us some coffee. Try Jack again, if you can."

Jack has been busy at work, his phone probably buried under a pile of manila folders and drowned out by the sound of stockbrokers yelling at one another.

She looks at her brother and then back at me.

I can tell it's not easy for her to leave.

Abigail, though, has always been my biggest supporter. Daddy's girl.

Right now, I couldn't be more thankful for that.

And after all the time it's taken for Nate and me to be in the same room without him running away, I'm sure she's feeling relieved.

However, I never wanted it to come down to the fact he *can't* run away.

"Sure, Daddy." She gets up and, as she passes me, gives me a kiss on the cheek.

I slide my arms around her and hold her close.

I hate myself even more for the three years Nate and I didn't speak.

Life is way too precious. It can change in the blink of an eye.

Thank god, I have a second chance.

She looks up at me. "You okay?"

She knows the answer to the question, but she's trying to be a good daughter and acknowledge that I'm not just her dad, but a person with feelings.

I'm not going to burden her with them, though. "Yeah, I'm okay. You go on now." I release her even when all I want is to have my arms around all my children from now on. That way, none of them can get hurt.

At least, that's what any father hopes, I suppose.

Abigail leaves.

Then, it's just Nate and me and the machines keeping him alive.

I go sit in Abigail's chair and hold my hands between my knees because I have no idea what else to do with them. "I'm sorry, Nate."

Nate's eyes are closed. There are scratches down one of his cheeks. And his blond hair is scraggly on the pillow.

I reach over and gently smooth it out. Once, twice...I stroke his forehead. "I'm sorry for...for everything."

I take his hand. It's limp and tired. But I won't let go.

"I know you hate me." God, I don't know if he can even hear me. But maybe I need to do this for me more than for him at this point. "And I deserve it. But..." I take a deep breath that hurts going in.

I blink and a tear rolls down my cheek. "I love you. I have always loved you, even when you hated me and wouldn't speak to me. Even when I threatened to disinherit you. I love you."

I dip my head down and take a measured breath to keep from weeping.

"I have never been good at showing it. I don't need you to forgive me. I just want a chance to show you I can be the father I should have been from day one."

I clutch his hand as hard as I can without fearing I'll hurt him. I lean my forehead against his.

It doesn't matter that he's an adult, going on thirty years old. He's still little Nathan. Still laying in his car-shaped bed, asking for a bedtime story, trying to keep his eyes open until he's snoring like a puppy on my arm.

"I'm here. Dad is here. Okay?"

Fuck the club. Fuck everything I've spent my life working on. It was always the wrong things.

This is the universe giving me a second chance to get it right, at least a little bit.

And I'm not going to waste it. "I'm going to be here every step of the way. I promise."

I remain there with our foreheads touching, tears gliding down my face.

And then his hand tightens in mine. Squeezing back.

I sit up, almost sure my brain is tricking me.

But there it is, his fingers tighten around mine.

When I look back at my son's face, his eyes are cracked open, gleaming. Staring at me.

We look at each other for a long time.

It may not be forgiveness, but it's a start.

24
———

SONIA

"WHAT DO YOU *MEAN*, WE'RE RUNNING BEHIND?" I PUT my hands on my hips.

The lead designer laughs like it's no big deal. "I mean that we're running behind. Do you want me to break out a thesaurus?"

The wine cellar encircles us. Except it doesn't much resemble the cellar anymore.

I feel like I'm standing in the ancient ruins of Pompeii from all the dust and rocks and mess that's accumulated the past few weeks.

"I have plans to close the club at the top of next week for you to put the finishing touches on–"

"We need two more weeks." He half shrugs. "I don't know what else to tell you."

I bite my lower lip to keep from bursting a slew of insults all over this man.

I haven't liked working with him from the start, but it's even worse when Edwin isn't around. And Edwin hasn't been around for three days.

My fault too. Which makes it worse. "You'll be hearing from our contracts department, then."

"Fine. Send them my way." He turns around to go hound some workers who seem to always be doing *something* wrong. As if they can afford to fuck up anything else now that they're running a full two weeks behind.

I storm out of the cellar.

I have been on edge since Nate walked in on Edwin and me. Scratch that, I am now so far off the edge and plummeting toward the jagged rocks at the bottom of the cliff, except I'm trapped in a freefall, and I don't know when the solace of death will come.

I run straight into Farley, almost knocking us both back to the ground."Whoa, whoa, whoa!"

"Oh, sorry, Farley, I–"

"Everything alright?"

I huff. "Um, no, I'm afraid not."

Edwin might be my employer, but Farley is my direct report.

And while I've always been afraid of disappointing Edwin, he's never indicated his disappointment. Farley, on the other hand, doesn't like it when things don't go his way.

"What's going on?"

"They need two more weeks."

"Two more–" Farley's voice is close to shriek- levels.

"*Yes*, two more weeks." I blow past Farley to continue down the hall back to the main members' lounge.

Farley's John Galliano shoes follow behind me, an annoying clicking that competes with my own high heels.

"So, what are we going to do about the club closing on Monday?"

"We're going to have to reschedule."

"We can't reschedule!"

I turn on my heel. "Well, there would be no point in closing when the project doesn't need the club to close, now would there, Farley?"

Farley's lips bunch up. He knows I'm right, and there is nothing to be done about it.

"But we've already informed all the members–"

"Well, we'll tell them the date has changed. See? Watch." I stomp out into the main member area and cup my hands around my mouth. "Closure date is changing. Be on the lookout for a notification on your member account!"

The people in the main area look at me like I'm crazy, but that's just fine.

Screw it. Screw it *all*. If the builders want to question me, and Farley wants to argue with me, and Edwin wants to ignore me–

I deflate a bit.

Edwin is ignoring me. Yes. In fact, he hasn't been to the club as far as I know since I ran away from his office.

It's my own fault. I deserve his distance.

It's broken my heart right in two all the same.

I have to do my job, though, which means pushing the pieces of my broken heart far away where I cannot access my feelings.

But since everyone wants to test me today...

Farley follows close at my heels as I head for my office. "Are you fucking crazy?"

"Maybe a little." I shrug.

Farley grabs my arm and turns me to face him.

"Sonia, I don't know what's been going on with you the past few days but you're acting..." He scans the room of members. "You know how we have to act around here. And it's not like that."

It's true. We follow a code of conduct at all times

despite whatever hell is going on in the background. "I'm sorry. You're right."

Farley's eyes soften for a moment.

Maybe I can tell him. Maybe he'll listen. We're friends, aren't we? Perhaps he'd listen and keep my secret and–

"So, what is the date, then? For the closure?"

Right...how could I be so stupid? It's all business. "I don't know, I'll have to look at my calendar."

"Could you let me know by five today?"

"Fine. I'll–" My phone starts to vibrate; I pull it out of the pocket of my slacks.

My heart falls into my stomach when I see the contact information. It's just a phone number without a name attached, but I know the number by heart. Attaching it to a name will make it seem too permanent. Too...awful.

If he's calling me, I know I've fucked up. "I have to take this."

Farley starts to protest, but I ignore him and head into my office, shutting the door behind me as I answer. "Hi, Bruce."

"You're late on your payment, Sonia."

My heart drops into my stomach. "Am I?"

I look down at the blotter on my desktop, the one that has a printed calendar on it where I notate things like meetings and dinners with Bridget. Days I'm supposed to pay the loan shark.

And sure enough, I was supposed to issue out a payment yesterday. "I'm sorry, things have been hectic, let me–"

"It's payment and a half now."

I drop into my chair. "I...what?"

"You're late on a payment, now you owe–"

"I can't give you payment and a half."

I swear, Bruce, the fucking loan shark, chuckles. "Then we can add it to your tab."

"I–" I lean my forehead on my hand. "I'm going to be paying you back for the rest of my life."

"It's a shame the daughter has to pay for the sins of the father. I know, it's not fair." Bruce sighs. "But those are the rules."

My eyes burn with hot tears. *More* tears.

I've cried every day since Edwin found out about me and Nate. And the crying is never cathartic. It's painful.

I hate that nothing is going right in my life. Will it ever? "How can I follow the rules when you keep changing them?"

"Life isn't fair, cupcake. And neither am I. Get me your late payment by the end of the day. Or else–"

"Let me guess. I owe you double."

"Now you're catching on."

As soon as Bruce hangs up, I go to my banking app, transfer everything in my checking account to his money grubbing hands, and then throw my phone across the room before tumbling into a fit of tears.

I'm trapped.

On one side, I have the debt, and on the other, a job that I need to keep in order to pay off said debt. And the one thing, *the one thing*, making it worth the vicious cycle, I've lost. Because I am a liar and a traitor.

I saw it in Edwin's eyes. The way he recoiled from me.

And with just a few days of not seeing him, I feel like I'm in withdrawal. Like he became a drug that I crave.

With Edwin, the world seemed easier.

I have taken care of myself for so long, even when I was with Nate.

Back then, I was taking care of Nate too. Playing the role of girlfriend and mom in one.

It took me this long, but I got to meet someone who can take the load off. Who makes me feel out of control in the best way.

And I've lost him.

I'm not sure how long I'm crying before there's a knock on my door.

"Sonia? It's Solomon."

I shoot up and look again at my blotter.

Shit, we have a meeting scheduled.

Solomon emailed me out of the blue about it yesterday, saying there were some things we needed to discuss regarding the operations of the club.

It was cryptic enough that I'm scared he might fire me even though I'm pretty sure that's out of the purview of his job.

I swipe the tears away and blow my nose with a tissue before forcing a smile. "Come in!"

Solomon opens the door to my office and stops. "You've been crying."

Fuck. "No, I haven't."

"I can come back later."

"Solomon, please, sit." I gesture to the chair across from my desk. "I'm fine."

Solomon smiles, a pitying look in his eyes. "I'm not an idiot, Sonia. I have a daughter, after all."

Once Solomon found out Bridget and I have become friends, he's been very paternal to me, even though we almost don't interact at the club.

His job is higher level, dealing with the finances and the nitty gritty numbers, which keeps him tethered to his desk most of the time.

"And Bridget–" He breathes a sigh as he sits in his chair. "She would kill me if she found out I saw you were crying and didn't ask about it."

I clasp my hands under my chin and force a smile. "I'm fine, Solomon. Really. If she threatens violence upon you, you can send her my way."

He furrows his brow.

"Now, please. What did you want to meet about?"

"Well, if you insist..." He readjusts in the chair, his long legs appearing unable to get comfortable. "I'm going to be taking over as interim CEO for at least the next month."

"W...what?"

"Edwin is taking a leave of absence."

Oh god, this is all my fault. "Is everything alright?"

Solomon clears his throat. "He's fine, but his son has gotten into a bit of an accident."

"Which one?" The nauseous feeling in my stomach tells me I already know.

"Nathan. While he was surfing. A freak accident. I don't know all the details, but–"

"Oh my god, is he alright?" Though I don't love Nate the way I used to, I would never wish ill upon him. I can't help but feel this is my fault.

Solomon nods. "Yes. I mean, he will be. He has a spinal cord injury that apparently is going to take some rehabilitation. Edwin wants to be there."

"Of course, he does." I'm unable to contain a smile.

He's a good man. A bad father wouldn't do that for his child.

"So, I'm going to make sure that everything is still going according to plan. As if he never left. And that means you and I should touch base about how things work around here since I'm not normally in the fray, as it were."

Tears start streaming down my face, and I turn from Solomon. "Sorry."

"Oh, Sonia..." Solomon comes over and pats my back. "It's alright. Everything will be alright."

I don't know what he knows or doesn't know. Not sure if his comforting is out of pity or out of a sense of duty.

Right now, it doesn't fucking matter. It feels nice for someone to tell me everything is going to be okay because deep down, I know the truth.

Nothing will ever be alright again.

25

EDWIN

"I have to admit, this is nice." Nate grins.

Jack, Abigail, Nate, and me, all in the same place. That hasn't happened in years.

And now that Nate is more cognizant of what's going on around him, it means a great deal more than having us all fawn over his half-comatose form.

Jack chuckles. "Yeah, I think that's the painkillers talking."

Abigail punches him in the arm. "Don't be a jerk. It is nice, isn't it, Natey?" She bats her eyes, squeezing Nate's hand.

"I'm injured, Abs, not five."

I am posted up in the corner of the room where I've been since I came to see Nate in the hospital that very first day.

Abigail fetched me a few changes of clothes so that I didn't have to leave.

And though everyone has encouraged me to go home and get some meaningful sleep in a bed instead of on a couch that is too short for my legs, I have been compelled to be with Nate every step of the way.

I know the doctor said he didn't hit his head, but from the way Nate is smiling at me from time to time, I have to wonder if we're dealing with a small case of selective amnesia that has just wiped out all the wrongs Nate feels I've done to him and replaced them with happy memories.

Or maybe Jack's right. Maybe it's the drugs.

"Knock, knock."

I turn to the door. "Come in."

A nurse with a blonde ponytail sticks her head in. "Hi there, I'm Laney Briggs, I–" She scans the room. "Oh my god."

Her face is somewhat familiar.

Nate's head bobbles on its axis. "Laney?"

"I... Oh my god, I had no idea that you were my client, I..." She smiles. "Hi, everyone."

I knew she looked familiar. It's been a few years, but she would circulate the club sometimes with Mason. They were together for several years before they had, from what I recall, a pretty nasty breakup which sent Mason packing his bags and following Nate across the country to California.

"Forgive me, I had no idea when the agency sent me over that I was coming for..." She continues to smile, though it's clear she's nervous. "This is weird, isn't it?"

Nate still seems to be having trouble comprehending what's going on. "Sorry, I'm on a lot of painkillers. Why are you here?"

"I called an agency to get you a live-in physical therapist for when you're discharged. That way you can just focus on resting and recovering. I wanted whoever was first available, and I guess..." I stand and go to Laney. "Good to see you again, Laney."

"You too." Her pale skin is now beet red.

"If this is uncomfortable for you, we're not going to make you stay, of course."

She shakes her head. "No, it's been years, I mean...as long as Nate's not uncomfortable with it, I don't mind."

I glance at Nate.

From the expression on his face, the sort of half-melted smile, I don't think she should worry about that.

"I'm fine with it."

"Good, that's good." Laney grabs a rolling stool the nurses use and positions it beside Nate's bed. "Then I'd love to talk through your recovery plan with you all, if that's alright."

Jack, Abigail, and I listen to every word as Laney explains what will be happening over the next few months while she works with Nate.

Good thing we're all on hand because Nate is struggling with his critical thinking. Not sure if it's the drugs anymore or having his eyes on a beautiful girl. However, I doubt Nate would ever make a move on Laney.

He's a better man than I am. He wouldn't date his best friend's ex.

And there I was, trying to date my *son's* ex.

Sure, I didn't know, but I can't shake the feeling that I should have.

"My goal for this plan is to have you walking within a few months, six tops." Laney's eyes are on Nate. "And since I'll be able to monitor you so closely, I have a lot of confidence."

"Sounds good." Nate smiles. "Real good."

She laughs and then looks up at me. "I think he might need some rest before this all really sinks in."

"That sounds like a good plan. Thanks for coming in,

Laney. My assistant will get all the details worked out, and we'll get you set up at my residence ASAP."

Nate's gaze flies to me. "*Your* residence?"

"Yes, of course." I shrug. "I have the space, after all." But that's not the real reason. I want to be there every step of the way, just like Laney, to make sure my son recovers.

I expect Nate to protest, tell me that he doesn't need my help. But he just smiles. "Okay."

I've never felt my heart so close to bursting at someone just saying, "Okay," until now.

Laney leaves soon after, followed by Abigail and Jack, leaving me and my son alone.

"Well." I break the awkward silence. "I'll step out, let you get some rest and–"

"No, Dad," Nate's voice is small. "Stay for a bit, would you?"

My body feels numb.

"I want to talk. About what happened."

I don't know if I can bear to talk about Sonia right now without losing it. But I will put that aside for Nate's sake. It's the least I can do.

I take a seat on the end of his bed. "Where would you like to start?"

Nate stares at me. His breaths are shallow. There's a lot of emotion built up in him.

"You can say whatever you need to, Nate." I'm so careful when I touch his shin, only to remember he can't move it away if he wants to due to the temporary paraplegia.

Before I can pull away, Nate says, "You can touch me, it's alright."

I smile. Big smile.

He smiles, a tentative turn of his lips. "Thank you for being here."

"Of course, Nate."

He blinks. "I never thought you'd be the kind of dad who..."

I raise an eyebrow. "Who would sit with his son in the hospital?"

Nate nods and tries to swallow. "I mean, even mom has only visited the past few days."

Clarissa has visited every day. And I know she's worried. But she hasn't been posted up here like I have been. Says it's too hard. And as funny as it might seem, I can't understand that excuse.

Of course, it's hard. He's our son. "I love you. It's as simple as that."

"It didn't use to be." His eyes fall to his hands on his lap. "Can't you understand how confusing it's been to go from my own father casting me out to you saying that you love me all the time?"

I close my eyes for a moment. Let out a long sigh. This is my own fault.

"I've always loved you, Nate. I just expressed it the wrong way. I thought I knew what was best for you. So, I tried to control you. And that's not love. I know that now. I'm just sorry that it took me losing you to realize that."

Among other things, Nate's disappearance has taken a toll on me in unexpected ways.

I buried it down so deep that I thought I wasn't feeling any of it.

The truth is, I was feeling all of it all the time. And the second I knew he was back in New York, I knew I needed to find him. To apologize. To fix things.

But Rome wasn't built in a day.

"You promise me you weren't trying to hurt me with the..." Nate licks his lips. "The Sonia thing?"

Just the utterance of her name hurts.

I shake my head. "Nate, I promise, I had no idea that she was your ex. I didn't even hire her. There was no way that I could have..." The details don't matter. "I understand if you don't trust me yet. But I would never have done that to you on purpose. Never."

Nate is silent, trying to size me up a bit.

I don't blame him. "If you can forgive me for –"

"Of course, I forgive you. You didn't know. Sonia, on the other hand..."

It's not my place to convince him to forgive her. But maybe with time, I can make him see that she just did the human thing.

She followed where her heart led her.

That's what I did too. And while it may have gotten me into trouble, I'm not sure I would change it for the world.

I don't have regrets when it comes to Sonia. As long as Nate can forgive me, why would I?

Nate looks out the window, his face slack. "I followed her here. To New York. I didn't know she had gotten a job at the club. All she said was that she was moving on to something bigger and better. And that didn't include me."

On one hand, I'm furious that Sonia didn't think my son was good enough for her. And on the other...I still feel like she was meant to be mine. How fucked up is that?

"We were together for almost three years."

"That's a lot of time."

My son smirks. "For you, maybe."

"Hey." I half-laugh. "I'm working on it."

"I wasn't the best boyfriend. In fact, she has reasons to think I'm some sort of–" He bites back on his words. "I didn't mean to hurt her. But I was so immature."

"Nate..."

"I was. I know that now." Nate swallows. "I haven't wanted to face it."

We look into each other's eyes.

I see so much of Clarissa in Nate, and I always have. Blue eyes, blond hair.

But I see a little bit of me now too. In the shape of his face and the edge of his jaw. The strong line of his nose.

And somewhere, deep in his eyes, a severe longing to be loved for once, just for being human.

"I went to California. I became a surfer. A beach bum. I literally used whatever money I had just to fuck around and...that's not a life. You know?"

"If that's what you want, then–"

"No, it's not what I want." Nate takes a deep breath. "I never wanted to work at the club because I didn't want to be like you, Dad."

Ouch. But I deserve it.

"However, what you've shown me just by being here... Maybe I've been wrong about you."

Nate reaches for my hand, and I take his. "You never have to do anything you don't want to."

He gives me a lopsided smile. "Maybe I could grow into it. As long as what's between us doesn't change."

I shake my head. "It won't. As long as I'm alive, it won't."

26

—

SONIA

Bridget elbows me. "I think you should talk. I know you didn't have bad intentions. But all Nate knows is that you left him and tried to shack up with his dad."

"Shack up with? How old are you?"

Bridget blushes and rolls her eyes. "Do you want me to try and get him to talk to you or what?"

In the two weeks I've spent away from either of the Lyons men, I've had the clarity I sought by coming to New York in the first place.

I need to leave my old life behind.

Other than the debts hanging over my head, I said goodbye to California for a reason. And that meant saying goodbye to Nate too.

However, I was cruel and went by things the wrong way.

I left him just to stick myself right into the life he left behind.

That wasn't fair of me. But I also know that I'm not going to be leaving the Lyons Club any time soon.

As long as I have a job there, that is.

And Bridget has been invaluable as my closest confidante, though she has been sworn to secrecy.

Here in the safety of my office, I can appreciate her offer to build the bridge between Nate and me.

"Yes, I think I do."

She smiles, and I know it won't be long before Nate and I are face-to-face.

I talk to my friend for a bit longer, but as always, work gets in the way and Bridget leaves.

THE LAST TIME I WAS AT EDWIN'S GORGEOUS penthouse was to comfort him about his son.

Now I'm back.

For Edwin's son.

Nate is recovering well from his injury.

I checked two or three times to make sure I wouldn't be too much of a strain on his recovery by coming to speak with him.

And I also made Bridget promise me that Edwin wouldn't be home. I can't deal with that right now.

He has been on my mind every second of every day.

If I see him, I'll lose all the progress I've made in letting go of him, which hasn't been much.

Or any.

"In here." The pretty blonde with the congenial smile leads me down the hall into the main room. She's dressed in scrubs that look extremely comfortable. She must be Nate's nurse or something.

She steps aside and allows me through.

My breath stops when I spot Nate in front of the big picture windows overlooking Central Park.

He looks over at me, smiles his easy smile. "Hey."

"You're in a wheelchair."

Nate laughs and rolls toward me. "Yeah, have to be for now."

"Oh, my god."

"Don't look so upset, Sonia. It's a great arm workout."

I breakdown. I didn't expect to. I thought it would be difficult to see him, but this...

I collapse onto an ottoman, tears rolling down my face. "I'm sorry, I'm sorry, I'm sorry."

"Sonia, hey, look at me." Nate rolls all the way to me and grabs my hands. "What are you apologizing for?"

"This is..." I gesture toward the chair. "This is my fault."

He laughs. "Don't give yourself so much credit."

"*Nate.*"

"Hey. Chin up." He tucks his fingers under my chin and makes me look in his eyes. "Unless you were my surfboard or whatever fucking wave took me out, this is not your fault."

I chuckle, though I still just want to cry.

Though my heart belongs to someone else, and regardless of everything else that happened that parted us, I still love Nate. I'm not in love with him anymore, but I will always love him.

He is deserving of that love, that fondness. "I'm sorry for other things, then."

"Care to elaborate?" He leans back in his chair.

Here we go. "Well, I guess I'll start with apologizing for how we left things."

Nate purses his lips. "It's fine."

"No, it's not fine. It wasn't fine. I...blamed you for things that were out of your control."

His eyes fall, hands fidgeting on his lap. "I should have known better."

"Maybe we both should."

We are both quiet.

Hard to believe the last time I was here, the halls were filled with lust, moans, and kisses between Nate's father and me.

"I shouldn't have sought out the job at Lyons. But it wasn't to get to your dad. I swear."

"It was to hurt me."

I freeze.

His head tilts. "Wasn't it?"

"It's more complicated than that." I gnaw on my lower lip for a moment. "It was to put the wall up between us once and for all. That you and I were different. You didn't give a fuck about anything. And I...well, I had to. And if the club represented everything you hated, then I wanted to be that too."

Nate furrows his brow. "You wanted me to hate you?"

"Yes. Because then you'd let go of me."

He is silent for a long time.

I shake my head. "But you followed me here. And you came to my apartment. And kept crossing boundaries I set and–"

"I'm sorry."

Now, it's my turn to be silent.

"I'm really sorry, Sonia." Emotion creeps up in his voice. "It hurt when you left. But that's no excuse for what I did. Following you here. Although, I think I had other reasons for it. You were just a good excuse. Or a bad excuse. I don't know."

A tiny smile creeps onto my face. If his staying at his

father's house means things are better between them, then that makes me happy.

I want Nate to be happy.

And more than that, I want Edwin to be happy. Reconnecting with Nate will bring him more happiness than I think he's ever known.

Even with me.

Nate looks into my eyes. "I hope, though, since you're still working at the club, that we can be friends?" There's a hesitant tilt to his voice.

I smile. "Will you be around the club?"

Nate shrugs. "I'm talking about maybe taking up a position there with my dad. *Maybe.*"

My stomach twists at the mention of his father. I don't even have to hear Edwin's name to feel thrown back into emotional chaos.

"That's great, Nate. I mean, if you're happy."

He nods. His eyes travel to the doorway. When I look over my shoulder, his nurse is walking down the hall, carrying something from another room.

Does he like her? When he catches me looking, he snaps right back to me. "Yes, I'm happy. As happy as I can be for being in this chair."

"Yeah, you're going to have to tell me all about that right now so I stop worrying."

Nate laughs. "Okay, okay."

Nate explains his injury to me. The moment it happened, waking up in the hospital, the whole plan for his recovery that was laid out by his physical therapist, Laney, who turns out is Mason's ex.

"Everyone's been really supportive. Really great. I have visitors all the time. My surfing buddies, Seth and Mason, Jack and Abigail." Then Nathan smiles big. "You."

I flush. "You're giving me more credit for this visit than I deserve."

He grins. "Well, you should come back. If we're going to be friends."

I nod. "Yeah. Friends."

It might take some time. But I don't want to throw away the years Nate and I had. He was good to me. At least for what he was capable of at the time. We were young.

Fine, we were young*er*. However, I've grown up so much since my dad passed away.

I didn't think Nate was capable of growing up like that. But I think he just did.

Nate clears his throat. "Um, I do have to ask, though–"

My heart plummets. "Nate, let's not–"

"I think it's only fair since I walked in on you kissing my dad that I get to ask you a question or two."

I'm surprised by how well-humored he is about the whole thing. Meanwhile, I feel like death thinking about the prospect of talking about Edwin.

"Fine. I guess it's only fair."

Nate leans on his elbow.

I still can't get used to him in this chair. My greatest hope is that it will be gone before I know it.

"So, how did that happen?"

"Nate–"

"I just...I mean, you knew about my dad. You knew how little I thought of him and the way he treated women and–"

"I didn't know he was your dad at first!" I sigh. "Before we were introduced. It's complicated."

Nate stares at me.

I'm expecting a slew of questions, jabs, and jokes at my expense.

Instead, he tilts his head to the side and smiles, "So, you

saw him across the room and just felt it, huh?" And he's serious. It's not teasing and it's not playful. It's real.

I shake my head. "I didn't know what I felt. I was confused."

"I'm not angry, Sonia."

"Well, you should be. It was a mistake. And whatever happened between your dad and me wasn't real. It was misguided, and we were..."

I huff. "I don't want to talk about the details. I just need you to know that it wasn't my intention to hurt you by doing what I did. I was just being...selfish."

But I wasn't being selfish. Not really. If I had been selfish, I wouldn't have resisted for so long. If I was being selfish, I should have wanted Edwin for his money or his looks. If I was being selfish, I wouldn't have cared about anyone's feelings but my own.

What happened between Edwin and me is...inexplicable.

I know one day the memories will be fond and dear to me. Right now, though, I want nothing more than to erase them from my mind.

Because as soon as it may be, for me, Edwin is already the one who got away.

"You're not a selfish person, Sonia."

"People change, Nate."

—————

27

EDWIN

I shouldn't be listening, but I am. To everything Sonia says.

And it breaks my heart to know that for the past two weeks she has been convincing herself that what we had was nothing.

Because for the past two weeks, I have been learning to accept that it was everything.

With Nate's forgiveness and our new bond, I have realized exactly what Sonia means to me.

A chance at the life I always wanted.

When Nate told me Sonia was coming over to speak with him to make amends, as arranged by Bridget, I was going to stay away. That's what Sonia wanted. She only needed to deal with one Lyons man at a time.

But it was Nate who convinced me that I should come see her too.

"She'll probably be annoyed because Bridget asked me to make sure you weren't home, but..." Nate ran his hands through his blonde hair that was growing shaggier by the day. "You two should talk. I'm sure there are things you need to say."

I was stunned by the emotional intelligence of my son. He didn't get that from me, that's for certain. And also the fact he has been willing to rise so far above what he first perceived to be a betrayal.

"I can tell that you miss her. Every time her name is said, you look so bereft. Like–"

"Like a lost puppy?" I forced a smirk.

Nate frowned and shook his head. "Like you're heartbroken."

And that's the truth, isn't it? My heart is broken without Sonia in my life.

I thought I would have to choose between my son and the woman I am falling in love with, maybe even love already. But my son is a bigger man than I have ever been. So, I don't have to.

Now, I'm here to tell her that not a day goes by where she isn't my first and last thought. And every thought in between.

Hearing her say that what we had was "nothing," though, breaks my heart.

I retreat to the front hall, sliding my hands in my pockets. Serves me right for listening in on them.

It was wrong, and I promised Nate I wouldn't. I just... couldn't help it if only for a minute.

Laney appears in the doorway to the kitchen with a glass of water and a fleet of pills, no doubt time for Nate's afternoon meds. "You okay?"

"Yes, fine."

"You're pacing."

I plant my feet. "I suppose I am."

Laney smiles and pats my shoulder as she passes me. "I'm going to get Nate ready for his afternoon rest."

That's her nice way of saying, "be prepared."

"Sounds good."

I watch her walk down the hall and then shake out all the nervousness in my hands. "Come on, Edwin. What are you afraid of? What are you worried about?"

The truth is, I have never in all my years done something as high stakes as this.

I've been in boardrooms and business meetings with the rich and powerful, seduced women, fathered children. And somehow, none of that measures up to the anxiety of this moment.

Gentle laughter and conversation comes from the other room.

Laney telling Sonia that time is up, she needs to get going.

Little does she know she's walking into a conversation she wasn't prepared to have.

That's how life is sometimes, though. You can't prepare for it.

Footsteps down the hall.

Sonia's voice reaches me. "Yes, it was nice to meet you, too, I'm sure I'll see you again." Her voice is music to my ears as it echoes through my home. "Bye, Nate!"

I wait for her, watch the hall, and when she emerges, it takes my breath away.

It's her day off, I remember. And that means she's just in her normal, everyday clothes, a look I have seldom if ever seen her in.

Dark hair down over her shoulders, a loose T-shirt, stylish jeans, clean white sneakers.

Beautiful.

Her expression, though, the affable one she was wearing for Laney, sours.

"What are you doing here?"

I try to smile. "It's my home."

Sonia pulls on the strap of her purse. "You weren't supposed to be here."

"I know."

"Then, why–"

"Nate thought we should talk."

Her shoulders tighten. "I'll murder him."

"Please don't, I have a vested interest in his survival." I half chuckle.

Sonia stares at me. "Edwin, I can't do this."

"You don't have to do anything, just let me..." If I can say what I need to, I can fix everything. I'm sure I can. At least, I think I'm sure. Oh god. "Let me just talk. Alright?"

She sighs. That's as much of a "yes" as I'll get.

"Sonia, I..." I take a few steps closer.

This isn't how I wanted to say this. In a moment of panic, where I have her cornered. But I've thought it over, really thought it through.

And it's a much better choice than coming back to reality, walking into the club, and doing it there while she's working.

That's what's always been the trouble with our relationship. Apart from the whole Nate thing.

But could that be a problem for me if I didn't know until it was too late?

"I am thinking of you always. I have tried to untangle my thoughts from you. Tried to grasp the idea of moving on. And I just can't. Because I love you."

Wow, the words were so much easier to say than I thought. They feel so right when I say them to her.

"Edwin." She shakes her head. "Not this. Not here."

"It's okay. Nate knows. He–"

Sonia tries to walk past me, but I intercept her, placing my hands against her shoulders.

"Let me go, Edwin." There is not much heft in her voice.

I know she doesn't really want to go before she hears what I have to say.

"Sonia, please, I have been falling in love with you. I never thought I was capable of these feelings. People would get married and fall in love around me, and I thought they were joking, I thought it was all some ruse."

She tries to step away again, but once more, I intercede.

"Life for me has always been work. They have been synonymous. And then I met you."

"I can't be your reason for changing. That's not how people work."

"Yes, it is. It's you, it's–" That's not totally true, is it? "Because of you, I have completely changed."

Sonia balls her hands up in front of her pressing on my chest. "I can't be your reason."

"It's not just you, it's...it's–"

Spit it out, Edwin.

I shut my eyes and take a deep breath.

It's time to let the truth come out.

"Just before my forty-ninth birthday, I was working late, overtime, as usual. I bent over to pick up a file." *Such a simple fucking task.*

My mind flicks back to the searing pain that overcame me that night, after midnight in my office at the club. "The moment I tried to get back up, my body gave out. My back it was—"

I can't help the shudder that takes over me. "I was frozen on the ground. I was alone and couldn't get to my phone, but even if I had been able to..." I take a deep breath.

Despite the physical pain I was under, nothing hurt as bad as knowing I was alone. "I would've had to call Solomon. And he would have come running, I know he would. He's a good friend. But...my children. If I had called my children, would they have come? Would they have rushed to make sure I was okay?"

She shakes her head. "Of course, they would have—"

"Maybe *now*. Because I've been doing the work. Because I make an effort with my children now. Because I know that life is about so much more than money and work. It's about love."

I stroke Sonia's cheek. Her eyes flutter shut.

It's about this feeling right now. "It's about *love*."

"Edwin..."

"I was lying on that floor for hours, immobilized, powerless, until my assistant walked in the next morning. I'm not sure anybody would have worried about me if they hadn't heard from me for days."

Sonia scoffs. "That's ridiculous, that's—"

"People who *matter*, Sonia. People like my children who didn't get nearly enough of my attention in their childhood, or friends that never get calls back or..." Tears start piling up in my eyes. "People like you."

Sonia moans like she's in pain. "You can't love me, Edwin, you can't."

"Nate said—"

"It's not just about Nate, and it's not just about my job.

It's about my life, Edwin. Everything is so messy. Every-thing is so—"

"Please tell me everything. I'll clean it up for you."

She breaks away from me, darting toward the front door. "It's not that simple!"

I break out into a sprint, slamming my hand on the door to keep it from opening. "Yes, it is!"

Sonia stares up at me. Her eyes wide. With fear.

Shit.

My chest heaves as I catch my breath. I tighten my hand into a fist.

"Yes, it is that simple. You don't know how far I would go for you. You simply don't understand."

Sonia's face hardens. "Your family...I can't be haunted by you like this anymore."

"What are you talking about?"

Her hand is still on the doorknob. She's ready to make an escape the second I allow her to.

However, I will stand here until my legs give out from under me, until she understands just how much I love her. How much I need her in my life.

"My dad, he...he was a gambler."

Was...

"My mom left us when I was too young. So, it was me and my dad. He had a regular steady job, sure, but he spent a lot of time gambling to try and make ends meet. And that was fine. At first."

Her eyes go to her hand on that door, and she frowns. "But it didn't take long to become an addiction, and suddenly, it wasn't just about making ends meet. It was about making the big win but ending up losing everything all the time."

A primal impulse rages inside me.

Sonia is meant to be taken care of. Not to make ends meet. Not to lose.

"He was still my dad, though, he was all I had. And I loved him even through all of that. I worked my way through college, paid for all of it myself..."

Sonia pauses and a small smile crosses her lips. "And then Nate came along. And things seemed good. My dad and him were friends."

Darkness clouds her eyes. "Too good of friends. I don't know if it was an effort to make my dad like him or if he had no self-awareness at all, but Nate became his enabler. He would sometimes even loan him money that I felt I needed to pay back and–"

I shake my head, thinking of what I would have told Nate if we'd been in touch. Maybe if I'd been a father, I could have spared everyone this heartbreak.

"The debts got worse and worse. And seedier and seedier. When Nate finally stopped giving my dad money, his addiction was worse than ever, so he went to loan sharks."

Everything snaps into place. Of course...loan sharks. They're holding her debts over her head. Calling her at all hours, demanding more and more money.

"Then Dad just couldn't take it anymore, I guess. One day, he came home and grabbed one of the bottles. Started drinking before dinner and was totally wasted and nursing the second bottle of whisky by the time I went to bed."

The sadness in her eyes crushes my chest and I just want to hug her, but the wall between us seems unsurmountable.

"He told me how much he loved me and apologized for the shitty life he gave me. I ignored his words. Ramblings of a drunk man."

Tears run down her face, and my hand twitches with

the almost uncontrollable need to reach out and touch her. Comfort her.

"You don't have to talk anymore. It's okay."

Her head shakes.

"I dismissed him with an 'I love you, Dad, but we'll talk tomorrow. I'm tired and I have to work early tomorrow'. Except, by morning, he was dead. And I didn't listen to him because I was selfish. Because I was tired. Because I was—"

I can't hold back anymore and reach out, but she steps back and shakes her head as she holds out her hands to keep me away.

"I didn't even have time to grieve him because that same day, a man approached me to let me know all of his debts transferred to me."

My hands are fists at my side, and I just want to run them through that guy's face, whoever he might be.

"How much is it?"

She shakes her head again. "It doesn't matter."

"Sonia, I can help."

"No, you can't." A fire blazes in her golden eyes. "I can do it. On my own. Like I've always done."

"But you don't have to." I reach out to her once more. "You don't."

"Please don't touch me."

I retract my hand yet again, wishing I could cut the damn thing off.

Her jaw is stiff, trying to hold back some of the tears as she speaks. "I broke things off with Nate then. But it wasn't a clean break. He felt guilty, and I was so alone and–" Sonia laughs a humorless laugh. "We were so stupid."

"You were grieving, that doesn't mean stupid."

"I'm still grieving. And you're..." Sonia's eyes glimmer. "You're *Nate's. Dad.*"

We stare at each other for a long time. What she just said is the absolute truth. It is something that will never change about me.

And the fact that she has been with my son is a fact that will never change either.

I don't care about any of that, though. As long as I have Nate's blessing, which I believe I do, all I want is Sonia. To protect and love her. To help her. To walk into this next phase of my life with her.

I swear she leans forward first. A micromovement. The tilt of her jaw, the incline of her chest.

I lean halfway in to meet her, and she doesn't draw away.

Snatching the moment, my lips caressing hers, trying to say everything I can't put into words in just a kiss.

I can fix everything. I can take care of you. I can be yours. I love you.

I slide my hand over the top of her head, a caress. A promise. *I'm here. I'm not going anywhere.*

Sonia jerks away and touches her lips as if they've been electrocuted. Her eyes fall to the ground. "How do I know you're not like him?"

"What?"

Sonia looks me dead in the eye. "How do I know..." She doesn't finish her sentence. She doesn't need to. I heard her the first time.

I've lost. I know there's nothing I can say or do to convince her that I'm different than my son.

He's from my body, from my blood. I'm the reason he is the way he is. That's how parenting works, even if I was lacking in that department.

My heart crumbles.

If I don't get away from her fast, it'll shatter me into a

million pieces. I step away from the door, no longer holding her in my keep.

Sonia rips the door open and disappears as fast as she can, leaving only the ghost of her mouth on mine, the aroma of her hair in my nose, and the distinct feeling that I will never, ever recover from losing her.

28

SONIA

CRYING ON THE SUBWAY IS A COMMON OCCURRENCE IN New York.

I've seen many people trying to keep their weeping to themselves as they rode the Q.

Now, it's my turn. I guess it was only a matter of time. A rite of passage.

I find a corner seat and sob into my hands.

I've broken my own heart leaving Edwin there like that.

So much of me wanted to give into him and say fuck everything. Take his money, take his love.

But I just can't.

Knowing what Nate did to me, I can't even fathom the potential for Edwin's betrayals when he's lived so much more and has so much more money.

Has he given me much reason to think that? No. In fact, I should be grateful he was willing to give me a second chance when I was the one who lied and betrayed him for so long.

However, the idea of him one day holding all that

money over my head, holding me captive to his will because I *owe him something...*

I am tired of owing anything to anyone.

I'm so screwed up in the head, it's like my thoughts are in a different language, words I once knew not making sense.

Through the din, the only words I can understand are, *I love him, I love him, I love him.*

That makes me cry even harder.

I realize halfway through my ride, I was so turned around I got on a southbound train instead of a northbound one, heading away from Queens. Just my fucking luck.

I miss my dad more than anything. And that makes me angry. Despite his addiction, he was loving. And funny. And always knew what to say.

I know he and Edwin would have something in common. They both have regrets about what kind of fathers they were.

Instead of backtracking and getting on the right train, I may as well head back to the club. It is closed until tomorrow afternoon, thanks to the never-ending construction of the whisky room.

A perfect place to clear my mind.

I SIP A GLASS OF WINE ON ONE OF THE LEATHER couches and check the time. Almost five in the morning.

The construction workers will be coming in around eight.

I ought to start considering heading home. Can't believe I didn't leave sooner. But one hour turned into two, one glass turned into two, and I couldn't bear the thought of leaving.

It's never been so quiet in the club because there's never a time in the day at least a few members aren't here, even in the wee hours of the morning.

I'm here all alone. And it's been nice.

I've spent my time indulging in all the amenities the members get to enjoy.

I mean, all I've done is vegetate on the couch and drink wine while watching premium television in the Media wing, but hey, I'm grieving for my life here.

"Okay, Sonia," I say to myself. "Time to get up."

I don't move.

"Time to get up, up, up."

Again.

"*Girl.*"

I lay there for another minute or so and then get the inspiration to launch myself up off the couch, leather groaning under me.

I shut off the television, the umpteenth episode of *The Office* I've watched in a row.

Then the world is silent.

The club being part underground is amazing for keeping out the noise of bustling New York City. But it's also eerie, standing here in the lowlight, not a single sound other than my breathing.

My head flies to the door.

What was that snapping sound?

Distinct enough that it captures my attention. Small enough that it could be anything.

I keep my eyes on the open door to the cinema and wait to see if it happens again.

I'm not one of those stupid people in horror movies who

feel the need to check every noise, thank you very much. I'll just stay right here.

One second...two seconds...ten...thirty.

Nothing.

Just the wine and my imagination.

Okay, it's official, I need to get home. Need to get into bed. I'm hearing things.

I walk out into the hall, overcome with tiredness. My bare feet feel cool against the long-tiled hallway. High heels dangling from my fingers.

Snap.

Again? What *is* that?

My stomach ties in a knot.

Calm down, Sonia.

Maybe it is just one of the construction guys who came in early to get something. Or perhaps a member forgot that the club was closed and maybe somehow the security protocol glitched and allowed a non-employee inside.

I wield one of my high heels in my hand, just in case, and call out in a friendly tone, "Hello? Someone there?"

I emerge from the hallway into the main member area.

It is empty and quiet. Even the usual waterfall feature embedded in the wall has been turned off while the members are gone, the usual babbling sound reduced to silence.

I look around. "Anyone here?"

No one to my left. No one to my right.

I drop my arm at my side, high heel clonking against my thigh. "You have to go to bed, like yesterday."

I head into my office but stop in the doorway.

Perking up my ears, I try to catch on the sound that stopped me, the tiniest bit of hissing. Like ghosts conversing. I look back over my shoulder once more. Nothing.

My heart is pounding in my chest, made even worse by the fact I know I'm creating fear for myself, half-drunk on wine and all alone.

I've got to get out of here.

Plopping down in my seat, I get my high heels back on, the office chair spinning with me. "Fucking shit." I'm unable to steady myself.

A snap. Actually, a click. And this one is close.

I freeze.

"Turn around," a gruff male voice says from behind me.

What the... I sit up straight, not heeding the order at first, shock infiltrating my whole body.

I'm not alone. I haven't been alone this whole time.

"Now."

Spinning in the chair, I catch myself against the desk, finding myself face-to-face with two huge figures wearing balaclavas. One of them holds a gun pointed right at me.

Is this Bruce's doing? Is he coming to collect now?

The panic button under my desk!

I start to reach for it.

"Don't you fucking dare," the other masked intruder says, a woman's voice.

I freeze.

I may be brave, but I'm not dumb. There's a gun pointed at me. *A gun.* The barrel is an empty chasm as might be my life if I don't cooperate.

"Hands in the air. No sudden movements," the man demands from behind the gun.

I lift my hands.

I'm shaking. I'm fucking shaking. Adrenaline pumping through my veins.

"What do you want?"

"You're going to do exactly as we say, got it?" The woman comes to the edge of my desk and leans toward me.

I try to look into her eyes to remember any small detail about her that I can recollect to the authorities when the time comes.

That is, *if* I get a chance to recollect with the authorities.

What if they just make me cooperate and then kill me? What if this is the end?

The man waves his gun at me. "You've got a safe in here."

My eyebrows lift in surprise.

The safe is a secret. In order to protect the club upstairs, money is kept down here in my office. No one knows this.

There's even a fake safe in the nightclub office to throw people off the scent.

"No, I don't."

"Don't fucking lie to us, bitch." The back of the woman's hand connects with my face, hard, and the sting hurts like hell.

How do they know?

"I'm sorry. You're right. There...there is a safe in here."

"Well, get up and open it." The bark in the man's voice is clear.

I push the chair away from the desk, then flinch as the woman's hand lands on my shoulder. "*Slowly.*"

How the hell do they expect me to think or be calm or act a certain way when they have a gun in my face?

However, adrenaline takes over.

I'm outside my body, watching as it moves, going to the safe, my hand opens the cabinet against the wall that hides it.

I punch in the code on instinct alone, an intuitive

memory underneath the main thought, *Please don't kill me, please don't kill me.*

The safe beeps, green light emitted from the display and the locking mechanism.

"Move." The woman shoves me out of the way by the shoulder.

I remain in the exact spot she shoved me to, up against my office wall, trying not to look the gun in the eye.

For a second, I consider if I can somehow escape, but the man is too big. His shoulders practically fill the entire doorframe.

I try not to watch as she collects all the cash from the weekend.

Weekend money is deposited first thing Monday morning. That's how we do it here.

With everything in my personal life out of sorts, I dropped the ball on that despite the club being closed.

Could the robbers know this? Or was this sheer luck?

Has to be luck, right?

I don't recognize the voices of the people, nor do I see any familiarity in their eyes.

"It's even better than we thought" The woman laughs.

I look at the woman. "You know there are cameras."

She doesn't respond.

The gun presses up against my side and a hand wraps in my hair. "Don't fucking speak." The man throws me back into my chair.

I remain frozen, still bracing from the fall, trying to think of all the ways I could have stopped this.

"It's a small fortune!" The woman giggles, swinging her bag full of cash over her shoulder and skipping over to the man.

I eye them while they talk in low voices. It's so quiet here their words carry over.

The woman looks my way. "We're not supposed to hurt her."

"She's going to call the cops right away if we leave her."

Her. Me. God, what do I do?

Edwin will be mad. God, he'll go ballistic if I die here.

If he were here, he'd save me. He'd find a way to stop this and save me.

He always protects me.

Edwin.

He told me he loves me twice now. And...

I love him. I love him so much, but he doesn't know that. Because I'm so stupid, and I never told him. Now I might die here.

But if I do, I'll never get to tell him.

And it will be all my fault.

I can't die. I have to live.

At least long enough to tell him I love him too.

I need to get out of here.

They seem distracted. And I'm hopped up on adrenaline and a little wine.

I make a break for the button under my desk.

The man fires the gun, and though the shot misses me, it's a warning I know I have to heed.

"Bitch."

The woman comes around the back of my chair and grabs me by the head, pulling it against the headrest of my chair.

"If you do something like that again..." the man breathes. "You're dead."

I don't move a muscle. I don't try to fight them when they tie my hands to the arm rests or bind my ankles together or put duct tape over my mouth. In fact, it's comforting.

They wouldn't need to do all of this if they were planning on just killing me.

"Come on." The woman checks the watch on her wrist. "We have to get out of here. Now."

She darts out of the room.

The man starts to follow, but then he turns back to look at me. A sneer on his lips beneath the balaclava.

I press my back into the chair, wishing I could get away, but I can't.

He swings the gun toward me. A crack of pain against my temple.

Darkness.

29

—————

EDWIN

The sound of the door closing after Sonia is the axe that rips my heart in half.

I can't breathe, can't think. I have to do something.

Stop. Breathe.

I am Edwin Lyons. I have accomplished everything I set out to do, so all I have to do is come up with a plan.

Whatever else, I love her, and I'll get her back. I have to.

My life will be empty and worthless without her. Dark.

I lock myself up in my office and wrack my head, trying to comprehend how I can fix this.

I am a businessman. Maybe this is why personal matters have always eluded me. I always think I can rationalize my way out of situations, convince people of things that would suit their best interests.

But in matters of emotion, things are not that simple. Not by a long shot. I've learned this now. And I hate it.

And that's where I lie with Sonia. I cannot convince her to be with me, cannot show her a pros and cons list and why it would be a good long-term investment.

That's not how people and human relationships work.

I learned that the hard way with Nate.

I've changed now, though. I am not the hardened man I once was. And I need her in my life.

When my daughter forces me to come out of my office to eat dinner, my children all watch me with sullen expressions.

Jack stares at me. "What's wrong?"

"He saw Sonia." Nate shakes his head. "Didn't go well."

Abigail sighs and places her hand on mine. "Oh, Daddy. Maybe it's for the best."

Over the past couple of weeks, my children have become privy to the connection I have with Nate's ex-girlfriend.

Two weeks doesn't make up for a lifetime of bonding, but Nate's injury has brought us close together.

Nate was the one to encourage me to go after Sonia if I really loved her, which was a shock, of course. Something about his injury has given him mental clarity, though.

I can't say I don't relate.

Jack shrugs. "She's too young for you anyway."

Nate stares at his brother after looking at me. "I think they'd be good together. Dad's got it more together than I do. And that's what Sonia needs."

I push my fork around my plate, unable to even consider eating. "Can we not talk about it?"

My kids all exchange looks.

Jack clears his throat, looks at me from across the table with a serious expression. "I think we've spent too much of our lives not talking about things, Dad."

He is right. So, for the next god knows how many hours, we talk and bond.

I learn what my kids want out of a relationship with me, and I express the same. I share the secret I had been holding onto until I told Sonia.

Which leads Abigail to click her tongue. "This isn't very feminist of me, but you should go after her."

Jack frowns. "She said no, Abs."

My youngest crosses her arms over her chest. "Well, if someone loved me as much as Dad loves Sonia, I'd want him to come after me."

I can't help but perk up at that. "Even if you said no?"

"Yes." Abigail nods. "Even if I said no. Because no means no, definitely. But every once in a while, when two people love each other, a no is just a way to put up walls. To protect ourselves from heart break. So, Daddy, knowing her, what is her no?"

"Thank you."

It's still the early hours of the morning, just going on seven. Way too early to pay a surprise visit, but I'm desperate.

I get to her apartment thanks to Nate's directions. A teeny five-story walk up in Queens that feels like hell on my knees, but I can't think of the pain now.

"Sonia?" I knock on the door. "Sonia, it's me."

Nothing.

"I know you don't want to see me. But I need you to." I am careful not to talk too loud to alert any of the neighbors to my presence.

Again, nothing.

Nate said this is a small studio. She can't miss my

knocking from another room. And it'd be just as impossible for me to not hear her moving if she was inside.

I pull out my phone and send her a text.

Another one. I've sent several since I left the house to come here.

Still nothing, so I call.

Nothing from inside. Not a buzz, not a ring.

Sonia's phone is always on ringer for business calls at all hours of the day.

That's confirmation she's not home. Where could she be?

I love Sonia, but I still have so much to learn about her. Where would she go if she wasn't home? Where does she spend her time?

All I know is her apartment and the office.

So, I head down to the Lyons Club as a last resort until I have more information.

On the car ride over, I text Bridget since she and Sonia have become close, but she doesn't seem to know where her friend is either.

I arrive before the construction crew is set to start.

The club is silent, and the lights are dimmed.

Sonia's blinds are pulled as if she's not there, or she doesn't want to be disturbed.

But the door is ajar, though the lights are off.

I creep toward the door. "Sonia?"

No response.

I lean my ear closer to the gap in the door. I swear there is a rustle or something inside. "Sonia?"

Aw, fuck it.

All at once, I push the door open and turn on the overhead light.

And my blood runs cold.

Sonia is tied up in a chair, gagged, blood dripping from a gash in her head. Her eyes are closed, head drooping.

I run to her. "Sonia! Oh, my god, Sonia!" I hope she wakes up, that this is all some kind of joke.

I cup her face in my hands. "Sonia? Sonia, honey, can you hear me?"

Her eyes wink open, but not much.

She groans into the tape over her mouth.

"You're alive." A wave of relief sweeps through me, though fear courses in my veins. "You're alive, you're–"

Sonia groans again, squeezing her eyes together.

"Fuck, you're hurt. Oh god, you're –"

The police. I need the police. I need to get her an ambulance. I need to fix this before it's too late.

I reach under her desk and smack the panic button.

"They'll be here soon, honey." I want to hold her in my arms, but I don't know where she hurts.

I start to tear the tape off her mouth, but she yelps in pain.

"I'm sorry. Too fast. I'm sorry. So sorry." I try to peel it off the rest of the way, millimeter by millimeter.

"The safe," she whimpers when her mouth is free enough to speak. It's taking all her energy to keep her eyes open.

"The safe?"

"They...they took..." Sonia's lips smack together as she tries to find words and the energy to stay awake.

I look across the room at an open cabinet. Inside, the safe door is open and any money in there, gone. What the fuck happened here?

"It's okay. It's okay. Fuck the safe." I stroke her cheek. She is more important. There's time for the rest later.

Sonia attempts to smile, but winces. The wound in her head glistens with fresh blood.

"You're okay." I force a smile as I whip a handkerchief out of my pocket and press it against the wound.

She moans, eyes rolling back with pain. Her wrists strain against their binds.

"I'll get you out of here. You're safe, I promise you're safe with me now."

I try to undo the bind on her wrist, but my hands are shaking, and the knots are impossible for my thick fingers to thread through. "The police will be here soon. We'll get you to a hospital and—"

Sonia's head grows heavy in my hand.

I look up to find her eyes have shuttered again.

"No. No, no, no. Sonia. Wake up, honey. Stay awake."

She doesn't move.

"*Fuck!*"

By the time the police officers arrive, I have undone her bindings and pulled her into my lap, trying my best to get her to regain consciousness, the blood-soaked rag in my hand starting to drip.

I refuse to leave her side for even a second.

"Given her CT scan, I'd say the damage is mild." The doctor's tone is pragmatic. "Worst case scenario, she might experience a bout of temporary amnesia once she awakens."

I slide my hands into my pockets.

We both look at the scan of her brain.

She's pointed out various details of it to me, but I haven't retained any of it. "When will she wake up?"

The doctor sighs. "Well, that is something we will have to keep an eye on. With injuries like these, it can often be hard for patients to awaken from sleep. It's a good sign that she came to when you found her. We just need to be patient."

I swallow. I've never been good with patience. Case and point, me marching up to Sonia's door this morning before seven am.

"She owes you a huge thanks, Mr. Lyons." The doctor touches my arm.

I attempt to smile, but I only grimace.

Sonia wouldn't have been in this situation if it weren't for my club. My money. Me. It's like I ruin every life I touch these days. "Thank you, Dr. Chen."

I return to Sonia's bedside after the doctor leaves. I've been beside her every step of the way, bristling whenever the doctors need space in order to check on her.

I want to be able to rescue her. Always.

But still, I've fallen short.

I sit at her bedside.

I can't believe only a couple of weeks ago, I was sitting in the same hospital next to my unconscious son. This is more tragedy than I would wish upon my worst enemy. I'm just thankful she's alive.

I grab her hand, warming it in mine.

There's a bandage across her head now. But other than that, she's still the same Sonia. Gorgeous raven locks splayed on the pillows, pillowy lips parted as she sleeps. Her dark lashes have created a slight sheen of mascara under her eyes.

Perhaps it is my fate to sit at the bedsides of those I love for not having appreciated the gravity of love for the past however many years. Perhaps I am doomed to this existence forever.

If that is the way it must be, then fine. I accept my fate.

My talk with Abigail sticks in my brain. I'm not just running after Sonia.

I'm sticking by her side no matter what.

30

SONIA

I wake up in what appears to be a hospital bed, my mouth dry.

The room is dark, illuminated only by city light through the window.

My head pounds with pain.

What the hell happened?

I was in the media room. But I was scared.

There's something about the safe. Did I open it? Why?

A man... pulling me by my hair and the barrel of that gun.

Shit!

Edwin. He was there. His dark eyes full of worry. His fingers to my mouth as he peeled the tape away. His words. *"It's okay. It's okay. Fuck the safe."*

I smile.

Underneath the window, there is a lump on the couch meant for visitors.

I squint and a few details start coming through, though they're blurry. A mess of hair, long legs jutting over the arm, a suitcoat used as a makeshift blanket.

"Edwin." The realization fills me with euphoria, though my voice is more of a croak.

He found me, saved me, *and* he stayed for me.

What a fool.

I love him.

"Edwin." This time, the sound is clearer.

His form moves, wriggling out of whatever sleep he's managed to find.

I almost feel bad, but not enough to stop. I need to see him. Need to tell him what I was so afraid I'd never get a chance to.

"Edwin, I'm awake."

Edwin pushes himself up from the couch and rubs his eyes. "Huh?"

I wait for him to come to, to realize this isn't a dream. It's real.

He blinks a few times, focusing on me. "Sonia?"

All I do is smile.

Edwin rushes to my bedside, sinking down onto the miniscule bit of bed and touches my face. "How are you feeling?"

"Okay. Alive."

He smiles. "Thank god for that."

I lift my hand up to touch his. It's like my limbs aren't my own. "I'm thirsty." My voice is hoarse.

"Oh god, yeah, of course. Here–" Edwin fetches me a glass of water at top speed.

He slides his hand around the back of my head, helping me to lift my mouth to the lip of the glass. "There we go."

My body unwinds as I swallow the water. "Mm. Good. Thank you."

Edwin returns to me after setting the glass aside, gripping my hands in his.

I look at him. "What happened?"

His smile falters.

"I was going to ask you that. I can put a few pieces together, but..." Edwin swallows.

He's in so much pain. I want to take it away. If I didn't hurt already, I would.

His eyes take me in as if he can't believe I'm right in front of him. "I found you tied up to a chair in your office. There was a break-in. The safe was emptied and–"

"I'm so sorry."

"Hush, I don't give a shit about that. You think I give a damn about a weekend of money compared to your life?" His thumb caresses my chin. "I'm just so glad you're alive. That you're awake."

"How long have I been out?"

"A while. But that's okay. The doctor said you had a mild injury. No long-term effects, hopefully. Though you might have a hard time remembering–"

"I love you." The words come out of me like a geyser that has just blown up. It comes with no rhyme or reason other than it must be said. It's the words I've been dreaming while I've been unconscious, the moment I lamented not being able to live for while the gun was pointed in my face.

Edwin's mouth opens, then closes.

He shakes his head like there are marbles that need to be knocked loose and then blinks. Each movement so small and average, yet on him, beautiful beyond belief.

And then he smiles, tilts his head to the side, confusion shining through. "What?"

I reach up for his cheek, though my limbs feel heavy. "I love you."

"Maybe you don't remember that the last time you saw

me, you told me you couldn't…" His voice trembles. "I don't want you to say something if you don't remember."

"I remember, of course I remember." Maybe not *of course* in these circumstances. However, it's emblazoned on my brain, the last time I saw Edwin. "You told me you loved me. I told you I couldn't love you back. Because I was scared. But then…" I trap a lock of hair at the nape of his neck between my fingers. "Then I was held at gunpoint. And I was so scared I was going to die. But only for one single reason."

Silence falls over us.

Hospitals are a special kind of quiet. The coming and the going of lives. Love hanging in the balance, desperate prayers asking for miracles.

Edwin and me… We're a little bit of a miracle.

"I didn't want to die not being able to tell you that I love you. It would have been my biggest regret if I'd–"

"Don't say it, Sonia, please don't" His voice is no more than a whisper.

I smile at him. "But I lived. And the first thing, the very first thing I have to do is tell you. I love you, Edwin. I love you."

His head droops down. He shakes it. And then he begins to cry. Tears rush down, over my hand.

"It's okay. I'm alive. I'm right here. Shhh…"

Ever since I met my Phoenix, things have been on unsteady ground. It's a constant state of wondering when the earth will open up and swallow me.

Now despite me lying in a hospital bed with a wound that has my head pounding, the earth is steady. At last.

Everything is sure and right.

I love him. And it is a truth I will live by regardless of

everything else. Of Nate, of my job, of the loan sharks, and all the fear.

My love for Edwin comes first.

"Please be serious." A pleading in his voice I didn't know he was capable of. "Please don't be lying or trying to—"

"I swear. I swear on everything. I've been trying to ignore it, trying to tamp it down. But I can't. I love you, and I want you to love me so bad."

Edwin leans over me, his lips ghosting over mine, so light it's almost not a kiss. "I love you. You know I love you."

"And now you know I love you too."

He hovers over me for a moment, then closes that tiny gap between our mouths. Hushed and hot, sealing us into forever.

There's a knock on the door to my room, a sound sharp enough to make my head throb.

Edwin draws away. "That's probably a nurse. Time for more pain meds."

"Thank god, my head is..."

Edwin hushes me with a thumb across my lip. "Close your eyes. Rest."

"I don't want to rest. I want to look at you."

He takes my hand and brings it to his mouth. "You'll have plenty of time to look at me when you're better." Edwin kisses each of my knuckles. "Forever, if that's what you want."

Forever is a very long time, a time I've never been able to conceptualize, not even with my own father.

Forever with Edwin seems impossible to avoid. So, I will give in and fall down, down, down for all eternity.

THE NEXT DAY, THE WORLD SEEMS CLEARER AND brighter, not just because the sun has come out.

Edwin is at my bedside. In his hand, a historical romance he bought in the hospital gift shop with a couple groping at each other in clothing that I know for a fact isn't appropriate to the era.

He's reading to me.

What kind of man reads to a girl?

The perfect man. That's the answer.

"Let's see..." He tries to find his place on the page.

Edwin has his reading glasses on. I'd never seen them on before. Says he just needs them for reading before bed or night driving. It's so damn cute to see them perched on the end of his nose.

"'*Hannah grabbed at his breeches and pulled until Everett was entirely exposed, his steel rod standing at attention.*'" Edwin stops. "I don't think 'steel rod' is a particularly sexy term."

"What would you call it, then?" I scoop up a spoonful of hospital mandated Jell-O.

Edwin grits his teeth in thought. "Probably what it is."

"You can't write the word 'penis' in a romance novel. Not when they're being sexy. That's so wrong."

He snorts. "That's ridiculous."

"Okay, think about it. If we were about to get it on–"

"Already off to a good start."

I roll my eyes, unable to keep from grinning. We haven't fucked nearly enough for my taste at this point, but I guess we have a lot of time to change that. "If I said, 'I want your penis in me,' how would that make you feel?"

Edwin closes the book, folding his arms over it against his chest. "Well, I'd get hard."

"Okay, well, would it change anything if I said, 'I want your cock in me'?"

One of his eyebrows rises. "Hard*er*."

"Case and point."

"No, not case and point, because I can assure you if you ever, ever, ever say that you want my steel rod in you, the opposite will happen, and I would even get flaccid."

"Oh, please. No, you wouldn't."

Edwin nods. "I would."

"If I'm naked in front of you, you're telling me you're going to go flaccid if I say–"

"The nakedness wasn't a part of the original terms."

I can't keep from laughing harder than I probably should for a hospital room. "You're impossible."

"Actually, *you're* the impossible one." Edwin cups one of my hands against my belly, leaning toward me with a serious look in his eye.

I narrow my eyes. "I have a feeling we're not talking about what we call your dick in bed."

"You'd be right about that." Edwin is unable to keep a smile from creeping onto his lips. "No, I'm talking about something else. Something you have been avoiding."

I reposition myself in bed, sitting up a bit. "What is it?"

"If we are going to be together..."

The word 'if' hangs in the air. I don't like it.

"I have to insist you let me take care of your debts, Sonia."

I knew this would happen. I'm in no position to continue refusing. "I want to work, Edwin. I want to keep my job, if that's possible."

"Yes, of course, but I can't have you indebted to a monster for the rest of your life."

"I'll pay you back."

He rolls his eyes. "No, that would be—"

"I'll *pay* you *back*." I sigh. "Look. I watched my father be in debt to everyone. The way he groveled, the way he tried to laugh it all off." I point my finger at my chest. "I don't laugh things off. I face them. Not only because it's what I've always had to do, but also because that's who I have grown to be. I don't want things fixed with a magic wand."

I hold the wand. I am the magic.

Edwin huffs. "If that's a term you're insisting upon, then fine. But there will be no interest whatsoever."

"Are you placating me?"

"Absolutely."

"Edwin!"

He leans in closer, his voice an excited murmur. "I've got money, Sonia. Not just a little stowed away, but *money*. The real kind. The world-shaking kind. Let me use it *for you*."

My lips curl up.

What woman doesn't want a man who wants to take care of her? To do anything for her? That would be insane to refuse. I just never realized how damn sexy it was. "Are you bragging?"

"Sonia—"

"I'm joking, I'm joking." I rub my thumb against the back of his knuckles.

Edwin's jaw hardens. "I know you don't want to feel indebted. And you wouldn't be. Just because I take care of your debts won't mean you are forced to stay with me."

I sigh. "But what if I want to stay with you?"

"Then who am I to say no to such a wondrous thing?"

Edwin leans in and kisses me. His tongue flips into my mouth and I sigh, content.

In a gap between kisses, I moan, "Yeah, I want your *steel rod.*"

He throws his head back in laughter. "See? I can't take you seriously when you call it that!"

I peck him once more on the lips. "I love you."

"I love you."

I WAKE UP FROM ONE OF MY MANY NAPS TO EDWIN talking in a low voice.

I look over at the door of my room where his back is to me. "She's asleep. It's not a good time."

"Please, Dad." Nate. "I want to talk to you. To both of you."

For some reason, I want to see Nate. Want to see how he's doing, hear his voice, have him see Edwin and me in the same room.

Because he needs to know about the love we share. The sooner he knows, the sooner he can begin to process.

"Edwin." My voice is raw, sleep-filled.

He looks over his shoulder at me, dark hair coiffed to perfection, though his stubble is now overgrown into a thin beard. "You're awake."

"Please let him in. I want to talk to him."

Edwin pauses, trying to measure if I'm ready for such excitement.

I know myself better than he does. And though I'm still managing the weakness in my body, my head has felt lighter and lighter by the minute. I'm hoping to be out of the hospital by tomorrow.

This conversation, however, can't wait that long.

Resigned, he opens the door wide.

Nate is rolled in by Laney. He looks well, though his face is wracked with worry.

"Hey, Sonia."

I slide my hand onto the side of the bed and adjust the backrest so I'm sitting up better to look at him. "Thanks for visiting."

Laney looks at me. "Don't give him too much credit. He had an appointment with his doctor, so it was just *convenient*." Her smile is playful and there is a twinkle in her eyes.

"*Laney*, that's not *why–*"

Her hand lands on his shoulder, caressing it. "I'm kidding, Nate."

Laney rolls Nate right up beside me.

His eyes find mine. "How are you feeling?"

"I'm..." As if by reflex, my eyes go straight to Edwin who stands now at the foot of my bed, watching the conversation. "Good. I've been better. But I'm good."

Nate smiles and follows my gaze to his father. "You've made up."

"You could say that." I let out a nervous laugh.

"So, what happened between you and my dad wasn't a 'mistake', huh?" He leans back in his chair.

I wince. "Can you not keep reminding me he's your dad?"

"I'm sorry, I think I've earned that right."

I sigh. "Fair."

"So, what's the verdict?" Nate observes me. Then Edwin. "Is this...happening?"

Edwin leans on the plastic footer of my bed. "I don't know, Nate. What do you think after I've been in her hospital room for three days now?"

Nate nods. I'm surprised he's so levelheaded about it. "Sonia?"

I hold my breath for a second.

I don't know if I'm ready for our love to extend into the real world, for everyone to know.

But then again, I'm not sure I have that luxury when our relationship has been so taboo and complicated from the beginning.

The ground is steady, Sonia. You won't be swallowed whole.

"I think I love him." I clear my throat as my voice breaks a bit. "I mean. I know I do."

Edwin's eyes are steady on me. "I love her too."

Nate laughs through his nostrils. "Ew."

Laney jabs him on the arm. "Manners, Lyons."

"I mean, it's gross. This situation is gross. And weird." Nate takes a deep breath. "But I...I believe you two, that it had nothing to do with me."

Though he made a lot of mistakes while we were together, Nate always had a kind soul. He can self-reflect better than anyone I know. Must be something about being one with the water and all the surfing.

I hope he doesn't lose all of that while being in that chair.

"Believe it, Nate." I reach out for his hand. "I promise."

Nate takes my hand and squeezes. "Okay, Mom."

"Ew! Ew, ew, ew!" I shake my head and wave my arms. "That's gross."

Edwin scrapes his hands over his face. "*Nathan.*"

"I think I have a right to a few jabs now and then for at least the next year or so." Nate shrugs. "But all of this is to say, regardless of how weird it is, I just want you to know I'm okay with it."

Laney pats his shoulder.

"Thank you, Nate." I smile. "Thank you so much."

"Call me crazy, but I just want you two to be happy."

I glance at Edwin. The rims of his eyes are red.

I smile. "How far we've come, huh?"

"Helps when you realize what life is all about, doesn't it?" Edwin smiles back.

I wish I could shout to the world that you shouldn't wait for a near-death experience to give away all the love in your heart.

Give it all away as soon as you feel it. Even if it feels wrong, even if it's strange or confusing. Love is worth it. Love changes everything. And if people turn away, they are the ones with the problem, not you. Because there is nothing wrong with loving.

"Yeah, it helps a lot."

I won't forget that as long as I'm alive. Not for a single, damn day.

31

———

EDWIN

IF YOU WOULD HAVE TOLD ME AS I LAY ON MY OFFICE floor with my back spasming that in a year time, I would be experiencing love so profound it would simply erase everything I have done wrong in my life, reset the clock, and give me a second chance, I would have called you a lunatic.

However, today, I have the woman I love and all three of my children all under one roof.

I insisted Sonia stay with me after her release from the hospital.

Thank god, she was amenable to that.

I'm not sure I ever want her out of my sight again after what happened at the club. That's something I'll have to work through.

Nate, of course, is still staying with me, along with Laney.

And, tonight, Abigail and Jack have come to visit for a big family dinner.

The club has been far from my mind these past few weeks, which was a mistake given what happened. Though I've avoided talking with Sonia about it apart from the one police interview I was privy to when they visited her in the hospital, I have been working behind the scenes to figure out what the hell happened and who is responsible for it.

Solomon has been leading the inquiry with employees while I sort out things with security.

I've been furious with Lourdes and the security team, even more so when they said that the security footage from the time of the crime displayed no one on the premises.

However, for the first time in my life, I put all that aside in order to take care of my family.

It is a motley crew, that is for sure, but there is a love and appreciation in the air for what we have.

We all know how easy it is to lose.

Two close calls in the matter of a few weeks. The fact we survived still intact and closer than ever is a miracle. To be around the table together sharing a homecooked meal, by a chef, but still, is the greatest honor of my life.

Sonia sits by my side. It puts a warm feeling in my chest to be at the head of a table surrounded by my family.

It's never been like this. Even a meal with my children. All three of them together has been a rarity throughout the course of their lives.

And I never had one of their mothers to sit beside me. Or a girlfriend or wife.

For once, we are *normal*. Oddities in how Sonia and I came together notwithstanding. And that we are also joined by my son's live-in PT.

It's our version of normal and that's good enough for me.

Sonia puts her fork down and sighs. Her plate is still full. "I can barely eat."

"Yeah, the meds will do that to you." Nate eyes a forkful of spinach, leaning his elbow on the table.

I have noticed he's lost a lot of muscle over the course of his rehabilitation.

Right now, all we care about is him walking again. The muscles will come back with time.

I smile at Sonia. "You don't have to clean your plate."

She pouts. "It's delicious, though."

"There will be plenty of delicious meals in the future, I promise." I place my hand over hers across the table.

All the eyes in the room snap right to my hand.

This is something they're going to have to get used to, Nate included. I will be as gentle as I can with the introduction, but I want to live my life. Want to rain affection down on the woman I love without worry.

Jack shakes his head. "This is weird."

Abigail looks at him, her mouth agape. "*Jack.*"

"Not in a bad way. It just is. I've never seen Dad actually like someone."

I take a sip of wine to calm my nerves. "I like plenty of people."

"Not in a hand-holding way." Jack frowns. "And of all people, Nate's–"

Nate throws a roll at his brother. "In the past, bro."

Jack harrumphs and picks the roll up from his lap, taking a bite of it.

I smile at Nate. How all my children are so mature compared to how I behaved at their ages is beyond me. Perhaps they had a "what not to do" example in me to look at.

Abigail looks between me and Sonia. "Are you going to keep working together at the club?"

Sonia and I exchange a look, and Sonia turns to her. "I mean, I'd like to. Of course, I need to recover, and if I'm being honest, the idea of being at the club again gives me heart palpitations, but..." She tilts her head to the side. "I'd really like to. If that's okay with you, Edwin."

"Of course, it is. I think we make a good team. Even better when we're not sneaking about and lying to everybody."

Nate stabs a piece of lettuce. "You don't think it will be too weird, the three of us working together?"

An overwhelming warmth spreads across my chest. Pride. "I think we'll do just fine. As long as it's what you want to do."

Nate shrugs a shoulder. "The Lyons Club is a family affair."

"You're not obligated, Nate. Not anymore."

He shakes his head. "I don't feel like it's an obligation. I think I...I'd like to give it a try."

"Good, good. That makes me...happy." The word "happy" is almost like a revelation when it comes to my relationship with my son.

Abigail waves her hands around. "Okay, can we move on from all the idle chatter and get down to brass tacks? Sonia, what do you put in your hair to make it so shiny?"

Sonia laughs while the boys groan.

I keep on smiling. Can't seem to stop.

The girls go back and forth about beauty techniques, guys cutting in every now and then with an obligatory joke that is shut down by a glare.

I love it here.

My house manager, Carlisle, appears at my shoulder and leans down. "Mr. Lyons, someone at the door to see you."

I frown. "I'm not expecting anyone." I don-t want to draw attention to me.

"Someone from the club. A Lourdes Morales?"

I shoot up out of my chair. "Thank you, Carlisle."

I button the top button of my jacket and give a nod to the table. "Just a moment, everyone. Some business I need to attend to."

My eyes find Sonia's. Her brow is perked in question. Best not to disturb her with the news that the Lyons Club head of security is here to discuss the incident that led to her injury.

Every time we mention the club, I can tell it puts Sonia on edge. Like there's a hair trigger inside her that might send her right back into the memory, back into all that fear that she was trapped in her last moments.

The memory that she might die without telling me how she really felt.

Before I go, I lean down and kiss the crown of her head, avoiding the bandage covering her wound.

I am very much looking forward to a lifetime of kissing her like that.

I'm more than grateful when everyone launches right back into animated conversation as I leave the room.

As Carlisle leads me down the hall, I do my best to quell my temper.

Lourdes has already gotten an earful from me. More than an earful. The stone-faced head of security looked near to tears by the time I was done tearing into her.

It wasn't fair, but I was upset at being told there were few clues as to what had happened. And knowing how good Lourdes is at her job, well...I just found it hard to believe that in the direst of times, she didn't have answers for me.

Keep a calm head. For Sonia.

I find Lourdes pacing in the front hall, back and forth. She's in her usual all black attire, including a black leather jacket and sunglasses propped up on her head.

"Mr. Lyons." Her voice sounds as if it's a novelty to see me in my own home.

I give her a curt nod. "Lourdes. Good to see you. This is unexpected."

"I apologize for visiting you at your home, but given the circumstances, I wanted to give you the information we've found as soon as possible." Her panther-like eyes are square in mine.

"Let's take a seat, then, and discuss." I gesture into the sitting room off the front hall, the one reserved for impromptu meetings and gatherings, not casual rest.

Lourdes follows me, taking a seat in a chair across from me while I sit on the white sofa, my ankle crossed over my knee.

"I want to apologize again for our lack of foresight on this issue."

"It's alright, Lourdes." I say that only because I know it's what Sonia would want me to say.

Shaking her head, Lourdes places her hands on her knees, knuckles turning white. "It's inexcusable. The fact this resulted in Ms. Hill's injury and has now incurred an obvious lack of trust from members is...well, all I can do is apologize."

I pause. "You're not losing your job, Lourdes." I threatened it, sure. Which was not gracious of me.

Lourdes throat bobs up and down.

"Now, what is it you've come to show me?"

She reaches into her pocket and pulls out her phone, tapping and navigating as she speaks. "I've gone through the footage again and again to look for things the police might have missed, finding nothing but the repeating sixty frames that tricked our security officer on duty into thinking that no one was in the club, including Ms. Hill."

The police are not good for much, but they were able to identify that somehow, there was the same clip being played on loop through the CCTV footage, a sample of a silent club. No one knew that Sonia was there, much less the intruders.

"However, I decided to do some backtracking myself while the police still try and figure things out and...well..." She holds out her phone to me, a video awaiting to be played. "This footage is from the late afternoon before the break in, sometime after all the members had left."

I take it and tap the small triangle to watch.

The footage is still and silent at first. A view of the executive office hall.

"What is this?"

"Just watch."

A few more seconds roll by. Then, there is sound. Grunting and the sounds of scraping metal. A face pops up on camera.

A face I know very well.

"What the hell?"

Lourdes is silent.

I watch as Farley's ugly mug is close up to the camera. He must be teetering on a ladder in order to reach. He curses to himself. Tampering with the equipment.

"Farley's behind this?"

On the footage, he smiles and disappears as the footage changes to the empty hallway as if he was never even there.

"I can't say for certain, however it's very clear he tampered with the security footage. Used a signal jam in order to replay the footage that led our security officers astray."

"Why? Why would he do this?"

Lourdes shrugs. "I don't know. But I wanted to show you before I showed the police."

I look at her hard.

I know Lourdes came to me before the police because sometimes, it's easier to deal with things ourselves rather than create a scandal. It great to know that she has loyalty to Lyons Club.

Farley might not, but Lourdes does. As do so many others.

"Thank you, Lourdes. This is...above and beyond."

She smiles, a simple twist of her lips to the side. "It is the least I can do, given what happened."

We both stand, and I go to her, placing my hands on her shoulders. "I'm sorry for the things I said. I was..." Angry is not an excuse. "Scared."

"I understand."

I make a mental note to give Lourdes a raise. "Let's keep this information between you and me for now. I want to deal with Farley myself."

Lourdes nods.

We say our goodbyes as I walk her out.

Once I am alone in the hallway, I pause to consider what I've learned.

Farley, my chief operations officer, has betrayed me. He put his balls into undercutting me and harming the woman I love. He's lucky we don't live in some lawless time because I think I have enough fury inside me to murder the guy.

When I turn to head back to the dining room, Sonia is standing in the hall. Her face is bereaved.

"Farley?"

My heart pounds. "You heard?"

She nods. "I had a feeling this might be about...that night. I wanted to hear. And..." She sighs. "Really? *Farley?*"

I hold my arm out to her. "Come here."

"He wasn't there. I would have recognized him. The man was too big, and the other person was a woman and–"

"He must have had co-conspirators, or maybe he hired the people who were there."

Sonia is quiet for a moment. "But why?"

I close the space between us, winding her in my arms, up against my chest. "Why does anyone do anything?"

Why did Sonia and I find each other? Why did we fall in love? Why did Nate change his mind about Lyons? Why did Sonia's father gamble his life away? Why, why, why?

Because of a need. Sometimes a need greater than our own understanding.

I'm not empathetic to Farley because of this. In fact, I loathe him deep in my blood-boiling soul. But I can understand. Just a little.

"It will all be alright. I will deal with it. All of it." That is a promise.

Her hands press into my back. Tight. Almost like she'll never let go.

32

———

SONIA

"I wanted to say goodbye."

I cross my arms over my chest and stare at Farley.

We are in the atrium of Lyons Pride. Almost half a year ago, I was here in my white dress, picking up my mask for the masquerade that changed my entire life, Farley wrapping his arm around me, welcoming me to the team.

"I...know it might take some time to forgive me..." His hands slide back and forth around the handle of his suitcase. "But I really had planned for them to break in the old-fashioned way. Not use you to–"

"Once you're done trying to justify their actions, then I'll forgive you, Farley."

His eyes widen, and then he tries to smile but fails. "I guess that's fair."

Hands sliding back and forth on his suitcase handle still, eyes to the floor, he adds, "Thank you so much for talking to Edwin on my behalf. I was so sure I was going to be locked away for the rest of my life."

"Yeah, well, jail wouldn't help, and this facility for immersion in cognitive behavioral therapy might."

Farley's been struggling with addiction. He's spent all his money on cocaine and party drugs and got himself into somewhat of a debt. A weekend's worth of cash from Lyons would be enough to let him start over.

"Again, I'm sorry. I don't know what I was thinking, but my drugged ramblings with my friends turned into half-assed plans that got you hurt, and I will never forgive myself for that."

Farley isn't a saint, but he's not a devil either.

"I want the best for you, Farley." I give him a small smile. "Regardless of everything, I want you to get better."

He smiles at me, a tentative pull of his lips, and rolls his eyes. "Aren't you a sweetheart?"

A car pulls up, visible through the big glass doors.

"Well, that's my ride." He spreads his arm. "Hug?"

"Fine." There was a time when I thought of him as my friend after all. Maybe someday I will again. He's the one who gave me the chance to come here, brought me to Edwin.

We hug. It brings tears to my eyes.

"Alright. Well, I'll see you on the other side." Farley puts two fingers to his brow and then salutes me. His eyes lift to the staircase above for only a moment. His smile fades.

I look up. Edwin stands above, looming with a vacant expression. He doesn't need to do anything extra to intimidate, he just does.

Farley hurries out of the atrium to the car that is taking him upstate to his treatment center.

Edwin comes down to meet me, his hand feathering my cheek. "You alright?"

"Yes, I think that was good."

"Good. I'm glad."

Both of us look into the open door of the nightclub. It's the middle of the day, which means all the activity is in the members' club, not here. The emptiness sends a bit of anxiety through my chest.

"Are you ready?"

I have been away from the club for a few weeks now. Far past the healing of my injury.

However, the emotional scars inside have been difficult to overcome. I still wake up some nights in a sweat from nightmares about the moment I thought might be my last.

Being near Edwin helps. A lot. Just sleeping next to him makes me feel leagues better.

Still, it can't fix everything.

Today, though, I'm coming in for a tour. To see the place. To feel it out. I need to know if I'm ready to step back into my role.

I've said goodbye to Farley, already sat through a security brief from Lourdes who has assured me all of the previous security protocols were firm and steadfast, but they've added even more to ensure everyone's safety.

It is clear, everyone wants me to feel welcome. And I do. "Yes. I'm ready."

Edwin wraps his arm around my waist, and off we go, up the stairs, passing the place we almost kissed that very first night, and into the members club.

Everything is back to the way it was that very first day I was here. Bustling and exciting, the haphazard wine bar moved back into the wine cellar since construction on the whisky tasting room is done. The waterfall is running, music is playing, and conversations abound.

Bridget rushes up to greet me with open arms, Solomon following behind her.

"Welcome back!" She kisses my cheek. "I've kept your seat warm for you!"

"Oh, joy." I laugh.

Bridget has stepped in as an interim manager for the club. Like father, like daughter, I suppose.

"We're all very happy to see you, Sonia." Solomon nods.

"Me too." I grin. "I'm so happy to see all of you."

"Let's do a walkthrough, huh?" Edwin tips his chin forward. "Lead the way, Sol."

Again, like my first day, I go through all the nooks and crannies of the Lyons Club. Members greet me left and right with hugs and well wishes, some of whom I didn't think even knew my name.

Everything is in good working order, as expected.

Bridget has done a phenomenal job.

And the whisky tasting room is gorgeous, worth every bit of frustration it gave me.

Edwin pours us all a small snifter full, and we cheers.

"To Sonia's *hopeful* return." Edwin's emphasis on 'hopeful' is hard to miss.

I know there is no rush. Everyone around me is so patient and kind. But I'm in a rush to get back. I want to leave the events of that night behind and pick up right when I woke up, looked Edwin in the eyes, and told him that I loved him.

"I'm going to take Sonia to the office, get her up to speed on everything." Bridget grabs my hand. "Where should we meet you?"

Edwin sips his whisky, then eyes me up and down. "I'll let her know."

And just like that, I know exactly where he wants me to meet him.

Edwin and I have been having sex, yes. But it has been

soft and careful. He hasn't wanted to break me or hurt me, for which I'm grateful.

But I want to be his again. Want to be his petulant little brat. I told him as much before we left the house today. I know he's been half-hard ever since.

It only makes sense that my welcome back would include a visit to The Underground.

Back in my office, I update Bridget on everything.

She holds my hand. "So, it's official as in everyone knows?"

"Edwin wants to hold a staff meeting to tell everyone." I flush.

My friend grabs my shoulders and squeals, jumping up and down. "This is amazing!"

I don't refuse her excitement this time. I have nothing to hide, nothing to fear.

Edwin is mine. Now the world just needs to know.

"Hasn't it been weird, though? Living with Nate?"

"Kind of? He's sort of always preoccupied with PT, and he's been working on applying for an MBA. Plus, he's kind of always distracted by Laney..."

Bridget waggles her eyebrows. "His nurse? That's hot."

"Oh my god, you're so gross." I smack her on the arm.

Nate might be my ex-boyfriend, but he's my current boyfriend's son. And I've come to see him that way. Not as a son to me, but as someone in my life who is, in essence, not a sexual being.

Living together, while strange, has also done wonders for our relationship.

"I knew it would work out." Bridget reminds me of that emoji with hearts for eyes.

I smile. I don't want to get ahead of myself, but I have to

say everything between Edwin and me has felt inevitable. Everlasting.

I'm the most confident and optimistic about a relationship I've ever been.

"Now, tell me. About the sex."

"I may have whisky in my system, but I'm gonna need a hell of a lot more before I give you details."

Bridget pouts. "Fine. My place. Next week. You in?"

I grin. "Sure."

***

Bridget eventually lets go of my ear, and, once I'm free, I head into The Underground. Quiet as usual.

Hazel is talking to the Dungeon Master. We greet each other with a hug. In my ear, she whispers, "Don't worry, I won't tell anyone."

Once our relationship is public, we'll have to be much coyer about using the facilities for our own pleasures.

I don't care if Edwin's the boss and there would be no way that punishment could be doled out by our HR department in the form of dismissals. My reputation and integrity matter to me. It's what made me so good at the job in the first place.

However, seeing as we're not public knowledge yet, I can let this one slide.

I go to room eleven, a lucky number. I rap on the door and Edwin's deep timbre answers, "Come in."

I touch the door handle.

Though it's cold, it burns me, makes me realize just how much I need this. Need to be tamed. Need to be reminded who I belong to.

Who I will always belong to.

I step into the room, find Edwin in all his suited glory, only the buttons on his coat undone.

"I hope you haven't broached the one drink limit." I eye his whisky glass on one of the black trunks of toys, the brown liquor muddled with glass.

"Already starting with the insolence, I see…"

I smile. "Just want to be sure we're following the rules."

Edwin walks over to me, stops only an inch away. None of his body touches me, and yet I feel a fire coming off of him. No wonder the doorknob was hot.

His black eyes are somehow blacker than usual, all pupil where there should be iris. "When it comes to matters like these, I always follow the rules." He lifts a finger and presses it against my sternum. "It's you who seems to have trouble with that."

I smirk and then peer around his shoulder at the St. Andrew's cross.

It daunted me the first time I saw it, but after realizing what I have managed to handle from Edwin, his sweet forms of torture, I want it.

I'm salivating for it.

I brush past Edwin.

He makes no move to restrain me, but he does cluck his tongue.

I approach the cross, stand before it with a smile, and then turn back to Edwin.

"What do you think?"

"About?"

I grab one of the cuffs hanging off the x-shaped leather pillar. "This?"

"We have to begin the scene, Sonia." He seems to be measuring his words and tone.

I tilt my head to the side, letting my hand drift down the edge of the cross. "Let's begin, then."

Edwin's eyes flare. A reminder, he is the Dom, he is the one in control.

But I'm feeling a little bratty.

"Take off your clothes. All of them."

I look at him from beneath my lashes. "Yes, sir." That is a demand I have no problem appeasing.

I undo the front of my blouse and remove it. Then the skirt, which falls to my feet, leaving me only in a bra, underwear, and high heels.

Edwin stands there. He does not grab his hardening cock, nor does he smile. Just watches.

But I smile. I can't help it.

His gaze still makes my heart race.

But I'm not scared and I'm not resistant. I want more.

I snap the bra off first, goosebumps breaking out across my skin, my nipples hardening. Then, I go for the underwear and let them drop too.

"Leave the shoes on." Edwin rounds the center table, coming toward me.

I let him overpower me, grab me by the wrists and slam me up against the cross.

I bend my head back with a hissing low laugh.

"Don't you dare drop your wrists," Edwin growls as he fastens one hand to the cross.

"Yes, sir."

Then, he fastens the other into place. "You're being way too agreeable. I'm wondering when you're going to turn the tables on me."

I grin, head lolling to the side, and lift one leg, wrapping it around his thigh, pulling his crotch flush to mine.

"Ah, spoke too soon..."

I grind my pelvis into his, my wetness coating the front of his pants. "Fuck me."

"You're moving too fast."

"Don't tease me," I plead. "Fuck me."

Edwin's face grows hard. He undoes the cuffs.

I'm confused, my heart falling into my stomach. "What are you—"

"The first time we were here, I told you what would happen when you talk back."

Edwin forces me to my knees.

I cry out as he grabs the back of my head and presses it into his crotch.

Through the fabric, I can smell him, the delicious saltiness of his cock and balls. I wiggle my face back and forth, the hardness pressing against my face, unyielding.

He undoes his pants, the button, the zipper, lets them drop to his hips. Then, he pushes the top of his boxer briefs down, revealing the length of his cock.

I moan, my tongue lolling out like I've been starving for too long, need to be fed his member.

I lap at the head of his cock, one tear of cum dripping into my mouth. I dart forward to swallow him up, but Edwin wraps his hand in my hair, jerks me back.

"Look. At. Me."

I draw my eyes up to his. His teeth are gritted so hard.

"Look at me when you take me."

I let my tongue cup the head and do not let my eyes leave his as I take him deeper and deeper into my mouth.

Edwin's mouth falls open, the corners of his eyes softening with an emotion I can't pinpoint. Surprise? Relief?

No. Awe.

He is in awe of how my mouth fits around him, how his cock slides in with such ease, nudging up against the back of my throat. How I suppress a gag and go in for more, more, more.

I lap him, lick him, working fast and hard to drain him.

"Mm, god, you are a pretty little slut, aren't you?"

I moan around him.

"You are such a good slut. My slut."

I smile.

Edwin cups the back of my head, pressing my face flush to his body, not allowing me to retreat from his cock. He starts to fuck my mouth, bucking. "Shit, you take me so beautifully—"

He releases his grip on me, removing himself from my mouth. His hard cock bobs, red and angry.

"Though I'm enjoying this punishment, Swan, you come first."

I come first in all things. In life. In sex.

"But I want your seed in my mouth."

"Not today. Not this time. You have to earn it."

Edwin hauls me back up to my feet, and I giggle. He flips me around, my naked body pressed against the cross. He fastens both of my wrists and my ankles.

I glimpse back at him. My cheek pressed to the leather. My legs are spread, showing him my already glistening center.

"Please, fuck me *now*."

He aligns his body with mine, pushing his cock between my lower lips. Our mouths a mere inch apart. The moment hangs in the air. Just a quick repositioning away from him entering me.

"No." He retreats from me, leaving my body cold and empty.

He crosses the room, back to me.

"*Edwin...*"

"How do you address me, pet?" He glares at me over his shoulder. "I ought to leave you there for a long, long time."

My eyes widen. "Is that an option?"

His stern countenance breaks. "Would you like that?"

I nod before my brain can catch up with my body. Somehow my body knows more than my brain ever has.

Edwin laughs low. The scene is broken, if only for a moment. "My god, I've got a lot to learn about you yet, don't I, baby?"

I squirm against the cross, my body in an unpleasant state of unsated arousal. "Please come back." My eyes flutter shut.

Rustling comes from behind me. Then a buzzing sound.

My eyes shoot open again. "What is–"

A cold knob is shoved between my thighs, a vibrator buzzing.

I scream, trying to crawl away from the toy, but locked completely in place. "Too much, too much!"

"*Color*, swan."

Fuck, even though the feeling is too much, it's everything. "Green! Green."

Edwin presses the toy harder against me, the vibrations causing my clit to scream out.

It wasn't ready, not prepared, but that's what makes it hurt so good.

The longer it buzzes, the more I settle into it.

A hand slides against my upper back, all the way to my shoulder. Then the hand descends, caresses each cheek in turn.

When Edwin pulls the hand away, the cold air from the lack of contact hits me, and a second later, a hand cracks against my ass.

My body jerks, my clit grinding against the vibrator.

I cry out from the torturous pleasure-pain.

"Beautiful. Now take your punishment and we'll see if you learn to address me once and for all."

His hand showers both my cheeks with crack after crack. Some slower, some faster, some softer, some harder, but all of them so arousing I lose myself in the sensation, not knowing where pain ends and pleasure begins.

"Fuck!" I squirm. "Sir, please, it's too much!" *But it's still green. It's still all so green.*

The vibrator increases to an impossible speed. My body is shaking, every muscle trembling.

With a final spank, he issues the ultimate command. "Come now, Swan."

The coil of arousal snaps apart.

I scream.

Edwin stops the spanking, caressing my cheeks as I come, but doesn't withdraw the vibrator.

I bristle against my restraints but only end up nestling myself tighter against the toy.

"*Again*," he growls in my ear.

I come again. Again. Again. I lose count.

The pleasure burns through me, ravaging the landscape of my body and sanity. My body is limp against the cross, held up only by the restraints and my sheer willpower.

"Please." Tears coat my eyes. "Please, I can't–I can't–"

The toy drops to the floor, and I sag.

Edwin presses his body up against my back, grinding his erection into my ass. His breath is labored like a wild bull charging at me. His teeth sink into my ear lobe, and I whimper.

"My swan..." He sighs.

Edwin licks his fingers and stuffs them inside me. I wail, body reeling with pleasure. "*Edwin!*"

"Wrong." His fingers move inside me, fast and untamed, pressing against my inside-most point, the one that burns when touched in the best way.

"S-*sir*."

"That's right. You call me *sir*."

"Yes, sir."

"*Good* girl. I like it when you're good."

He withdraws his hand, leaving me panting, pressing his body flush against mine again.

Edwin places his mouth next to my ear. "But I also have to admit, I like it just as much when you're bad."

Before I can respond, Edwin thrusts his whole length inside me.

My body jumps against the cross, the cuffs rattling in my ears. I want to grab him, hold onto him.

But I am at his mercy.

The wanting, the needing, ramps up my arousal.

I buck my hips the best I can while being this restrained.

Edwin is in complete control, his hands locking on my hips as he drives into me from behind.

He determines the speed and the depth of his thrusts. Faster. Slower. All of him, circling his hips to feel the constriction of my walls. Retreating to leave me begging for him to come back.

Edwin grabs my thighs, pinching them hard. "Fucking *mine*."

"Yours."

Grabbing my chin, he twists my head to the side. Our eyes lock together. "Yes, that's right."

"I'm yours." A whimper. A pledge. A vow. "Yours, Edwin. Yours, yours, yours."

Edwin kisses me hard and fast, then presses the side of my face into the leather. "Oh, my *fucking* GOD."

I hit the apex of my pleasure, screaming against the cross. I clench around him, and I just know from the way we pulse together he's not going to last.

Edwin's head dips back, mouth falls open. Hair a complete wreck. And he roars as he comes, the way a primal animal does as he claims his territory.

It's what I am from now on. It has been decided not just through our words but through our actions. I have laid down my body for him, given him every part of me. Given him control when I have spent so long trying to control everything.

Someone else, at last, can take on my burden.

Edwin touches my cheek. "Sonia."

Our eyes meet. The scene is over. It is just us. *Us.*

"Crying."

I don't feel the tears that wet my face until he points them out. "Happy." I smile. "So happy."

Edwin releases my bindings and, the second I am no longer held up by them, I tumble into his arms, a shock of whatever is left of my body now that I have descended into complete and utter pleasure.

"My good girl. That's what you are." He kisses my temple and carries me to the bed.

I nod.

He rolls me up in a blanket and gives me some water and a square of chocolate.

"You need it after the scene. Take it."

I open my mouth and take it straight from his hand.

"The brat can be tamed." Edwin scratches his hand through my hair. "But only for so long, I'm sure."

We both laugh, a flurry of kisses and cuddles. "Yes, I've learned my lesson. For now."

"Don't you worry, my love." Edwin forces another sip of water into me. "I'll be happy to teach you a lesson again."

"Thank you. For freeing me." I smile.

I have been freed because of him. From my debts, from my past, from my fears.

And now I am ready to fly.

"Always, my Swan."

33

EPILOGUE

EDWIN

Nate and I are out to dinner, a tradition we started in an effort to rebuild our relationship outside of the business.

He spears a cherry tomato onto his fork and pops it into his mouth. "So, how are things with you and Sonia?"

I sip some wine. "Amazing. How are you feeling about all of this? It can't be easy for you."

"Easier than you'd think. Dad, I've moved on. You know that. I love you both, and I want you guys to be happy. You know you're not getting any younger–"

"Fifty is the new thirty-five."

Nate laughs. I love watching him so free. "Fine. But here is the moment of truth. Do you want to marry her?"

My cheeks are on fire.

"Oh, shit. You do! Dad. You have to ask her!"

"Nate, I really...don't want to rush anything." A complete lie.

I have wanted to rush everything from the second I saw her, my Swan, at last year's masquerade. Wanted to wrap my arms around her, never let go, take her all the way into eternity.

Hard to wrap my head around the fact that it will be a year in two weeks. Already? Only? It's like time has flown but stood still since I met her.

Nate rolls his eyes. "You had my mother pregnant after an hour of talking to her."

"Not exactly how things went down, but–" I gulp my wine.

"Oh, my god, Dad, listen. You've been living together for almost six months now. It's time."

I clear my throat. "I should discuss it with Sonia first."

"No need."

I quirk an eyebrow. "Why?"

Now it's my son's turn to blush. "She may or may not have dropped a hint to me."

My stomach drops. "A hint? To you?"

"Less of a hint and more of a plea. For me to get in your ear and push you to propose."

"Sonia asked *you* to convince me to propose?!"

Nate has a smug smile on his face. "You know Sonia and I talk. We're friends."

I shake my head in disbelief. "You're a better man than me, Nate."

I have no idea how I would react if I were in his shoes, but Nate has been surprising me at every turn.

"No, I just want you both to have your happy ever after. You deserve it, Dad. And so does Sonia. So, it's time to get a ring and pop the question." He grins.

"Cheers to that."

"LET ME SEE IT ONE MORE TIME."

I open the box and show it to Solomon. "Would you like one too?"

"Mm, rubies really aren't my color." He peers into the ring box. A smile creeps onto his face. "She'll love it."

"I hope so. Otherwise, I have Bridget to blame, since she helped me pick it." I snatch the box back with a wry smile.

Bridget's taste is unmatched. Plus, she and Sonia have turned into the best of friends.

Solomon grins. "How do you feel?"

I step in front of the mirror in the corner of my office, straightening out my suit jacket. It's hard to believe that I was standing in this exact spot one year ago today, before the last masquerade, lamenting my life and choices. Today, it is the complete opposite.

"Nervous." My smile defaults into a grimace. "Is that normal?"

Solomon laughs and pats my shoulder. "Plenty normal. Hard to believe after all these years and all these children you've never even managed a proposal, Ed."

"Don't remind me. Masks?"

This year's theme is precious gems. I feel quite sneaky choosing this, considering my plans for the night.

Instead of a phoenix, I have a mask meant to represent diamonds with a clear, sparkling finish that would look corny in hands any less adept than our mask makers.

I put my mask on and then admire Solomon's emerald mask. "Green is your color, my friend."

He slaps my back. "Thank you. I think so too."

I check my watch. "Sonia should be arriving soon."

"Oh, fantastic. I'll get into place to greet her, then."

"Thank you, Sol."

I've managed to finagle my way out of arriving with

Sonia by claiming business. Always business. I could tell she was a bit disappointed. My only hope is that the real reason will make up for it.

We both leave my office, Solomon heading out to the front staircase while I head to the upper level of the nightclub.

Everything is already underway. Music grinding, people dancing, drinks flowing.

I rest my hands on the railing and take in my domain. Whereas last year, I felt numb about the club, this year, I feel so much pride.

Because everyone is here.

Abigail and Seth are doing an atrocious version of the robot on the dance floor while Jack sits at the bar, chatting up a woman who I think might be too old for him, although, I should probably hold my tongue seeing my own situation puts twenty years between Sonia and me.

Which brings me to Nate.

I scan the room, but he is nowhere to be found.

I bite my lower lip.

He promised he'd be here. He said–

A hand lands on my shoulder. "Hi, Dad."

I grin at the sight of my son. "There you are."

"What, did you think I wouldn't show for your big night?"

I shake my head and embrace him. Tight. "I'm so happy you're here."

"Had to find you before the big moment. There's a sneaky glint in his blue eyes. "How are you feeling?"

"Everyone keeps asking me that."

Nate throws back his head in laughter.

He's kept his blond hair shorter, although still a bit shaggy for my liking. He's stepped into his role at Lyons, working as our new vendor liaison, which allows him the freedom to travel for work rather than making him feel stuck at the club all the time.

We are making it work, and it has been seamless.

He's got the Lyons charm but his mother's affability, and he's served Lyons well in his tenure thus far. "You're about to propose, Dad. That's a big deal."

"Thanks for being here."

"Wouldn't miss it for the world." Nate's eyes fall to the lower level. "And there she is."

Sonia emerges from the front hall into the club and my heart leaps into my throat.

Her ruby mask suits her so well, just as I expected, creating a stark contrast with her dark hair. She wears a gold dress; a Grecian goddess stepping down from Mount Olympus.

"Wow."

Nate laughs. "Man, you've got it bad for her."

"Is it obvious?" I don't take my eyes off my bride-to-be. I hope.

"Yes. Never stop, Dad." Nate pats my shoulder.

Solomon and Bridget walk on either side of her.

Bridget served as the distraction to keep Sonia occupied and unsuspecting.

"I'll go alert the musicians."

"Thank you."

Nate rushes off ahead of me.

The timing all has to be perfect.

I watch Nate approach the band leader, Jack and Abigail are now alert.

Bridget and Solomon are walking Sonia to the dance floor, all the waiters serving champagne avoid her just as I instructed.

It's time.

I descend the stairs as the music peters off and emerge onto the dance floor where people are clearing a path for me.

I stop at the very center and take a deep breath when my eyes lock with Sonia's.

She's frowning. Looks to her right and left for support from Solomon and Bridget, but they, as instructed, have scrambled off to the viewing gallery.

It's just me and her, the only two people in the world.

Just like that first moment we saw each other, not knowing how the courses of our lives were about to change.

I hold out my hand to her. "Come on. I won't bite."

Sonia laughs. "I don't know about that."

I laugh too. She's right about that. I have bitten from time to time.

Sonia is hesitant as she steps onto the dance floor. "What's all this about?"

"I think you might have a bit of an idea."

Her mouth spreads into a closed-mouth smile.

I clear my throat. "Thank you all for coming tonight to the annual Lyons Masquerade. I have spared you from the absolute mortification that was last year's theme."

"I liked last year's theme," Solomon grumbles from the crowd and Bridget shushes him.

"I appreciate you giving me a second chance to make it up to you all." The crowd chuckles. "Theme notwithstanding, last year's masquerade turned out to be the most important moment of my life. Other than my children being born." I look into Sonia's eyes once again. "It was the night I met Sonia Elaine Hill."

Her brow is already knit together tight to keep from

shedding the tears glistening in her beautiful golden eyes. The smile only grows by the second.

I pull off my mask.

A moment like this requires us to be face to face.

"I hope you'll forgive me for removing my mask. It will only be for the moment, I promise." I look over at Sonia. "You too, sweetheart."

She hesitates, then pulls off the mask, revealing her true face to me.

I remember a year ago how she refused to show me her identity. Now, I know all of her. There is no need to hide.

"Sonia and I had to overcome a lot to be together. Many of you know her as one of the managers around here at Lyons. Just one of our many hiccups. But when the universe calls out to you, you can't let trivial things like the boundaries of being boss and employee get in your way."

This is it. The moment.

I sink down onto one knee.

Part of the crowd didn't see this coming, some shocked gasps resounding through the club.

"Sonia, the past year has taught me a lot. But the most important lesson was that even if you wait a single second, you have waited too long to tell people you love them. You have to start as soon as you feel it. I have spent every day since I met you loving you. Probably before that too."

Sonia blushes, touching her cheek.

"You are the best part of me. You've shown me how to be a better man. And a better father. And I don't want to spend another day of my life without you as my wife."

"Oh my gosh." A tear rolls down her face as she hiccups a laugh.

I open the ring box, letting the diamonds and rubies glitter like they're somehow magic. Sonia's jaw drops.

"Sonia. My swan. Will you marry me?"

There is an enthusiastic "aww" from the crowd.

She nods before she speaks. "Yes, yes, of course."

I take her hand in mine as all the witnesses applaud.

Electricity shocks both of us, an intensity we have never known. Not since the beginning.

Knowing how precious both the moment and the woman in front of me are, I slip the ring onto her ring finger.

I can't believe I've waited so long to do this. That it took me so long to figure my shit out. I can only be glad that somehow my soul waited for Sonia.

"I hope you like–"

Sonia grabs me by the face and pulls me into a deep kiss.

I slide my hand around her waist, pressing her to me, making it clear to everyone that this woman right here is all mine and will be forever.

The band begins to play some jazz number.

I don't even remember what I requested from them. All I can feel, all I know, is Sonia's lips on mine, unwilling to let me breathe or break away.

When she pulls away, her hands still press to my cheeks. She grins. "You tricked me."

"I had to. It had to be a surprise."

She smiles, then her lips caress my cheek. "You are the best man I have ever known."

My heart flutters. "Working on it."

"No, Edwin, listen to me." Her amber eyes harden in mine. "Not many men can learn to love the way you have. Not many men are willing to admit they've neglected loving in their life. You are...so special."

I can't help but smile. "Oh. Well."

"And I love you. And want you to take me downstairs and do absolutely depraved things to me."

My dick leaps to attention. "Oh, that can be arranged."

"Alright, masks back on!" Abigail announces as our friends and family crowd around. "Moment's over. Time to dance!"

"Fine, fine. You win."

Sonia and I exchange a knowing smile before putting on our disguises again.

For now, we celebrate with our friends and family, but when the time comes, we will escape to our underground haven where I'll take care of her until the early morning hours.

As we dance, and laugh, my eyes are on her, and with my ring on her finger, I know.

Sonia Hill is just as *mine* as I am hers. Forever.